ROBIN INCE is a multi-award...
author. His book, *Robin Ince's Bad Book Club* was based on his
tour *Bad Book Club*. More recently he has toured *Happiness
Through Science*, *The Importance of Being Interested*, *Robin Ince
Is In And Out Of His Mind* and *Blooming Buzzing Confusion*.
Robin is currently hosting *Book Shambles* with Josie Long.

JOHNNY MAINS is an award-winning editor, author
and film historian. He has written three collections of horror
stories, the introduction to Stephen King's 30th anniversary
edition of *Thinner*, and manages to fit all that in around his
job as a Homelessness Officer.

DEAD FUNNY ENCORE

MORE HORROR STORIES BY COMEDIANS

EDITED BY
ROBIN INCE
AND
JOHNNY MAINS

SALT

CROMER

PUBLISHED BY SALT PUBLISHING 2016

2 4 6 8 10 9 7 5 3 1

Concept of Dead Funny © Johnny Mains & Clare-Louise Mains 2011 & 2016
The selection and order of this anthology is © Johnny Mains & Robin Ince 2016
Individual contributions © the contributors, 2016

Johnny Mains and Robin Ince have asserted their rights under the Copyright,
Designs and Patents Act 1988 to be identified as the editors of this work.

*This book is sold subject to the condition that it shall not, by way of trade or otherwise,
be lent, resold, hired out, or otherwise circulated without the publisher's prior consent
in any form of binding or cover other than that in which it is published and without a
similar condition including this condition being imposed on the subsequent publisher.*

This book is a work of fiction. Any references to historical events, real people or real
places are used fictitiously. Other names, characters, places and events are products
of the author's imagination, and any resemblance to actual events or places or
persons, living or dead, is entirely coincidental.

First published in Great Britain in 2016 by
Salt Publishing Ltd
12 Norwich Road, Cromer, Norfolk NR27 0AX United Kingdom

www.saltpublishing.com

Salt Publishing Limited Reg. No. 5293401

A CIP catalogue record for this book is available from the British Library

ISBN 978 1 78463 039 3 (Paperback edition)
ISBN 978 1 78463 052 2 (Electronic edition)

Typeset in Neacademia by Salt Publishing

Printed and bound in Great Britain by Clays Ltd, St Ives plc

Salt Publishing Limited is committed to responsible forest management. This book
is made from Forest Stewardship Council™ certified paper.

Robin dedicates *Dead Funny* to Pamela Ince who pretended not to notice when he kept stealing money from her purse to surreptitiously buy the *Mayflower Book of Black Magic Stories* and *Pan Horrors*.

Johnny dedicates *Dead Funny* to Michael Brooke for helping to add another string to the bow. A dear friend, indeed.

CONTENTS

INTRODUCTION

STAND UP COMEDY can be an act of trepanning without the use of a drill bit. The furious demons that build up throughout the day are cast out in front of an audience with the aid of wild gesticulation and stupid voices. The easy day is not always the best one for the comic, a few spikes of antagonism at least can generate the necessary frustration and umbrage to sharpen a performance. It is cathartic and addictive.

The greatest frustration is when an annoyance can't seemed to be turned into jokes or routines. Once, the basement flat I lived in flooded with sewage, destroying many of my possessions, soaking 1000 vinyl LPs, turning my horror poster collection to a stinking mush. That night, I went on stage and performed an impassioned set about why you should never try attain anything beautiful as in the end, someone will shit all over it. I attempted a similar routine a few nights later, but it wasn't as effective. Even as the effects of the deluge were still being felt, the routine was becoming flimsier. The greatest annoyance of the destruction of my flat wasn't merely the loss of possessions, it was its failure to generate a routine with longevity. However the horrible the incident, the stand-up looks at the destruction or horror and wonders, "is there some good material in this?"

In June 2015, I started a stand up sabbatical. After ten years of touring, I began to see hints of madness, and not the useful kind. I wondered how the loss of this nightly release would affect me. Would I sink into a world of absurd images, rail at the sky, and gibber and shake between eight and ten PM every night, or would I just sink into a chair and enjoy a silence, turning down my inner monologue because I didn't need to feed off it so much.

Within 48 hours of my (almost) farewell gig, I decided I would spend the next six months working like a 1940s pulp writer. I don't mean creating a religion that will take Hollywood by storm; that is further down my to-do list, I would just attempt to write a short story every day or two. I would learn about writing by banging my head against walls until stories fell out. What I have found intriguing is that my stand-up brain is now dormant. Where once each delightful or hideous experience would be processed into some rant or pun, now they were stretched and warped into elements of a story. Many of the stories will be deleted or placed on a pyre, but for now, I am just typing until blistered. My story in this volume was the first product of this process. In a moment of playing with my son in a park, I imagined the worst, and then pounced on it, hoping that my fear was not a solitary one but would tap into the paranoia of parents and child minders.

Talking to readers of the first *Dead Funny* at events and bars, some expressed surprise that the stories were not only lighthearted fables with a dash of cannibal offal or bloodletting. Some of the stories were really rather grotesque, others were haunting and melancholy. Some of the stand-ups had found a new drill bit of catharsis in writing stories for a horror anthology rather than gags for the immediate laughter and approval of a crowd. I hope that this is true of this volume too. Some writers return, Stewart Lee, Rufus Hound and myself, but most are new. With the exception of one comedian, everyone I asked said yes. It seems the sort of comedians I hang around with are the sort who have something ghastly lurking in their imagination, and sometimes it is stupid too. We are stupid, ghastly people, after all.

One surprise in this anthology of stand-up comedians may be the inclusion of a story by Alan Moore, the alchemist and soothsayer of Northampton. Johnny and I have made an exception as I once tried to destroy the mystery and reputation of Alan by luring him into the standup arena. I asked him to join me for a series of Christmas events mixing scientists, comedians and musicians. I even forced him to sing the theme 'Saturday Morning Watchmen' (a delightful parody to be found within the internet). It seemed I was on course to turn the respected writer of *Lost Girls*, *Promethea* and *From Hell* into a cheap turn like the rest of us. Sadly, a backstage conversation at the Hammersmith Apollo involving Hugh Grant and his imaginings of what Alan's beard may entail curtailed our attempt to ruin Alan's reputation by turning him into a team captain of *8 out 10 Cats*. Alan has returned to Northampton where we meet once a month and record our podcast, *Blooming Buzzing Confusion*.

This may be the last *Dead Funny* for a while. I hope it is both horrible and silly and that you are surprised by what lies within. I hope we are back some day for another volume, either before or after the next apocalypse.

Finally, thank you to Johnny Mains for making this possible and to my son for the new sense of paranoia and panic that goes with unconditional love.

ANOTHER INTRODUCTION

GETTING THE FIRST *Dead Funny* from the initial concept to print took three years. As briefly mentioned in my foreword to the first book, after Robin agreed to come on as co-editor, I asked quite a number of publishers if DF was something they would be interested in. *Horror doesn't sell. You've got a good concept there, Johnny, but horror is dead.* Then the stars aligned and Salt came on board, and it was a frantic race to get to the finishing line and to get the book out. There were a few mistakes along the way, but when the book was finally in my hands made the whole journey worth it. To have an *utterly* unique anthology, to try something that has never been attempted and breaks new ground, is something that the horror genre should be proud of. The old dog *can* learn new tricks.

As an editor, it's hard to be objective about a book after it's been published, a whole different thing whilst in the middle of it, but picking it up for the first time since it was let loose, I'm happy to find that it's a *very* entertaining book. Some of the stories take me back to the joyful *Pan Horror* era, and others slip into an urban weird territory that contemporary readers are currently enjoying. Of all of the reviews I've read about *Dead Funny*, none of them have called it a *boring* anthology. I am quietly relieved. I'd rather have polar extremes of feeling than a simple, meh, it was okay.

On November 2, 2014, *Dead Funny* was launched at the Bloomsbury Theatre, to a sell-out crowd of around 500 people. This was not your traditional book launch. My co-editor and friend, Robin Ince, brought together some of the contributors and other talents to put on a night of entertainment like no other. With Robin as Ringmaster, Charlie Higson, Josie Long, Stewart Lee, Rufus Hound, Danielle Ward, Reece Shearsmith all held court. I watched the whole show from the darkness of the wings, quite dazed that something that I had help create had somehow ended up as this.

After the show had ended, honest punters lined up to buy their copies of the book to have them signed by the talent. We sold a good number of copies, I even got to sign a few of them, and I was already thinking about the work needed for book two.

Robin agreeing to come back on board has been the icing on the cake. He is a great man and has been very tolerant of me, this fish out of water, swimming around in a comedic world I know nothing about. He's a good friend and I thank him and all of the authors for their patience during this process, which has seen a few delays hit it. Publishing is never an easy process, but it's what makes the end result all the more sweet.

Welcome to the Encore.

DEAD
FUNNY
ENCORE

DATE NIGHT

AS APARTMENTS GO, it was unremarkable. An unquestionably rented, one bed, basement flat; open plan-ish, not damp but ingrained with cold. From the outside it looked lousy but had, in the last year, been smeared with paint of forrestal nomenclature ('Canopy', 'New Bracken', 'Mossier'), welcomed a real-wood floor and expensive curtains. What little there was in the way of furniture was antique, functional and less ornate than it might have been. The modern morass of cables and incandescent plastics, hidden. The rest clean and wallowing in the pervasive aroma of essentially oiled candles. Whoever lived here had taste – or had at least met someone with taste and copied them.

Thick velvet drapes thwarted the external, urban din, lending the place an air of sanctuary. Inside, tonight, just two sounds could be heard. 'Janus Plays Telephone' by The Landau Orchestra, and the low whirr of a fan oven. The only soul capable of hearing either was sat in the bedroom, tying the clean laces of polished shoes on new-socked feet. Stef, dressed now, but not long from the shower, could still feel its heat on his skin, how his surface molecules jostled with recent antagonism; the stinging, surface vibration that matched the butterfly thrum of his gut. Stef was excited, inside and out.

Not that he'd show it. He checked his watch. Not long now. Final inspection.

The bedroom? Check. He re-plumped the duvet and all was right in the room. Linens were fresh, woods polished, lighting muted, surfaces uncluttered. A swift glance into the bathroom confirmed it was as he'd left it: steamy, but gleaming. Check.

The hallway. Not much to inspect, save for the front door, some coat hooks, a lacquered Sheesham dresser and the black, lidded vase which sat atop it. As part of the interior design, the jar worked; its brown-black curves in harmony with the drawers' hue and the wall behind it. Looked at directly, however, it was revolting. Not ugly, but repulsive, repellent – it had some indefinable property that quietly ordered the scrutineer to look away. In short, a thing that didn't want to be stared at for too long; Stef knew how it felt.

The lounge-kitchen-dining room was next. The small kitchen was catalogue-tidy, the only signs of ever having been used being the two regimented bottles of red (one open) sitting on the side and the warm illumination of the oven. The table was set for two, dressed with tea lights, runner and a single poppy in a thin glass vase. With only two diners tonight, the spare chairs could, he supposed, have been moved, but to nowhere tidier than leaving them where they were. Besides, one of them was broken – the lightest nudge and the damned thing toppled forwards, legs in the air. Its inelegance irritated him, but the alternatives were either repairing it, which Stef felt had an air of manual labour and was, thus, beneath him, or throwing it out, which would skewer the visual symmetry. As he started toward the lounge, his belt loop snagged on the chair and down it went. Stef took a deep breath, slowly closed his eyes, clenched and unclenched his teeth, opened his eyes, exhaled and righted it. It was galling how often this happened but, after tonight, he doubted he'd give tinker's cuss.

He straightened the print of Francis Bacon's *Pope Innocent XII* hanging above the armchair, made a millimetric adjustment to the fall of the curtain and turned to observe his handiwork. In this flat, Stef had set a stage, and tonight's performance was an improvised two-hander called *Give Me What I Want*. If all went to plan, the curtain call would be taken some hours from now with him sated and this immaculate apartment, attentively finessed, covered in blood.

The knock at the door came six minutes later than agreed. Opening it, Stef quickly ushered in his companion for the evening.

"Hello. Do come in," the warmth considered and affected.

"Thanks."

She was pretty. Dirty blonde, with dark roots, pale blue eyes and just enough make-up to look like she wasn't wearing any. Slim, a little taller than average and with an ironic, weary cynicism that emanated from her as surely as her perfume. She handed him her long leather coat, and he took her in. Stiletto heels, skin-tight, oil-slick jeans and a white linen shirt under a red satin corset. He immediately thought how good she'd taste.

"Camilla," she said, offering a cheek.

"Jacob," said Stef, kissing the cheek and failing not to become distracted by her extended neck and the imagined-audible throb therein.

"Sooooo . . ." she said, underlining the awkwardness of two strangers standing silently in a hallway and, in doing so, breaking it.

He came to. "This way," he said, waving her towards the lounge.

3

Camilla gazed about, taking in the spotlessness of her surroundings. "Wow. You've been busy. Trying to impress someone?" She smiled, eyes widened sarcastically.

He smiled back. "And what makes you think it's not always like this?" he asked.

"Oh, y'know. Single man. Flat this tidy? You've either got a missus or OCD. Or . . ." she struck a pose ". . . you're trying to impress some smoking-hot chick you just met on Tinder . . ." The end of the sentence was lost to self-mocking laughter.

"Well, maybe one of those," he replied, nodding, consciously aping her geniality – though in truth, he was irked by the teasing, gentle though it was. "Drink?"

"Sure, why not? You only live once," she laughed. "Red?"

For someone who'd never been here before, this girl sure knew how to make herself at home. Stef fetched two tall wine glasses and the open, breathing claret.

"So, you said you work in events," started Stef and, when that was met with a raised eyebrow, continued, "On your profile."

"Oh, yeah. Events. Well, you know what Macmillan said about those, dear boy."

"Sorry. Macmillan?" he asked.

"Prime Minister in the fifties. He . . . oh, look, it's not . . . never mind. Irrelevant. Sorry. Crap joke. Let's talk about you. What do you do?" she quizzed.

Setting down a glass of wine next to her, he replied, "Theoretical Physics,"

Camilla burst out laughing.

"What?" he asked.

"Nothing! Nothing. Just . . . 'Theoretical Physics'," she

4

repeated, air quotes included. "Ah, look. I'm sorry. You've made this huge effort and I'm ruining it. Sorry."

"No, no. It's fine," he lied, taking a large pull of the claret and immediately looking back to the bottle, readying the imminent top-up.

"Let's start again. Please," she pleaded, eyes brimming with amused apology, head tilted. That neck again. That neck. The most bestial part of him revved, the prior prissy indignation overridden, the slate wiped clean.

"Of course," he replied. "So, where are you from?"

And so: dating small-talk. Conversational lubricant oiling the machine that turns strangers into bedmates. Every date, at its heart, asks the question "Shall we fuck?" and now the negotiation as to whether these two would or not had begun; increasingly, it seemed they would.

He wanted her. And he wanted to wait until she was least expecting it, to sink his teeth into her lissom throat and for her to succumb.

A set of used dishes and two empty bottles later, Camilla made a move to the sofa, and the broken chair, sensing a golden opportunity to throw itself to the floor, took it. Stef silently cursed, audibly apologised for having a 'rotten, bloody chair', and stood it back in its place. He was trying to look slick and broken chairs weren't slick. Yes, it was only a minor thing, but he'd wanted this evening to be faultless. It was deeply unimportant, he knew that, and yet it rankled; a hairsbreadth scratch on this new-Bentley of a night. This was what he was thinking when it happened.

Taking to the sofa, Camilla had accidentally pulled down the woollen throw that sat upon it and, not wanting to blight the neatness of her surroundings, turned to put it back. In doing so, the taut white flesh of her neck shone like daylight through stained glass. Irresistible. He travelled the distance between them in a single step, and before she knew what was happening, his teeth were pressing down into the flesh of her jugular.

"No," said Camilla, tutting.

"No?" spluttered Stef.

"No," she confirmed. "You've rushed it."

"Rushed it?! We've been sat here for two hours! I've been 'domineering, but not too cold or unkind'. Come on! This was exactly like you said!" Camilla stood.

"It's meant to be a *seduction*, Stef. The moment you strike ... that's deep stuff, y'know. We've barely made it to the sofa! It's a really intimate thing. I mean, you of all people ...! When you bite, it should be because, deep down ..."

"... you want me to," chimed Stef, his eyes rolling. He was cross now: at the situation, at her, at himself. He knew he'd charged in, but he'd honestly thought, the way she'd adjusted the throw, that she'd been telling him to go for it. Clearly not. His frustration now stripped away the role he'd been playing all night.

"Yes, Stef. Yes. Because I *want you to*," she repeated, crossly. "Look, I know it's not easy, but it's important."

"To you," finished Stef, who immediately regretted it.

"Yes! To ME. Which *should* be enough of a fucking reason! But apparently not!" She was shouting now. "Do you know what happens when a vampire bites – not feeds – *bites*?"

He did know. He'd known for about two years, since they'd first talked about it. When it came to vampires, Camilla was encyclopaedic. Before he'd met her, Stef could honestly say he hadn't given the undead much consideration, but in the twenty-six months he'd known Camilla, this had changed. Drastically. *Twilight, Nosferatu*, seventeen different some-things of *Dracula, Nadja, Only Lovers Left Alive, Byzantium*, all watched in their first three months together. The reading list was similarly themed. *Salem's Lot, The Compleat Vampyre*, the complete Anne Rice, *30 Days of Night, The Strain*; the various lores criss-crossing and cross-referencing, the 'lifesty-lers' trying to make canon of it all. The online forums. The club nights. And then the blood. First as a donor and, after that, as a drinker; the surprisingly powerful religiosity of the ritualised letting and feeding slowly taking on real meaning for Stef, giving him power and purpose. Life was not as he had previously understood it. Now there was this. And now there was her.

Camilla had been encouraging throughout and the nirvanic reward-fucks she dispensed for each new transgression ensured that now, fourteen months since his first taste, he was a fully-fledged sanguinarian. In fact, of late, he'd started to wonder if he was more into it than she was. Thinking back, he could recall plenty of times she'd egged him on, but was struggling to remember any time she'd properly been in the thick of it. The abiding image he had of her at 'the gatherings' was of her on the sidelines, looking *amused*. Not captivated. Not intense or devoted – more like she was trying not to smirk. At home, nestled together, binge watching *True Blood*, there wasn't a whiff of it, but the moment they socialised he felt her fall away, play the supportive girlfriend rather than the active protago-nist. It niggled. He didn't want to make a mountain out of a molehill – especially considering that these doubts only really jagged into him when they were with the others, performing some rite or other, and he just couldn't bring himself to start a 'where we're at in our relationship' chat with blood dripping down his chin. He loved her utterly, but if she found him silly now, could he bear it?

Then, one day, someone on fang.com uploaded *The Compleat Compleat Vampyre*, which purported to be the unedited transcript of Jackson's masterwork, containing – from what Stef could tell, as he clicked swiftly through it on his lunchbreak – few differences from the published version. Indeed, the unseen material contained in the .pdf had seemingly been dropped for being either boring, badly written or bonkers. It may not have taught him anything new about vampires, but it certainly gave Stef a newfound respect for editors. And then the Cruormphora.

It wasn't a jolt or a slap in the face. It was more like he'd been walking whilst staring intently at his phone, heard a door slam behind him, looked up and realised that he'd accidentally wandered into an industrial freezer, his brain now tasked with processing both the location and its meaning against a rising tide of bubbling *what the fucks*.

A Cruormphora. The most singularly valuable and powerful item in all of Blood Magick. What little was known about them had been revealed to Ottoman torturers in 1457; corroborated, two centuries later and under similar circumstances by a guest of the Spanish Inquisition. Both deponents stood accused of being in service to vampires and both, after several weeks of firm encouragement, confessed, revealing much thereafter. The hierarchy, rites and intentions. The killing, the undying and the sex. What these men revealed, two hundred years apart, formed the foundations on which every vampire story since had been built. With one crucial omission – the Cruormphora.

Both men attested that the vampires would have sacrificed themselves by the legion to protect these 'blood urns' – not vessels for holding blood, but rather solid, jar-shaped totems, made of pure vampire cruor; the genesis of each being Sekhmet's black ichor. Sekhmet – "Mistress of Dread", "Lady of Slaughter", "She Who Mauls", "Mother of Blood" – the Goddess of Vampires. These unholy grails, connected by deep, primitive magick, formed a network which powered a global vampiric cabal. There were thirteen legitimate courts of vampires, each had its own Cruormphora, and each court ordered nothing without first giving their urn full consultation.

This was all that was known of them. Apart from these two testimonies, not another word, picture or description of the Cruormphora existed anywhere. Stef could immediately see why the editor had chosen to remove the entry from the book. Introducing an object so central to vampire lore without being able to expound upon it looked half-arsed. Indeed, Stef would have dismissed it as the olde-worlde bullshit it so clearly was, were it not for the fact that he knew he had one sat on top of the sheesham drawers in his hallway. Some things are understood by our brains, others by our gut. How could Stef be so sure? He just was; the truth of it burst through him, alongside too many questions for any of them to take prominence or make sense, but they all pointed to her: Camilla.

When they'd moved in together, the place was unfurnished. Interior design had never really interested him, but she'd approached the task with gusto. Seven days from signing the lease, their ugly duckling of a flat was a swan. He had never asked where any of it had come from, accepting her murmured 'eBay', 'storage' and 'charity shop' as true. So, was it possible she had just chanced upon one of the most important objects in all of magickal history? Yes. Probably. Were the odds overwhelmingly against it? They certainly were.

His plan to play it cool evaporated the moment he arrived home. Pushing open the front door, it was the only thing he could see. However hard it urged him to look away, knowing now what it was, its power seemed obvious and irresistible. How could he *not* have known? And in that moment, he realised that he'd never touched it; the thought of doing so now made his heart race. Holding his breath, he slowly reached out a hand, felt something foreign inside his head tell him not to, ignored it, pushed on and . . .

"Shit!"

Camilla, stood next to the sofa, was watching him through the doorway, had seen the gap between his fingers and the jar all but disappear. Now it was her turn to have too many questions. "How are you . . . why have . . . what have you . . ." the tumult of disbelief tumbling out of her. "Shit!" she repeated.

Silence, and in it, a look between them: "How?"

Camilla moved first, pushing past Stef, grabbing her coat and making for the front door. "Wait!" he started.

"Shut the fuck up," she snarled. "Not one. Fucking. Word. Come on."

They got in her car and drove, the atmosphere between them reminding Stef of the day his mum had caught him smoking outside WHSmith's. Camilla's fury was so strong that even though he'd done nothing wrong *per se*, he knew the diplomatic thing to do was keep schtum. Forty silent minutes later, they parked in, what a townie like Stef would describe as, 'the countryside'. Not that he could see much of it, the night's slender moon and low cloud conspiring to cloak anything beyond the immediate. Camilla's door was open before the handbrake had fully locked, and she had a foot on the ground before the headlights had lit their last. There was a decent distance between them before she called for him, the tone identical to one taken with an unruly pet. Five minutes of wordless marching later, she turned, a minute after that, up ambled Stef. They stood in a clearing, her glaring, him wary. When she spoke, it was weighted and deliberate. She'd had an hour to cool off, but every syllable burnt with fresh intensity.

"How do you know about the Cruormphora?" she asked in such a way that he began to wonder whether she'd brought him here to kill him.

"PDF," he replied and, from the look she shot back, realised that this had utterly failed to satisfy her. "Fang.com. Someone uploaded an unedited . . ." but that was as far as he got before she interrupted.

"Fucking, internet fucking . . . fucks," she stammered. "Fuck!" This eruption coming as a scream. "Can't leave well a-fucking-lone!" She pulled out her phone and started angrily tapping, the eerie screenlight turning her face B-movie monstrous. "Have you shown it to anyone? Flagged it up?" she asked as she typed.

"What? At work? Who would I tell? Jesus, Mills . . ."

"What about online? Or any of the Blood Magick lot?" She looked up from the screen. "Have you uttered one word of this to anyone, Stef? And don't fucking lie to me." She held his gaze.

"No. I swear."

She exhaled, her relief palpable. "Well, okay. We're not out of the woods yet, but . . ." The typing continued.

"Well, no. The exact opposite, in fact," said Stef, gesturing to the trees.

Distracted by her typing, the joke nearly missed her – "Wha . . . ?" then landed, the utter silliness of it (coupled with the relief that he hadn't told anyone about the Cruormphora) blowing much of the tension between them away. If she could have laughed she would have done, but instead settled for muttering "You dick" as her phone whooshed its email-sent whoosh. She looked at him. "Right," she exhaled again, "so."

"So," repeated Stef.

The cloud lifted a little and the moonlight crept through. They looked at each other. The panic dissipated and breaths were taken. Scores of questions answered in the other's face. But not all. It was Stef who spoke first.

"How do you have it?" he asked.

"It's a long story," she sighed. "Too long." She knew she was going to have to tell it or lose him. Hell, she may well lose him anyway. Either way, it'd change things between them and the realisation tore her heart a little. A tear fought its way from her chest, out through her left eye and zigzagged down her cheek. "You remember, when we met, you asked me about when I was younger?" Stef nodded.

"Yes. You made me promise not to ask you about it again. So I never did." It was true. She had. And he hadn't. "You said that you'd spent too much time being someone you didn't want to be. That it was all too painful and sad and that you wanted to live the rest of your life with no link to any of it. You said that if you told me about it, it'd keep a little bit of it alive and just knowing I knew would mean you could never love me because you'd never trust that I could properly love you back." His near-perfect recall of the conversation made her sadder still. "It was our second date. And when you said it, you looked so . . . beaten, that I promised to never ask again."

For the entire duration of their relationship Stef had sickened himself with imagining what awful thing had befallen Camilla. Every godawful news story made him wonder if *this* was what had happened to *her*. Incestuous abusers, paedophile rings, cults, war crimes . . . Stef couldn't hear about the world's worst without wondering whether Camilla had first-hand experience of it. Whatever she's buried, he thought, let it stay down. But he'd been wrong. Her desperation to start anew wasn't out of victimhood.

"Stef," she started, "I'm a vampire."

Given their extra-curricular activities, you could forgive Stef for feeling confused, or laughing, or doubting, but he didn't. The way she said it, the shame she gave the word, her eyes, he knew. For logic's sake though, he thought he'd try to argue.

"But there's no such thing as real . . ." He stopped. Before him now, barely wearing Camilla's clothes, stood a demon. The face a contorted abomination, somewhere between bat, piranha and gargoyle, the skin grey and mottled, her hands now talons, wracked scythes. Nosferatu.

Stef, knowing he must, took it all in. "Right," he said.

"Right," the creature hissed back.

That night, she'd told him everything. She was pure vampire, had never been human. Had been born before countries. Had spent millennia doing what she was born to do. Had torn the throat from kings, paupers, babies, grandmas, hookers, eunuchs and priests. Had turned townships into ghost towns and worn flesh like jewellery. That it had all changed. That it was the advent of the printing press which had predicated a new cautiousness in vampire kind. That a culture of disguise and assimilation had been fostered. That the thirteen formal Courts of Vampires had disbanded in favour of a more nimble, less detectable, organisation. That without an enforced hierarchy, the empire petered out. That there were fewer vampires in the world now than there had almost ever been, but that the survivors were "the sanguinarian version of UKIP, harking back to a glorious past that has nothing to do with glory and almost everything to do with power." That they had all been around too long. That, without an end, stories have no meaning. That she'd inherited the Cruormphora. That, even though its power had long since waned, you did not talk about them in their presence – "Hence driving out here." That she was bound to protect it, even though its residual magic did that anyway. That, when he was sleeping, she left the flat and fed on people who wanted to die. Mainly people about to jump off tower blocks. Sometimes people in nursing homes. Occasionally, just for fun, "some city cunt walking out of a brothel into a Porsche." That there had been no new Vampires for the last hundred and sixty years. That the problem with living so long was that eventually death was the only thing you hadn't tried. That, by the time Bram Stoker put pen to paper, the party was not just over but that anyone who'd been to the party had pretty much forgotten it had ever happened in the first place.

It was a lot to take in. Stef tried to appear stoic, and were it not for the fact that his girlfriend was a purebred, millennia-old vampire who could smell human emotions like a fox smells fresh bins, he might have pulled it off. The truth was, over the last two years, he'd become so deeply embroiled in the world of vampire fantasy that, confronted now with an entirely contrary set of vampire facts, he felt . . . lost. It was like the lead singer of the Bootleg Beatles meeting Paul McCartney, only to be told that, actually, John Lennon and George Harrison killed *themselves* because they'd suddenly realised that everything about The Beatles was shit. And that he agreed. And so did Ringo. So much of his world, invalidated in a single conversation.

"But, if you're so over the whole 'vampire thing', why get me in to it? Why come to the club nights?" he asked, his sense of betrayal adding piquancy to his delivery.

"Stef," she started, "I'm a monster. I am death and nightmares. The time of my kind may be over, and fuck, I'm glad it is, but that doesn't mean there isn't a part of me that doesn't . . . miss it. Like an old ballerina watching *The Red Shoes*. There's comfort in nostalgia. But then . . . seeing how into it you were, it made me think, like, maybe, you could," - a short breath - "love me. Not the girl. The monster. Me."

He looked at her. She looked at him. "Change," he said.

"What?"

"Change. Let me see you again."

It was no effort to oblige him, and she did. He stared. She felt a little judged but, as part of her confession, endured it. "Right," he said. "The thing I don't get is, why do you care? You want to be 'loved'? It's just not very . . . vampiric, is it?"

The laugh that met this question sounded like hot acid being poured into a rat's nest. When it spoke, it was beastly. "So bored. So jealous," the creature rasped. "Never got to choose. Born to kill. To defile. Humans choose. To be good, to be bad. Resented it. Freedom. So jealous. Fed the Cruormphora, asked it if I might choose. It said such magick did exist but not tell me where. Would not lose its favourite daughter. I did not wish to be human, just I wanted the power to choose."

"But why?! You had it all! Immortality, power, magic . . ."

"Monsters are born, but true evil is chosen. I wished to excel."

"So," Stef continued, "what changed?"

"By the time I had the magick, killing was so boring. By the time I had the magick perfected, I despaired. Must become something - anything - other than what I was. So bored. So sick of it. So sick of me. Had to choose. Chose. . . . this." Stef now looked once again at Camilla, albeit a Camilla whose clothes were stretched to all hell. "And then I chose you. I have seen a billion lives, and ended millions in the worst ways imaginable. There's absolutely nothing special about you, Stef, not as far as anyone else is concerned. But I chose to feel what humans feel. And how I feel when I'm with you - when you're not being a dick—" she smirked and he laughed "—is as good as being human feels."

That night in the woods they had kissed and made up. Had both felt so battered by the night's revelations that they agreed to ignore its ramifications for now. He told her it would all be okay, that nothing would change, and she did her best to pretend she believed him - but, with a sad inevitability - here they were, three months later, arguing.

"It's meant to be a *seduction*, Stef. The moment you strike . . . that's deep stuff, y'know. We've barely made it to the sofa! It's a really intimate thing. I mean, you of all people . . . ! When you bite, it should be because, deep down . . ."

". . . you want me to,"

"Yes, Stef. Yes. Because I *want you to*. Look, I know it's not easy, but it's important."

"To you."

"Yes! To *me*. Which *should* be enough of a fucking reason! But apparently not! Do you know what happens when a vampire bites - not feeds - *bites?*"

"Of course I do!" he shouted back, "That's the whole fucking reason I'm doing this!" He was right, it was.

In the twelve weeks since they'd driven home from the woods, Stef's imagination had gone into overdrive. Here he was, a boy whose wildest dreams just crashed from 'outlandish fantasy' into 'achievable reality.' Charlie Bucket with a vermilion ticket. How could it not change things? How could he - he who had spent countless hours dreaming what it would be like to be a vampire! - now have a way of becoming one and just pretend he didn't? Oh, it had changed things alright. Camilla now held the keys to the kingdom and Stef just had to convince her to hand them over and let him in. It was proving to be trickier than he'd hoped.

He'd first broached the subject in bed. They had 'tried something'. Specifically, he'd chained her to the bed, she became her monster-self and he fucked her, dressed as Van Helsing. He said some truly fucked up things to her, the beast hissed some ancient curses back at him and the sound she made when she came - which she did. Hard. - broke two windows and the screen on the microwave. It seemed as good a time as any to ask her a favour.

"No."

He let it lie.

A week later, he tried again, this time at dinner. They were having a conversation about going on holiday, possibly taking the train down to Budapest and visiting Vajdahunyad Castle. It was odd booking a holiday with someone who had not only been to every place on Earth, but had murdered and eaten at least a half dozen people while she was there. Somehow, Stef sensed, CenterParcs just wouldn't cut it. Hence Vajdahunyad.

"But you've been before?" he asked.

"I've been everywhere before."

"Jazzy cow."

"What?"

"Well, that you've been everywhere. Seen it all, done it all. All that time."

"Well it's not like I was on an episode of *Coach Trip*," she countered. "I was Death Incarnate, I wasn't there for sightseeing."

"More bite-seeing," he offered.

She rolled her eyes, then, unable to help herself, snorted a laugh. "You're a dick," she teased, eyes sparkling.

"And you're an ancient killing machine," he said, pushing his chair back and swaggering toward her, "but I still think you look pretty with my cock in your mouth."

The broken chair fell.

"Leave it," said the seated Camilla, pulling him towards her and tugging at the loose end of Stef's belt. "Make me look pretty."

His blood rushed immediately to where it was needed and she seized it happily. If there was one thing Camilla had scorched into her DNA, it was lust. For centuries, hers had been gleefully sated by human blood and acts of depravity; she now applied the same zeal to fellating Stef. His eyes rolled backwards, he had to concentrate on standing as her tongue spiralled and her head bobbed. She felt him getting harder in her mouth, could feel his balls tightening. A minute later, it was nearly done.

"Bite me," he grunted. The surprise of it broke her rhythm.

"Bite me!" he repeated, grabbing her hair into his fist.

He looked down at her, she looked up at him, her fangs reflecting the lamp behind him. She hissed. He felt the sharp points tear into the shaft of his cock and he came as she fed.

"Oh my god . . ." he panted, in the recovery period between cumming and being normal again. "Fuck yeah . . . woah . . . Thank you."

"You're welcome," she replied, the heel of her hand wiping trace amounts of blood, spit and cum from the corners of her mouth. "You dick." She couldn't resist.

"So, when does it kick in?" he asked, wincing as he saw the two neat puncture wounds in his slowly drooping cock.

"When does what?"

"The changin . . ." He immediately realised there'd been a misunderstanding. Then she did, the post-sex high evaporating almost immediately.

"I didn't *bite you* bite you. I just . . ."

"No. Right. I know, I know," he interrupted, the knot of disappointment, apology and gratitude tightening in his chest. He tried to look nonchalant, but it was too late. He grabbed some kitchen towel, wrapped it around his rapidly shrivelling penis and pulled up his jeans.

She watched him, but her thoughts were elsewhere. She knew how much he wanted it – how much he thought he wanted it. Based on what they'd read and watched together, she could hardly blame him. Being a vampire looked cool as fuck. Who wouldn't want that? She opened her mouth, ready to make him understand, realised he never would and shut it again. She could still taste him, all of him, and he tasted good. Would it really be so bad if were . . . maybe . . . no. No. No! She absolutely could *not* start down that path. Her kind were in 'managed decline'. That's what they called it, 'The Dynastag', the last council of her kind. Their time had passed. Humanity had made its own monsters. They had their instructions. No new vampires.

It's very hard to love someone and not give them the thing they want, even when you know it's bad for them; indeed, especially then. She was starting to waver. She absolutely mustn't. But she had.

She tried, instead, to explain it all to him. That it wasn't up to her, that the reality of what he was asking for was a million miles away from what he'd thought it would be, that he should trust her – he was better off this way. He said he understood, and he did. He just didn't agree. And for the last ten weeks, this was all they'd talked about. Him trying to convince her, she trying to convince him. She thought she could put him off by describing how unbelievably horrible it was to transform from human to vampire. Not like in the movies where the bitten "goes a bit damp and sweaty for ten minutes, then jumps up, fangs out shouting 'Let's go!'" It could take days, sometimes weeks, and every minute of it awful.

First came the pupal stage, the host body inverting, former flesh becoming gory chrysalis. Once it solidified, the bones and organs began their reconditioning, learnt how to form and reform for future shapeshifting – profoundly painful lessons but, once gained, initiated the final, tertiary phase in which the viscera knitted back together; the vampire within perfectly conscious as each synapse burned into the network. Agonising days later, the new creature would emerge, starving, naked and wracked - like they'd awoken in hospital after a near-fatal car crash. It was a process that had to happen in perfect darkness, and under careful supervision. Once bitten, immortality was conferred quickly, but there was no guaranteeing the thing alive at the end of the process was a vampire - unless it was properly cared for. Camilla shuddered. She'd seen a few fail and, even as a creature that revered sacrilege, the memory of them turned her stomach.

Stef listened to her. He nodded. "But I'd be here. With you. You'd look after me, right? And then . . ." he trailed off.

There was no reasoning with him. She may as well have tried talking a teenage girl out of the boob job she'd been saving up for; the truth of the short-term utterly lost to the glorious (imagined) result.

The week after, she changed tack. "You keep talking about this like it'll bring us closer together," she protested, "but the opposite is true. Most people can't spend more than ten years together! How do you know you won't hate me in five? Or fifty, let alone five hundred?! You become a vampire and the one thing you can be sure of is that there's no 'happy ever after.'"

"There were no certainties when I thought you were human," Stef reasoned, "but I still wanted you. 'Worry about the end, and you'll never begin,' my grandad used to say. Who knows where any of us end up, Mills? That's not the point, is it? We love each other for as long as we can. That's all anyone can do." He was kissably close to her now. "And what if you're wrong, eh? What if we *can* love each other from now till the end?" - his face now level with hers - "If two people ever could . . ." - the end of his sentence lost as their lips met. He was talking shit, of course, but it was romantic, and enough of what he said was sufficiently true that she kissed him back rather than call him on it. Who knew what was around the corner?

Every couple negotiates – which carpet? Car? Threesome? Eight weeks of negotiations later, she threw him a bone.

"If I *were* to bite you – *big* if – I'd need to know what kind of vampire you'd be. In the old days, the noobs'd go mad. Feeding frenzies, blood baths, the lot. You couldn't be like them, Stef. I couldn't bear it if you became some . . ."

"Twatula?" he proffered. She sniggered.

Fuck, she knew this was wrong, that she really shouldn't even be considering it, but who'd ever know? And then she'd have him. This funny little boy. Forever. Ish. A week later and there he was, trying to prove himself.

"It's meant to be a seduction, Stef. The moment you strike . . . that's deep stuff, y'know. We've barely made it to the sofa! It's a really intimate thing. I mean, you of all people . . . ! When you bite, it should be because, deep down . . ."

". . . you want me to,"

"Yes, Stef. Yes. Because I *want you to*. Look, I know it's not easy, but it's important."

"To you."

"Yes! To *me*. Which *should* be enough of a fucking reason! But apparently not! Do you know what happens when a vampire bites – not feeds – *bites?*"

"Of course I do! That's the whole fucking reason I'm doing this!"

"And don't I fucking know it, eh? Needy, needy, needy. Is there any chance, just for once, you'd think about what I want?"

"What you want, Mills? What *you* want? Before I met you I

couldn't have given a shit about vampires, blood magick, or . . . or . . . any of it! I'm like this *because* of you. I want this *because* of you. All I did was think about what you wanted and it made me like this. You lied to me, but when you told me the truth, I kept loving you. So now what? 'No Stef, sorry', 'No Stef, ooh, it'll be very sore', 'No Stef, I'm not allowed – even though no-one'll ever know'. I can't do this! I can't stand you judging me and telling me I'm not up to it. Because if you think . . ."

Camilla zoned out. She couldn't blame him. The whole 'being bitten by a vampire' thing was never meant to be a test, wasn't something that could be passed or failed. The monsters of old were creatures of instinct. They appeared from shadows, slashing, biting, tearing. Gurgling, throat-ripped fathers would see their bleeding daughters desecrated. Pregnant women wailed as their sons were cleaved from within them, tossed to and fro, dismembered and eaten. Forcing Stef to prove he could hold himself to a higher standard than any monster ever had, had been her way of ensuring he'd fail. Then she wouldn't have to bite him and this would all go away.

Except it wouldn't – and then what? Would Stef ever take no for an answer or, now that he knew the truth, would he go looking for a vampire who *would* turn him? He was unlikely to find one but, with everything he now knew, his would be the kind of search that would raise alarms with the Dynastag and they weren't exactly renowned for their kindness or compassion. Maybe biting him was the only way to keep him safe?

It could just be attrition from the weeks of arguing but, increasingly, she'd felt like biting him *was* the right thing to do. It wasn't what she wanted, but she'd be lying if she said there wasn't a little part of her that wanted to see what it'd be like. Them. Together. Feeding and fucking. Then, maybe, they could get back to having a laugh. Snuggling on the sofa with a box set and a barely conscious snack. It could be good. It could be great. She zoned back in.

". . . whatever it takes, Mills, whatever it takes. I mean it. I can do this. Give me the chance. I deser . . ."

She was right. There *was* a difference between biting and feeding. You didn't need to be a vampire to feed. Anyone can make a cut and suck blood out of it. But *biting?* That was different, that was a skill, a calling. Morphing fangs into ivory needles, champing straight through the throat into the spine, piercing the spinal cord and regurgitating thick, changing blood directly into the host's central nervous system. She had done it before, was never going to do it again, but . . .

He never saw it coming. The force of her swept him off his feet and she pinned him to the wall, tasting the fear as it flashed through him. "Still got it," she thought, the metallic tang of blood now giving way to the milkier flavours of Stef's spinal fluid. He went limp. She was in. From deep inside, her ichor surged up and injected home, the work it had to do began instantly.

Her teeth retracted and Stef slumped to the floor, conscious but spaced out, trying to focus, to find her eyes, to thank her. He looked, and felt, drunk. This was the happiest he had ever been and was desperate to thank her but had all the coordination of a twelve-pint drunk. Eventually, with her help, he struggled to his feet, slurred out the only words he could string together – "Love you" – and flung his pursed lips at where he hoped her face was, before falling heavily into the armchair.

Camilla looked at him and felt herself at once both lover and mother, muttered an old, dark prayer that he would endure the pain to come and sighed audibly. She felt relieved. No, she felt . . . hope. The recognition brought out an involuntary snort of laughter. It was true. However much she'd wanted to tell Stef why he couldn't be a vampire, now that he was going to be one she felt . . . happy. The infinite possibilities of this new arrangement clattered into her mind. All that lovely killing and fucking and feeding and kissing and box-setting and laughing and piss-taking and teaching and snuggling and killing. She could deny her true nature all she liked, but now that the idea of sharing it with Stef exploded into her imagination she had to confess, she rather liked it. She looked down at the pallid, jerking boy in the chair and a paroxysm of joy swept over her. If she could have caught her reflection she'd have seen a dirty blonde, with dark roots, pale blue eyes and a smile that could outshine stars. The world was theirs.

How quickly that face changed.

The sound was low and faint, deep and rumbling. It was a sound of foreboding. And it was coming from the Cruormphora.

Panic shot frozen knives all through her. Stef heard it too and murmured but she shushed him. She had, at most, ten minutes to get him the fuck out of here before the things making that noise burst out of the ancient black-brown jar, demanding unholy satisfaction. She grabbed Stef's phone, tapped open the taxi app, and in the time it took to load, felt despair fill her like poured mercury. However, all was not lost. On the map glaring at her, was the icon of a black cab just three streets away and in a speech bubble hovering above it: '2 mins'. It took her just twenty seconds to set the destination and press 'order', but it still felt too long. She lifted Stef effortlessly, carried him to the hallway and opened the front door. The cold night air rushed in and Camilla cursed again. He wasn't dressed for this. She checked the screen. The cab would be here in one minute. From the other end of the hallway, the Cruormphora sounded once more.

The same noise, but louder now. They were getting closer.

Camilla set the reeling Stef by the open door, ran through into the bedroom, flung open the wardrobe and grabbed the thick winter coat he'd been wearing when they'd first met, the loveliness of the recollection at odds with her current terror. She span on her heel and ran back through the living room, catching the table with her hip as she did so. The crockery jumped, the cutlery clinked and the broken chair began to fall, but Camilla was back in the hall before it landed.

"Fucking chair . . ." mumbled Stef, as the hated furniture banged down. The cold air had sobered him up a little and Camilla was grateful for this small mercy. "Whazgoin'on . . . ?" he asked, his sweaty face crumpled with confusion.

Camilla pulled the jacket onto him and got him to his feet as she answered. "Listen Stef. *Really* listen. I can't explain now, but there's a cab that's going to take you back to the woods. Yes?" she asked searching for any sign that her words were registering, and when no confirmation came, she shook him, hard. "Yes?!"

"Woods. Yeah," he repeated, his swivel-eyed head lolling.

"You've got to get yourself into the clearing, Stef, where we had our talk." Her delivery was urgent, but her tone was all primary school teacher sing-song. "It's really important, Stef. The clearing. It's the only place you'll be safe . . ." but he'd passed out. She slapped him. With a moan, he came to, just as the telltale squeal of Austin FX4 brakes told them his taxi had arrived. Stef's phone dinged confirmation, Camilla slid it into his coat pocket, pulled up his hood, and together they stumbled up the concrete steps toward his getaway car.

Inside, the lid of the Cruormphora started to rattle. They were nearly here.

As she slid Stef into the back seat and clicked his seatbelt closed, the driver piped up. "Uh, no. Look, sorry love. I can't take him. He's smashed to pieces. If he throws up in here . . ." But Camilla had already slammed the rear door shut and now strode to the driver's window.

"Listen to me," she fizzed, every word a punch. "He's in trouble. There are people, coming here, now, who'll kill him. He's done nothing wrong. The only person who can stop him dying is you. Open the windows, take him exactly where it says on the app and if you come back here tomorrow, I'll give you three hundred quid. Okay?!"

"I can't open the windows, love. They're not electri . . ."

Camilla yowled frustratedly, yanked open the door nearest Stef and grabbed the window winder.

"Listen, baby," she barked as she wound, "this'll only be for a couple of hours, okay. I'm going to come and get you. Just get to the clearing."

Stef had a brief moment of clarity. "Yeah. Got it. Clearing. See you in a bit. Love you."

"Three hundred quid?" asked the cabbie.

Camilla slammed Stef's door. "Yes! Go!" and the driver, newly motivated, obliged. As the cab pulled away, Camilla hurried back towards the flat, weighing up her options as she ran. When the Dynastag got here, what was her move? Play it cool? Diplomacy? Claim that the dying magic of the Cruormphora had misfired? That seemed believable, she'd presumed the thing exhausted, hadn't heard a peep out of it for almost a century. She damned herself. How could she have been so stupid? She'd got lost in the spur of the moment and . . . fuck. Fucking fuck.

She could hear the rattling lid as she descended. For the first time in a long time, she was grateful of her years. She was ancient, indeed, one of the very first, arguably *the* first – if you didn't include her mother, Sekhmet. Had this not been the case, the odds of reasoning with The Dynastag would have been zero. Their usual methods left little room for constructive conversation. No, her heritage accorded her some respect, and with Stef out of the way maybe – just maybe – they'd get away with it.

As she closed the front door behind her, she tried to focus. When they apparated from the Cruormphora, she must play her best 'Hey guys! What the heck are you doing here?' card. She needed to seem calm. This was all some crazy misunderstanding – one that could be sorted out quickly and peacefully. She could, perhaps, more easily regain her composure were the Cruormphora not vibrating like it was sat on a washing machine. Suddenly, the sound of thunder. Camilla removed the lid of the blood urn, shying from the heavy black smoke that now blew out. She centred herself, breathed deeply and became the demon. Monsters should be met by monsters.

Yet, she had been right – or half right. The Cruormphora was indeed exhausted. She had not fed it in a very long time, being content to let it wither, and wither it had. The work being asked of it now by The Dynastag was simply too much. It could feel them pushing at the other end, trying to force their way through, but its magick was too weak. The harder they pushed, the less stable it became, until with their final, raging push The Cruormphora could give no more. It exploded, not into pieces but into dust, a mist of ancient blood and sorcery, the silt immediately omnipresent.

The force of the eruption smashed into Camilla, catching her entirely off guard, hurled her backwards through the doorway into the lounge. When she landed, it was not on the table that Stef had lovingly set, the sofa that they watched Buffy on together, or the floor that they had endlessly fucked on. It was on one of the legs of the broken chair, which ripped into her back, through her heart and out of her chest. She made not a single sound, nor ever would again.

Why was everything so loud?

Why was everything so bright?

Where was she?

She would be here soon.

Stef bobbed back into consciousness. It would be fleeting, but in this brief window, these were the thoughts he clung to.

What were all the other voices?

Men's voices.

Wait. Where am I?

"Listen, just . . . if anyone comes looking for 'im, maybe . . . y'know, don't grass 'im up."

"How do you mean, Mr . . . ?"

"Nah, sorry Doc. Just call me John. I don't wanna . . . I just brung 'im in . . . I don't wanna be on no form or nuffin."

"Okay. John. What do you mean 'grass him up'? Is this man in danger?"

"I dunno. Dunno 'im. Just picked 'im up. His bird said there's people after 'im. I'm not gettin' involved. I think she might have been in on it. She wanted me to take him to the woods. Look, I'm not gettin' involved. I just . . . well, I couldn't just dump him in the middle of nowhere. Not when 'e's all . . . *fing*."

"No. Well. Thank you for bringing him in, John. Are you sure you can't give a brief statement to the Police? If he's in trouble, if you truly want to help this man, the police will be best placed to . . ."

"Nah. Leave me out of it. Sorry. I ain't . . . nah."

The first voice grew fainter. Then footsteps.

"Right. Hello? I don't know if you can hear me . . . Can you speak to me? Can you say your name?"

Stef could not. A sigh, the snap of a latex glove, then the sheer, burning agony of his eyelids being prized open, bright torchlight flooding in.

"Jesus! Nurse! Jesus! Jane! JANE! Get hold of Simon in quarantine. Tell him we need an isolation room. I don't know what this bloke's got but . . . Jesus!"

The pain overwhelmed him, he could focus no longer, and in that moment Stef died.

What awoke, nine days later, was not Stef.

But it was hungry.

ISY SUTTIE

UNDER MY SKIN

March

Current List of His Rules For Me
- Don't leave wardrobe door open
- Don't mention any exes, even if it's to show him in good light
- Don't disturb him in bathroom. I wouldn't like it, would I?
- Make sure to lock patio door and windows at night
- Don't turn the corners of his books over to mark my place
- Don't ask for sex in morning until he's had his orange squash
- Keep raw meat on top shelf of fridge or it will contaminate other food
- Keep weight below nine stone
- Don't blow nose at table – leave room and shut door
- Don't sigh whilst emailing
- Don't say the following when he gets in from work:
  "Alright?"
  "Are you ok?"
  "Good day?"

"Bad day?"

- Remember: he will tell me about his day if he wants to. He doesn't need prompting.

APRIL

Just came back from the Cavendish. We were with Julie, Simon, Ali and Anna. He kept calling Anna Hannah but she didn't correct him, which was really sweet of her. I think it's hard for him to remember all the names of my uni mates because (a) I've got so many! and (b) his mind just doesn't work that way.

He's so creative that it's not that he sees the world in a topsy-turvy way, like an artist in a clichéd film would, it's that he is so absorbed in his work that he's really good at being black and white about his opinions in 'the real world'. He doesn't dither about whether to buy steak or chicken, or what coffee to have – it's like he saves all the softness inside him for his painting. He can be quite ruthless in everyday life, which I admire.

Like tonight, Julie was saying how she's planted loads of herbs in her little roof garden and that bugs eat the leaves of some plants but not others and she doesn't know why they pick those particular leaves. It's really annoying her and she doesn't know how to stop them from doing it. She went on about it for ages – people suggested putting pesticide on them but Julie said you can taste that in the food. Someone (ok, me!) made a weak joke about pestocide.

Then he did that laugh of his which is really loud and funny like he's putting a full stop on things. "Ha! Ha!" Ali said maybe the bugs are jumping from leaf to leaf and it's just about which leaves are next to each other and she trailed off.

He was completely silent and I thought oooh, maybe we'll get a painting inspired by this in a few days – little insects and close ups of green and yellow half-eaten leaves, maybe some rotting ones in the background.

We went out for a fag after that and he said he was annoyed with Julie. I noticed he was very white, which is the way he always goes at these times. His lips look ultra-luscious and red when he's angry, like he's a boy who's been eating blackberries in a fairy tale. "Why", I said, "Because of the bug thing?" "No", he said, "She hasn't bought a round yet, she's so busy talking about the fucking bugs, and now it's our turn again." "Oh, she's always been like that", I said. "She once charged me 76p petrol money when she helped me move house." "Why would you be friends with people like that?" he said. "I just don't get it." "We go back ages", I said. "Don't let her get under your skin. She used to hold my hair back when I was hammered throwing up, she cooked me loads of food when I was ill, she's just not great at money. I think her parents brought her up weird. Like, once she turned up to a dinner party with a loaf of bread and a paperweight." His lips went redder – or did he go whiter?

When we got back to the table I could see he was really trying to be nice to her but he was carving into the table with his keys so I said we should come home. He's just said we can't see her again. We can see the others but not her.

MAY

Additions to His Rules
- Walk one metre behind him at all times. (Some exceptions: tying shoelaces, stopping to chat to neighbour, gawp at moon, etc)

- Don't see parents more than once a month. (A few exceptions: Christmas, birthdays etc)
- Don't interrupt him in arguments - if I do he can't be held accountable for his actions and I know this, so don't do it
- Don't clear throat at table - leave room and shut door
- Don't say the word, "Cooeee", even as joke
- Only listen to Mozart
- Don't initiate conversations with men unless they're family members
- Don't move in bed once he's asleep - if he's tired he can't paint properly
- Go on exercise bike for an hour a day
- Don't wear hair in ponytail - makes me look like librarian
- When clapping/waving, tense arms so upper arms don't wobble
- Email HR at the end of every week with my list of complaints about Norma otherwise they will never do anything - this is for my own good

JUNE

I'm a bit drunk! Will try and remember everything.

Firstly, we're in Alicante. It's really sunny. Good, good, good. I'm not tanning of course, pale twat that I am!! He is. We were simmering all day. Little dances towards the big row then back again. Very colourful dances. Foxtrot, polka, waltz. Not initiated by me, of course.

We started drinking early. At lunch, he said I was smiling at the waiter (I was smiling at a Spanish baby). He said I should put different types of food from my plate on my fork rather than eating each type separately, which is what I've always done since I was a kid. Then you can save all the roast potatoes til last, like pudding. To prove he meant it he ordered me paella even though my steak had already arrived. So because I was tipsy when the paella arrived I picked out all the chicken then all the peas etc. His face did the fairytale blackberry thing but I felt great because I thought, it's like popping a spot, we've got to go there, and it'll burst and be awful, but then we'll make up and it'll be gentle and feel new and I'll kiss his blackberry lips again and again. He walked off and I stayed there. This is insane because when that normally happens I leave too and follow a metre behind, but I just thought fuck it, I'm on holiday, I've got a pile of shrimps here to be eaten. Also, we hadn't paid. I ate a few shrimps and looked at the baby and my heart was beating so fast. The baby was smiling at me and I smiled again and I thought, I know I look beautiful, I just know. I felt magnetic. One of those moments like in a film.

The waiter came back, who *was* good looking, and I knew he was turning on the charm like he was pressing go on a funfair ride and that I was just another pale freckly English girl and because I knew, I didn't care. I ordered a double G and T and he brought it to me and said he was about to finish his shift and he sat down and said my name Davide (or something like that). I said my name's Anne (I don't know why I didn't say my real name) and he said you saving shrimp 'til last and I said yes like roast potatoes and he didn't get it but he still laughed and I thought that was nice.

Then I had two more double G and Ts and about half an hour had gone by and the clouds looked bloody excellent in the sky, just so Spanish. Davide (or whatever) asked where my husband was and I laughed because we're not married and then he came back (where had he been?) and pushed Davide's chair hard, and he said something into Davide's ear and Davide ran onto the beach and away. He looked at me and he was shaking and crying, and he said come here now Charlotte and hugged me so tight that I could feel his blood in his veins and I could see the rest of my shrimps over his shoulder on the edge of my plate with a bit of lime which was melting in the sun. I thought if I could just have those last few shrimps my life would be utterly perfect but we came back without them and that was better because you should always be left wanting a little thing in life to make you have a will to live.

When we got back to the hotel, he tied my ankles together with the rope from the curtain in our hotel room and then he put me in the bath and he said, "I'm going to have to tie your wrists together too but I don't know what with" and we were both actually laughing about the situation. Eventually he settled for my USB cable. It was weird because I was just thinking about the shrimps I'd left behind and then I said I need a wee but he didn't say anything so I just had to do it in my dress. I was in the bath anyway so it didn't go on anything else. He finished tying my wrists and he leaned close to me and said "I'm under your skin, no-one else is", and I thought we were probably going to have sex and I was worried about us damaging the USB cable as it's Norma's from work. But he just left me in the bath for I think probably three hours with a chair and things against the outside of the door so I couldn't get out and unfortunately by the time he came in for me I had weed again but by then I didn't care as much about my dress, it's old anyway. Then he said you won't ever talk to a waiter again will you and I said no and he untied me and got me out of the bath.

Then we had the most amazing night. We ordered room service and I ate a salad with lots of different things on my fork and it was so nice – watermelon and rocket and white cheese and ham. I don't know why I didn't do it before – all these lost years! We drank wine and smoked fags on the balcony and talked really honestly about stuff and he said if I followed the rules he wouldn't have to do anything and I do get that. I said I am human though I am going to forget sometimes and he said if you loved me you wouldn't forget and I said I do love you, I really do. He said that he loves me too, so much that he can't bear the thought of me dying or leaving him. I'm under his skin and he's under mine and we don't need anyone else. He takes it as a personal affront when I disobey him because he wants to protect me.

I can't believe someone loves me this much. When I was growing up all the boys at school were total shits – they would just use girls and not even know their surnames. I just feel so lucky to have him and that he has forgiven me. Then we watched *The Wire* and he's fallen asleep on the sofa. He looks so gorgeous. I'm sitting on the balcony writing this and smoking and I honestly have never felt so alive. I'm not sure what the rules are about whether I should wake him so he can go to bed properly. I think I'll just let him wake up naturally and then I won't have done anything wrong by not waking him. I just went to the toilet and the USB cable and rope are still on the floor and I looked in the bath and thought, oh I was lying in you earlier this evening. It's just a bath!

Early July

Additions to His Rules
- Don't look at his paintings unless he says I can, even at his exhibitions
- Wear the outfits he has laid out the night before (not the Spiderman costume – that was a joke – but he waited til after I'd worn it to the supermarket to tell me so)
- Within the house, address him as 'Sir'
- Don't eat sugar or cook anything with sugar in it
- Keep asking for pay rise by sending hourly emails to my manager until she responds
- Don't address Norma apart from on email (somehow he always gets the truth out of me even though he's not there)
- Send half-hourly texts whenever I'm away from him to inform him of actions and what time I'll be home
- Always let mobile go to answerphone and don't call anyone without his permission
- Let him deal with all my emails
- Have private health check every three months (savings)
- Have all moles on my body removed in case they turn into skin cancer (costs £250 per mole so doing monthly with savings)
- At dinner table, always do things in same order: sip, take mouthful of food (different types together on fork), clasp hands in lap for ten seconds whilst chewing and swallowing. Repeat
- Delete all males' phone numbers from my mobile, even tradesmen and Dad (doing this tomorrow – secretly memorising Dad's mobile)

JULY

Funny how punching a wall can lead to slapping a face. Good old Rimmel.

LATE JULY

I lost his iPod. He didn't do anything but has given me 2 'debits'. When I get to 15 it's going to be bad, he says.

AUGUST

Julie's getting married today but we're not allowed to go. Joked that she would at least be buying the rounds at her own wedding but he didn't laugh and gave me another debit. I'm on 13 now. These are the things I've got them for:

- Initiating conversation with lollipop man (1)
- Leaving wardrobe door ajar (1)
- Losing his iPod at the beer festival (2)
- Making us late to meet his family for lunch (1)
- Telling Anna about how he eats the bones of fish because he considers it a weakness and waste of time to pick them out (1)
- Not telling HR about Norma making me work 'til eight (2)
- Putting raw meat on the wrong fridge shelf (1)
- Asking if we can go to my sister's housewarming (not classed as special occasion) (1)
- Writing his name in his mum's birthday card rather

     than giving it to him to sign (1)
- Keeping shoes on in the house (half)
- Forgetting to take his library book back (half)
- Making the joke about Julie buying the round (1)

It's nice of him to give me the halves as he's trying to help me. I just can't help messing up and I'm trying my best. I feel like sometimes I try so hard, it causes me to mess things up. We never leave the house now apart from for me to go to work, and it's straight there and back. He paints and works out all day. We're under each other's skin, like he always says. Two peas in one pod.

LATE AUGUST

I'm on fourteen and a half. Slapping a face has become hitting an arm has become raining blows onto face and body. And I'm not even on fifteen debits. He says it'll be worse than I could ever imagine, that it will make Alicante look like a holiday. Which it was. I didn't say that, of course.

SEPTEMBER

Everything's fantastic again! My life is such a rollercoaster, which is what I always wanted when I was growing up in my boring old town. He's so calm and his lips don't go blackberry red anymore. He's even letting me listen to Kraftwerk all I want and sometimes I do things in a different order at dinnertime and forget to clasp my hands while I'm chewing, and he doesn't say anything. We watch *The Wire* every night and he doesn't even get angry when I have to pause it to work out the plot or get a drink. The first time I pressed pause I braced myself for the rain but it didn't come. His arms just stayed lovely and floppy. We had a big hug that night.

OCTOBER

I've started replying to my emails again and answering my phone. His parents ring a lot and I say we can't see them at the moment because he's working on the biggest painting of his life and can't be disturbed. They, like me, are very proud of him. When I go to work I leave him with a tray of food and a glass of orange squash but when I get home he doesn't seem to have had much of it. I've started talking to Norma again and stopped emailing HR about the pay rise. Leon from head office came into work to give a presentation and he looked round the room at all the different people and smiled at each of us and I smiled back. Been feeling a bit sick but it seems to go by lunchtime.

LATE OCTOBER

I've cancelled my monthly mole removal appointments and three-monthly health checks and bought a new dress! It was on my way back from work and I just had to get it. I've gone up a size - must be all the sugar I've been letting myself have! It's black with tiny purple Christmas trees on it. I knew he wouldn't like it but he hasn't been laying out my outfits recently so I had to do it really. I showed it to him and he didn't seem to mind too much. I've stopped going on the exercise bike apart from on Sundays, and I wore my hair in a ponytail today and Norma said I looked nice. We're nearly at the end of series 3 of *The Wire*. I have to say he looks more engrossed in it than ever.

NOVEMBER

Everyone keeps saying I look radiant. I wear the Christmas tree dress every day (I can wash and dry it on the radiator in an evening) and keep putting my hair in a ponytail. His parents have started knocking at the door and shouting through the letterbox but I just hide under the table like I used to when the rain came.

Current List of Charlotte's Rules for Him
- Stay sitting on sofa while I'm at work/pub/party
- Don't get anything from the fridge while I'm away
- Listen to Kraftwerk on repeat while I'm out
- Don't ever say again that *The Wire* is a modern-day version of *King Lear*
- Don't answer the door to anyone at all
- Wear your Spiderman outfit when I tell you to
- Leave the raw chicken on top of the cooked chicken in the fridge
- Don't ever say again that *The Simpsons* is a modern-day version of *King Lear*
- Don't do any painting
- Leave the wardrobe doors and the drawers open
- Stop smelling so fucking disgusting!!

DECEMBER

I'm going to so many Christmas parties that I feel bad I'm

not spending much time with him, but he's just so antisocial it's embarrassing. I bumped into Julie at one of them and we made up. When people ask after him I say that he's working on his paintings, but he never does anything, the lazy fuck. He's smelling pretty bad now as he hasn't showered for months (these creative types!) so this morning I wrapped him in cling-film (six rolls) and moved him into the spare room so he can be more comfy and so I can give my nose a break. I lifted up the valance (God I love that word) and he fitted really neatly under the bed.

After that I went and met Mum and Dad for lunch and they ordered wine and I said I'd not really felt like drinking lately and Mum said you look radiant and I said not you as well and she winked and I winked too. Then Dad said come here now Charlotte and hugged me so tight, and I could feel his blood in his veins and I could see my pile of roast potatoes over his shoulder, and I thought I would die of happiness.

CARNIVAL

SHE WANTED TO be Carnival Queen. Ever since she was a little girl and first saw the float going by, bearing a passingly ugly teenager glumly waving at the crowds in polyester frills. To Becky, this was the most fantastically beautiful creature she had ever seen. Wreathed in (plastic) flowers, on a garden chair, gliding through the cheering crowds as if she brought actual joy in waves. How was the lorry transporting her? It was not the lorry that moved her. But clouds. The crowd breathed in and sighed unanimously. This may as well have been an angel from heaven. With a perm. She was chewing gum, Rebecca remembered. The height of glamour. To think, when you were grown up you could chew wherever and whenever you wanted. Becky's mum commented that 'that girl' worked at Sammy's Fish 'N' Chip shop. But Becky couldn't consolidate that grumpy, greasy teen in a stripy hat, stenching of vinegar, with this divine being. A couple of 'runners-up' perched behind her in peach meringue dresses, like disconsolate toucans. They looked annoyed. As well they might be. They could only sniff at glory, in its wake. "She only got it because her dad's on the council," said Becky's mum. She shook her head, disapproving. Becky started thinking about how her dad could join the council. But she stopped in her tracks, held her breath. The

Queen was looking at her. Could it be? Becky looked behind her, to either side. No one else. Yes, she had to be, she *was* looking at her. Did she imagine . . . a nod? In slow-motion, the Queen threw something underarm. What could it be? It arced through the air. Becky felt as only a hopeful bridesmaid can feel, willing the bouquet to fall her way. A token of permission, of approval, bestowed by fate, that she, yes she, would one day be Carnival Quee . . .

It hit her in the eye. "Goarrr," Becky grunted involuntarily. No one seemed to care. Her eye streaming and squinted, Becky bent to pick up the token. It was a penny. Dirty, chewed almost. Seemed like the Queen had been sick of people throwing coppers at the float and decided to get her own back. The float had nearly disappeared round the corner now. The mundane crowd now losing interest, drifting away. Some brats on parental shoulders crying, on a come-down from their candy-floss high. The helium balloons beginning to sag. The world had returned to reality again. For a moment, a fairy had swept through their midst, and now everything in the town looked that bit more shitty again. The concrete flower beds, the ugly shop signs, the reek of cheap pork from the butcher's. Becky put the penny in her pocket anyway. Mum and Dad were beckoning her home.

The noise of the fairground geared up and Becky could see flashing lights on the horizon. Flashing purple, pink and green. Her parents had decided she was too young for all that. Instead she could only dream over her fish-fingers.

Eight years later, Becky was on track. She'd had her ears pierced. She wore legwarmers. Every morning she would carefully squeeze any whiteheads using thumbs, and then generously apply an excruciating spot treatment, followed by lashings of orange concealer. Concealer that concealed nothing, but certainly provided a distracting feature in the centre of her chin. Like a tiny stupa in the Nepalese capital of Kathmandu, viewed aerially. Her freckled face was then outlined with a clear circle of orange powder that didn't cover her ears. Like a guide: "Look here. Locus of face." She chewed gum, religiously.

She'd picked her 'runners-up'. These were her friends, Kayley and Emma. They weren't as pretty as her. They were just slightly off. Kayley had a massive nose, but was slim. And Emma was a bit fat, with a pretty face. Becky encouraged her to finish off her Wotsits. Daily. Otherwise there could be a fucking disaster. Becky wasn't the prettiest at school. But she was just girl-next-door enough. She knew from eight years hard study that they didn't choose the high fliers or the beauties. They chose those who they felt would never leave.

Hagford was a medium-sized town, redeveloped in the sixties. An uninspiring central high street had been surgically enhanced with a concrete post office and a huge hotel at one end, worthy of *Bergerac*. It was like a stranded 80's yacht covered in pigeon droppings. Any of the original buildings, little thatched cottages, had been almost squeezed out like rotting teeth, clinging on only by the skin of them. This was the street up which the carnival processed every single year, descending to the fields and the fairground. It was some kind of ancient tradition from pre-Magna Carta 'Hag Ford'. Past the clock. Past the pond. Past the newsagent's. Past the odd knick-knack shop, Bits 'N' Pieces. Past the shoe shop, Shoe-Inn, fed with a regular stream of Hagford Comp pupils who end up working there, managing it, then dying in a care home on Ducking Lane. The same route, always, that took the floats anti-clockwise round the town, through the residential streets, Dusky Arbour, Hallow Road, Dark Lane and Black Cat Drive. Ancient names for brand new boxy houses. Identical estates of orange brick. Freshly mown lawns and barbecue sets. All so that everyone can get a look. At the procession.

The buzz at school was growing. The excitement of the fair, and the floats. The school football team was going to do 'Thriller', but dressed as American footballers. As if this was supposed to be sexy. Some of the teachers were going to do a 'pop star'-themed float. The thought of Mrs Carr gyrating on a vehicle made Becky feel sick. It was totally only so that she could wear those leather shorts she inexplicably wore to play a fairy in the school panto. Becky wouldn't stoop to such fripperies. Her eyes were firmly on the prize. Queen. Only Queen.

The fair was a whole other matter. Virginities had been lost, life partnerships formed, children conceived, drugs and belongings exchanged willingly or not, along with various venereal infections. All on this very site. The fairground in Grim's Fields. It was a place where legends were born. Anything could happen. A friend of Emma's elder sister had run away with a fairground worker, for example. If Becky was this year's Carnival Queen, she would have her pick. Nick Bumble would be in the palm of her hand. She would hold sway over that fairground. She would be all-powerful. She would go on as many rides as she liked. And eat hot dogs. And parade around, knowing she was Queen of that small town. She'd make them spin the waltzers faster. And she would scream and scream.

Her window was small and her time was now.

Then she saw her. The new girl. Walking down the school corridor. Someone had said there was a new girl. But she hadn't thought much of it. An 'old Hagford family,' Becky's mum had said. Come back to the town with a new business. Or something . . . she wasn't pretty. Or tall. In fact, it was hard to describe her. If Becky had known the word, she would have known she was being hit with 'charisma'. She stared. The girl walked past, a lopsided smile on her face. One eye larger than the other. And a different colour? Long black hair. A pointed chin. And her walk was funny. Jittery. Like she belonged to another universe. Becky looked around her, was no one else seeing this? All she saw were soppy grins. "Hi, Rue!" said the head of the football team, Nick Bumble. He was tall and had all the latest sportswear. Rue smiled back and nodded. An annoyingly enigmatic nod. She waved a hand in front of her face. Nick Bumble seemed enchanted. Becky dropped her coursework which was in a folder she'd bought from Athena. Rue had gone. What the hell was this? How could something *change* in Hagford? At the eleventh hour? It was unforgiveable. Becky felt a sinking feeling in her stomach, she couldn't put her finger on why. She went into the girls' loos and checked her stiff-hairsprayed fringe-crest, dabbed some more concealer on the stupas. She looked at herself. She was still girl-next-door, still Shoe-Inn material. Still in line for coronation. That hadn't changed. So why was she worried? She sprayed herself liberally with Sure and went to class.

That afternoon after school, she and Kayley dawdled on the bench of Talisman Square, checking out the local talent and eating baked potatoes out of polystyrene boxes with plastic forks. They scowled at some eleven-year-old girls as they scurried past mouselike. This was *their* territory. A concrete square with some benches in it. When they'd finished, they went to browse Bits 'N' Pieces. Normally they'd shoplift something, but there was literally nothing to steal amongst this shit. Windchimes, greeting cards, ornaments, plastic flowers, gemstones. The fat purple-haired shopkeeper was reading *Bella* really slowly and clutching a Lucozade, unmoving. Like a melting Madame Tussaud's. Kayley was laughing at a resin figurine of a bulldog with a sign around his neck saying *Mummy I've done something Naughty*, which alluded to a dogshit rendered in resin next to him. Becky's eye landed on a book. Strange sort of a thing to be in Bits 'N' Pieces. The longest bit of text they had in there was usually *You Don't Have to Be Mad to Work Here But It Helps*, written on a loo-roll holder. The book was called *Past Hagford*. It was clearly second-hand. Becky flipped through it gingerly, she didn't know why, she hated old stuff. Photos of Hagford streets, when there were still horses and carts. An old drawing of the fields. A story about witches. An ink etching of the pond, with a strange contraption suspended above it. A long plank of wood, a lever, operated at one end by a man in a Guy Fawkes hat, and at the other, a seat, on it a woman. One eye bigger than the other, a wonky mouth. The water seemed to ripple. The woman's hair to blow in the wind escaped from her cap . . .

"Becky!" shrieked Kayley, in her ear. She'd found a card that when you opened it played the theme tune to *Steptoe and Son*. Kayley thought this was hilarious, and pretended to hobble around in time to the lolloping tune.

"Ha," said Becky drily, "we should give that to Rue."

"Oh . . . but Rue's lovely," said Kayley, not noticing Becky's scowl of incomprehension.

"You'll wear the battery out!" said fat, purple hair, clamping the card shut. "Are you going to buy that?" she said, nodding to the book in Becky's hand.

"Oh, no. I just wanted to see my house, that's all."

"Well your house wouldn't be there, would it?" snapped the shopkeeper. "Your house is new. The old one burnt down. To the ground. Had a curse on it, apparently." Well, Becky found that hard to believe, surely they would have mentioned it in the estate agent's catalogue. "Your house," said the shopkeeper, poking her in the hip with a long sparkly purple nail, "belonged to a horrible man. He used to torture women. Hundreds of years ago. But I suppose you aren't interested in history these days, are you. Just yourselves and what shoes you're going to buy."

"Actually," said Becky, "we're both doing GCSEs in history. We're just not that interested in old bags." Then she slammed the door triumphantly with a tinkle of plastic wind chimes.

Then they went to the shoe shop to look at the sort of shoes they would wear to sit on that float.

Swimming day. Becky had scrounged together enough for a Bounty from the vending machine. Rue glided past, swimming kit in hand. Involuntarily, Becky let out a hiss. Rue did not turn, but Emma exclaimed in surprise with her round pudgy milk-maid face. "Becky!" Becky looked at her, a little surprised at herself.

"D'you want some of this?" she said, proffering a bollock of Bounty. Emma gobbled it greedily. "Easy", thought Becky. She didn't even have to try.

Becky glared down the row of swimmers, in Speedo swimsuits and goggles, lined up, drily, not to dive until they'd heard teacher's instructions. Rue stood in what seemed to be a sacking ensemble. Was that even allowed? It didn't even look like a swimming costume, more like a sealskin, or some other organic material. It covered most of her body, thigh to neck. But at her waist, Becky could see a small rip in the fabric. And some kind of strange marking. Not a birthmark but a . . .

The teacher blew the whistle. Rue smiled lopsidedly in an enigmatic fashion. Becky pulled her swimming costume out of her own arsecrack uncomfortably. "Now, for your survival awards, I hope you've got your spare clothes from home?" nasally intoned the teacher.

"Yeees" drawled the teenagers.

"I want you to put these on over your costumes. The idea is to remove the additional clothes and climb out of the pool unaided." A rustle of plastic bags as the teens got out their 'additional clothes'. Becky had brought her brother's shirt and trousers. No way were her clothes going to get marinated in David Lloyd's piss, who was the boy who lived in a council flat and stank. Of piss. He was at the shallow end, because he couldn't afford to swim. Well out of Becky's league at the deep end, but you never know. Piss spreads, like evil. Rue had brought some kind of 'goth-gown', a heavy black number, with pleats and a high collar. Becky nudged Emma, and snorted. Emma didn't respond. But then she did have an extra layer of fat, a nudge wasn't necessarily detectable. Becky bent and whispered to Emma, "Watch this."

She was going to totally freak that freak out.

The whistle blew and the teens plunged into the chlorine-acid water. T-shirts and skirts billowed. Becky, holding her nose, felt the water seeping under her polyester. She opened her eyes painfully. It looked like a really bad underwater disco. David Lloyd was pathetically doggy-paddling. Emma had already started taking off her rather too saucy dress, like an underwater striptease. And Rue was hanging like a dead thing, arms hanging down, as if she was enjoying it. Becky fixated upon her prey, and struck out underwater, like a schoolboy shark, in shirt and trousers. Giggling to herself internally, she grabbed hold of the corner of Rue's long, black dress, and tugged on it firmly. Becky was a good swimmer. She had stamina, the teacher had said. That was what she was good at. The long game. Rue had begun some gentle movement towards the surface. But jolted against the pull of her gown. She swam up, and up. But could make no progress. Becky gripped on, crablike, gleeful. Then Rue turned. Looked down at her. Suddenly, with surprising speed, Rue was gliding towards her. Now she was face to face underwater with Becky. Those uneven eyes. The dress billowing out behind her like ink from a squid. Without so much as a bubble or flinch, she smiled. With that lopsided grin.

Becky burst out of the water painfully, gasping for breath, scrabbling to get out of her clothes. She swam to the edge of the pool and pulled herself out, shaking. White in the face. "You okay, Becky?" said Emma, 'caringly'. Everyone was staring at her, humiliatingly aghast. Becky looked down at the black mass in the pool. Suspended, like a dead body, like a horrible octopus of terror, like a creeping Cthulhu of dread, like a horrid wig of . . .

"Well done, Rue!" said the teacher. Becky jumped. Standing next to her, smiling enigmatically, was Rue in her swimsuit. Strangely dry. The black mass in the water was just her dress. "Letting yourself slip a bit there, Becky," said the teacher frowning. "Not your usual standard. You were the last to get out. Last ones don't get first place!"

It was Carnival day. Becky had cried all day and all night, and four days and nights before that. She wasn't going to go, she told her mother. When they'd made the announcement, Becky had shrieked, and fallen against Kayley and Emma. Like James Brown after a long concert, she'd had to be guided out of assembly. Panting and swooning. Kayley and Emma were both runners-up, of course. The bitches. Becky wished a pox upon both of them. They both rather prudently avoided talking excitedly about their dresses and the Carnival Queen in front of her. If she saw them on that float she'd shriek "fat ugly honk-nosed cows! Wonky-eyed HAGS!" at them and would have to be dragged away screaming, pointing an accusatory finger. Why couldn't everyone see it? Were they blind? Was this not the ugliest collection of crows ever dragged together since panto? The girl group Bewitched couldn't boast a lower looks rating. "I'm not GOING!" she tantrumed, Frisbeeing a cereal box across the kitchen, Puffed Wheat radiating out like a Catherine Wheel.

"Well, they'll be coming right past the house," pointed out her dad, eating a sausage. "If the mountain won't come to Mohammed . . ." Becky squealed and banged her head against the door. Why was he bringing religion into this?

"It's because her family are bringing new business," said Becky's mum, stroking Becky's perm in a consoling manner. Becky swatted her hand away.

"It's not new business," said Becky's dad, slurping on tea absently, "it's old business. Very old business."

But curiosity was getting the better of her. And competing

with that, revenge. She stared at her tear-streaked orange face in the toilet mirror. It looked like Tatooine. It was a bog-faced Cabbage Patch doll face, perfect for Carnival Queen. She'd practised the smile. It was going to improve her marriage chances. I mean, it was like a dry run, right? If Nick Bumble couldn't see what she'd look like in a meringue, if he couldn't tell people at work he was married to a former Carnival Queen, it just wasn't going to happen. Becky pushed the soap down the plug hole, its slime oozing out between her fingers. Her destiny had been wrenched from her. If Rue started working at Shoe-Inn this summer, that would be the final straw. Why did they choose her? Why did people like her so much? What was this power she had over everyone? They'd said she'd been chosen for her 'considerable charm'. Charm?! Where did 'charm' ever get you in Hagford?! Not a currency here. But everyone had been fooled. Spellbound. Everyone needed to see Rue for just what she was. A dirty, downright, evil, loathsome . . . Becky's eyes fell upon the bottle of bleach next to the loo.

In the distance, Becky could hear the 'Thriller' music. She leant against the wall, pulling her sleeves over her hands. She'd dressed in funereal black. Like Robert Smith with a deathwish. People had started to gather outside their houses. Families with prams. Old people smiling, holding little flags, their collections of pennies ready to throw. Everyone beaming with excitement. The marching band were approaching at the front of the parade. Becky watched cold-eyed as Vicki Bailey twirled her baton in the air and dropped it, scrabbling in the gutter to pick it back up. God, this town was shit. Becky's mum and dad had brought out fold-up chairs and were on them eating hot dogs. The offending weapon, Becky had slid inside a bucket in a bush. She felt like Lee Harvey Oswald, except she didn't know who that was. She'd ignored the lesson and done doodles of Garfield. The football team was approaching. Faces painted grey, zombie-like, shoulder pads and American football helmets. Half of them were already sitting down on the float doing nada while the other half did 'Thriller' dance moves half-heartedly. They were already zombies, thought Becky, so that was accurate at least. Nick Bumble was sat leaning on one arm, gazing out glazedly, like a bloody Athena poster. Becky called his name, did a little wave, but nothing. Why was she now invisible? She had important stuff to say to this town. Important stuff to give. All of her. All of herself. They didn't seem to see her sacrifice. She had status. She had had status. Once. Now she was just nothing. A pleb. A forgotten pleb. Nick picked his nose and craned back towards the floats behind him. Becky knew what he was looking for. The Queen.

A hush descended. The Carnival Queen float was approaching. Wreathed in flowers. They were playing classical music to accompany it. The lorry float glided, every now and then jerking and jolting, the polystyrene ionic columns wobbling dangerously. Becky grabbed her Toilet Duck nervously. A Toilet Duck for a total toilet. Rue wanted to sit on a throne? Okay then, this is what you get. She'd ruin those dresses. She'd ruin those wonky eyes. They'd see the real evil come out in this girl. The whole town. This would flush her out.

The float was jerking parallel to Becky's house, Kayley and Emma waving at the crowds. The crowds cheering and blowing kisses, throwing pennies which Kayley and Emma caught in a bucket and a toy fishing net. The back of Rue's head, waving at some kids. 'I know what you are', thought Becky. And then, as if she'd heard . . . Rue turned. Everything stopped. Becky was looking into Rue's eyes. And they were black. It was as if her face had jumped out independently and was now right in front of her own. As if her cold eyes were burrowing into her soul. Anger. Anger so potent, so baleful, it struck terror into Becky's soul. Fury. Cold fury. But Rue's mouth was smiling. Becky, limply poised with the bleach, looked around her. The music was silent. The crowd were unmoving, suspended, doing nothing. Then Rue began to get off the float. Slowly, jittering, black eyed, she approached. Becky was paralysed, unable to run. She looked at her parents and they were just smiling at the float, ketchup dripping onto their laps. Rue was still approaching, clambering over the wall, right up to Becky's face.

She spoke to her, her smiling lips barely moving, but her words as clear as day. "I am going to hunt you. I'll give you a one-day head start."

The procession had moved on. Nothing but a few smatterings of pennies and ice-cream wrappers littering the floor. Becky jolted out of her reverie, the unused bleach in her hands. The sun was going in and her parents were folding up the chairs. "I've got it all over me!" complained Becky's mum, rubbing ketchup off her batwing top.

"That was good wasn't it?" said Becky's dad. "The 'Thriller' float was excellent. They really did look dead."

Becky watched the sun dipping beneath the neat rows of houses, and heard the beginning ominous strains of pop music as the fair started up. She waited, still fearful, then hypnotically clambered over the wall, down towards the High Street. "Going to the fair are you?" her dad called out.

"Don't be too late!" shouted her mum.

Past the post office, past the Shoe-Inn, past 'Bits'N'Pieces now displaying a Closing Down sign. Ducking Lane to the left, Hallow Road to the right. Past the town clock and the De Launcey Hotel, she gathered speed. A little old man with stick and flat cap banged shut the door of his thatched cottage as Becky walked past, like he was trying to keep the plague out. Breathless, she didn't know why, Becky followed the copper trail down Widdershins towards the pond and the fields, the pop music getting louder as she went, like her heartbeat, tribal drumming before a ritual. Clouds were gathering and thunder rumbled loudly before a loud CRACK. Becky edged round the pond. It was humming with energy. Black. The dark clouds reflected on its surface. Now Becky could hear screams from the fairground. She could see the mechanical arms rising and falling above the trees, rag-doll bodies in their clutches popping up and then down again, legs flailing. She swallowed. She'd always loved rides. But now she felt like a cowardy custard. Stupid. She thought to herself. Banging herself on the knee. She plunged through the nettles and approached the fair from a secret location to spy what she could spy.

From behind the sticky goose grass and wild hellebores, squinting, she could make out the waltzers. The carriages swung round and round. The riders pressed back centrifugally to their seats. But no screams flung out. Becky edged closer. All the funsters were glazed-eyed, unmoving, mouths open. They were dead. Becky looked up at the metal octopus, swinging people round, her eyes closed as she was spattered in the face with blood. Sightless eyes swung close to her. In the distance, there were screams. The Fun House people screamed in genuine terror as they tried to escape an unseen menace, slipping over comically on schizophrenic travellators. A girl, dragged backwards by her foot through a crazy door, its jaws clamping back and forth around her, her screaming as it did so. Then silence. Becky watched from behind an empty burger van as Rue emerged. She glided out, in her blood-spattered peach frock, a lop-sided grin on her face. And then up the hill towards the Old Oak.

It was beginning to rain now. The fairground creaked, eerily silent other than the mechanical moans of the rusty machinery. Becky could not believe her eyes. She had witnessed the decimation of a whole town, townspeople sacrificed on big metal moving monoliths, painted on the sides with bad pictures of Madonna and Tina Turner. Candy floss half-eaten, abandoned on the ground. No sign of the fairground operators, just the odd set of fingers decorating the bushes from where they'd been flung, severed by machinery. Tears and snot dribbled down Becky's orange face, mingled with rain. There's no way she would have done this if she was Hagford Carnival Queen. She would have just given out a few sweets. Kayley and Emma were both dead on a swing boat. Emma's guts hanging out like streamers from the carriage. Under the Old Oak, at the top of Grim's Hill, Becky could make out a figure. In shoulder pads with an American football helmet swinging in one hand. He was smoking a fag. Nick Bumble. This was where they would have had a snog, had things been different. But approaching the tree was a jittering figure, dressed in peach.

Becky ran, as fast as her legs could carry her. This was the most unselfish thing her stocky little freckled legs had ever done. She was going to stop it. Stop her. Rue was reaching the tree, Nick was turning to greet her, he was smiling, holding out a fag, she was taking his hand, drawing him closer, her face to his face, her grin to his grin, opening her mouth, wider, wider, wider. Becky screamed out. *BANG!* A huge explosion of thunder. Lightning forking down to the Old Oak. Burning Nick to a frazzle, still gripping the helmet in one hand, though now looking truly dead, falling flat to the ground like a Pop Tart. The Old Oak left looking like a twig used to toast marshmallows. And Rue turned to Becky unscathed. Her eyes jumping out at her over a hundred yards. Words in her ear, "I'm going to hunt you."

The fair was a place legends were born. Anything could happen.

So Becky ran home and packed and left that night. And still she roams, from town to town, working in a shoe shop here, a Bits 'N' Pieces there, getting older, getting tireder. But she can't ever stay long. No friends, no family, no prospects. She can't ever become one of the townspeople. Because she's being hunted, see? And she's only got a one-day head start.

THE VAULT

THERE'S SOMETHING ABOUT churches I just can't resist. I'm not religious; quite the opposite, but when travelling I often find myself drawn to these great piles of stone and solitude. They are at their best when empty. A congregation spoils the mood – a reminder of the human aspect of religion that I cannot stand, but the building by itself suggests the divine without the need for mediation.

I like small village churches most of all. The sense of human history; the tattered flags of local regiments; the pews named for long-dead worshippers. Then there are the hints of our pagan past. It's a fact now over-rehearsed by zealous atheists that most old churches are built on former heathen sites; that the transition to Christianity was made more smoothly by adopting certain traits of the Old Religion:

"You celebrate the reawakening of nature on the spring full moon? We can accommodate that. Here. Have an egg while I tell you about Jesus."

One of the great pleasures in life is the visible unease of an ancient rector upon being asked to explain what the Green Man is and why it's in an Anglican church.

I'm not sure I'll truly enjoy a walk around an old village church in quite the same way ever again.

✂

I hadn't planned a church visit. I was performing in a small town on the Suffolk coast in October of 20 – and I'd set out for a walk along the coastal path from my bed and breakfast to the only place in town that served vegan food. The father-and-son owners of the B&B were overbearing and didn't posses a single social skill between them. They came from another age. Few things make me feel part of the great history of British show business than staying in cut-price digs, and these characters were worthy of an anecdote on Parkinson if only I'd been famous in the Eighties.

"You'll be wantin' food, I espec'," said the father. His languid voice carried a bizarre air of menace even when offering help. He had the solid build of an old boxer and his face was of a type they just don't make any more. His son looked like a hired heavy in an episode of the *Sweeney*, but had a naive sweetness to his temperament that suggested he didn't know his own strength. This made him even more intimidating. I've read *Of Mice and Men* . . .

"Er, food? Yes, well . . . I'm vegan," I apologised, finding myself on the back foot.

"Ah," was all the bruiser could say.

"I'll find something in town, thanks." It was late afternoon and I needed something before my show.

A useful app on my phone suggested a greasy spoon a few miles down the road that offered a simple meal. The direct route would take me there in ten minutes, but a more meandering path took in the cliffs and seafront and I fancied earning my appetite with a bracing walk.

After a detailed explanation of how to operate the front

door and after being furnished with two keys on an oversized wooden keyring I ventured out onto the quiet road. The smell of the sea and the sound of distant gulls was suitably stimulating and the iron-grey autumn sky lent a brooding atmosphere that made me feel enjoyably gloomy. The town centre lay directly to the West. I struck off towards the South.

The road curved around to the right, parallel with the coastline which imposed itself on the terraces from a distance of at least two hundred yards. I kept a stiff pace for ten minutes or so, following the curves of the cliffs and trying to guess the age of the houses. After a while I spotted an entrance to a church yard on the other side of the road. A tattered arch led through to a small burial ground which was virtually derelict. The few ancient tombstones were obscured by weeds, as though nature were making a concerted effort to reclaim them. In most cemeteries this effect would be romantic; in London's grand Victorian cemeteries the ivy lends a gothic beauty. This yard had an atmosphere of abandonment, almost of despair.

I checked myself for these feelings. The season descending into winter can often drag my mood down until I spot the obvious link. I walked briskly on, hoping the exercise would stir up my humours.

The church was large and impressive, and as decrepit as its grounds. Scaffolding covered the east elevation, though it looked almost as old as the building itself and there was no other evidence of works being advanced. Standing back to take in whole church I was struck by the unusual design. I'm generally quite good at telling the rough period of churches, but this was beyond me. It looked . . . *incredibly* old, but I couldn't slot it into any particular period. It wasn't Gothic, it didn't look Norman, and it was much grander than the only Saxon church I've visited, in Bradwell-On-Sea in Essex. That one is tiny; this was huge. I took a few pictures with my phone, but the dim light prevented any clarity.

Walking around the West side there were more graves, these less encumbered by weeds. I tried reading the epitaphs but they had been so eroded due to the site's proximity to the sea it proved impossible. As a bank of dark cloud moved overhead and the gloom deepened even more I was struck by a sense of the alien. I've been in scores of church yards and cemeteries in my travels. Normally I find them comforting. That feeling was totally absent here. I felt unwelcome.

I tried the main door and found it locked. As I was about to walk away I heard a distinct scuffling sound from deep within the building. The hair stood up on the back of neckxcsx. I'd been sure I was alone. I turned around and pressed my ear to the door. I strained my senses, listening far inside.

Nothing.

Nothing but my own heartbeat and my own breathing. I held my breath and tried to make out what was inside.

A bang on the door made me jump out of my skin.

As I gathered my fragmented senses the door unbolted and pulled open from the inside. A tiny, ancient man with a weathered face stared at me with beady, sunken eyes.

"You from the Council?" he asked, his voice cracked and high.

"No. Sorry, no I was just looking."

"Church is closed, lad. Vandals."

"Oh, sorry to hear that," I offered.

"Fucking kids." The swear-word was incongruous.

"Nothing's sacred any more. The council are s'posed to be comin' round to look at . . . woss-the-word," he flailed with gnarled fingers, ". . . *assess* the damage."

"Can I come in, look round?" I surprised myself with this boldness. I was still full of adrenaline from the shock of the noise and I was curious to see the damage. There was a long pause. The wind blew through the crack in the door.

"Yeah alright. Come on. I 'aven't got long though. You might 'ave to let yerself out."

I ventured inside. "Is that okay, leaving the door unlocked?"

"Door doesn't lock, lad." He pointed. There was no bolt.

As my eyes acclimatised to the darkness I saw a few crude tags sprayed on the walls. It was the usual crap: FROME and GAZ and DARREN IS A BENDER. The scrawl wasn't enough to undermine the stark grandure of the interior. It looked even bigger on the inside; a common trick of church design. The usual feeling of a higher presence, the awe induced by the high ceiling, the feeling of being outside while being inside was still there. More so than usual, in fact.

"It doesn't look that bad," I said. My voice echoed around the walls.

"Downstairs. They did something in the vault. Voodoo or Satanists or some such. Rock music kids, you know. Your lot. Hmm." He amused himself by tarring me with the same brush.

The door to the crypt was a dark rent in the wall. Square and inky black.

"Can I have a look?"

"Help yerself, lad. Yer more brave than what I am, hmm. No light down there, see? Hmm."

❧

I pulled a torch from my bag. My prepper geekery means I always have the right tools for the job, at the expense of sexiness. The stairwell was colder than the body of the church, and my breath was visible in the beam from my light. The remains of a broken bottle crunched under my feet.

The vault was a total wreck. Bottles and cans were strewn on the floor. A fire had scorched one of the walls. The remains of what looked like a series of rituals were everywhere. Candle stubs, incense. A cheap plastic skull. The walls had been painted – not just with spraypaint as upstairs, but crude, obscene murals. A symbol was repeated on several walls. Like a pentagram, but with eight points, not five. It looked familiar. I was sure I'd seen it elsewhere that day.

As I looked more thoroughly there seemed to be several layers, several different elements. I wondered if it was the work of the same people.

There was a lot of writing in characters I didn't recognise. I attempted more photographs, my torchlight making them stark and grainy. I had a friend who could possibly tell me what these meant and I felt the need to record them before they were cleaned up.

I shivered. The cold was biting. The rector called down the stairs. "I'm off, lad. Close the door after you." Now I was alone I felt the unease I had felt outside. A *something* sense of hostility from the building itself. I should get the rest of the graffiti recorded and get to my –

Shit. I had been so distracted I'd completely forgotten about my gig. I looked at the time. Seven o'clock. No time for food. I needed to run.

I turned and knocked over a small stool. The noise ricocheted off the walls. It was so loud it made me realise how silent I'd been keeping. A noise in a dark corner inflamed my already heightened nervous system. I flashed my torch and caught a flicker in the air between me and the wall, just for a second. I needed to get out. The building was playing tricks on my brain.

Something slammed into me from behind. My torch clattered to the ground and smashed. I launched myself at the stairs. A blistering pain made me cry out as a piece of broken bottle stabbed into my foot. I fell backwards, hit my head on the wall and knocked myself out.

I woke up in darkness. My head was pounding and bewilderment fogged my brain. I felt around for my bag and found my phone. I shined the dim screen light about me. It barely pierced the darkness, but it was enough; I was back upstairs in the main body of the church. The crypt door was shut. I made to stand up and searing pain exploded up from my foot. I sat back down and listened intently. I was alone. I looked at my phone for the time. Nearly midnight. I'd been out for hours; missed my gig.

I looked at the crypt door again, and noticed two thin parallel lines stretching from the door to my heels. Someone had dragged my upstairs. I left as quickly as my injuries allowed.

The rest of the night is less clear. I was losing blood from my foot and I passed out more than once on the way back to my digs. I vaguely recall an argument with the father about my late return, but then there is another gap in my memory. In the morning I left as soon as it was light and headed home. But there remains something nagging about that night. Something I saw before falling asleep . . .

In the familiar surroundings of my flat things seemed normal again, and I felt sheepish about my overreaction. Looking back it was clear that I had filled any gap in my recollection with the worst-case scenario. Obviously I had taken myself upstairs in the church. The mood of the place was making me invent fanciful notions.

After I had cleared my inbox and squared things with the promoter of my missed gig, I emailed my friend Alex – an occult scholar – my pictures of the graffiti. He responded immediately.

From: Alex Cummins (bellweather@mail-o-serve.co.uk)
Sent: 04 October 2009
To: Andrew O'Neill (destructo9000@netmail.co.uk)

WHERE THE FUCK DID YOU FIND THIS?!
This is like the Rosetta stone or some shit! Some of it is Sumerian, then there's Hebrew, some of it is Enochian. No idea what the rest is. I've never seen those characters before. Let me do some digging.

I told him about the church and the rest of the graffiti. Over the next couple of days Alex asked more and more questions. Which wall was the East? What time of night was it? Had I experienced anything unusual? I was amazed he was taking it so seriously, and I was still hesitant to tell him the details of my night. I felt silly

Alex decided he had to visit the church. I gave him directions (it didn't appear on Google Maps) and I told him to stay in the B&B:

You HAVE to stay there. It's like a Tom Waits song

come to life! The church is just down the road – turn
left out the hotel and follow the road round. For some
reason it's not on Google Maps. I hope it's all still there!

He took lights and a proper camera and recorded everything.
A lot was new since my visit:

From: Alex Cummins (bell_weather@mailserve.co.uk)
Sent: 05 November 2008
To: Andrew O'Neill (destructo9000@netmail.co.uk)

The graffiti shows four separate stages of development.
They start out as just teenage heavy metal stuff like pen-
tagrams and even the word SLAYER (!) But then they
get more and more sophisticated, with the Sumerian
mixing in with Hebrew (which is an odd fit) and then
the Enochian, which is the magical language of angels
revealed by John Dee and Edward Kelly in the 16th
century. The final one was tricky to decode, but apparently VERY similar characters have appeared in sites
in Denmark and Norway – on the coast too. So clearly
there's a local cult who are using the vault for rituals,
and they have made contact with something which is
then guiding their ritual work. This is so awesome.

Oh, and a friend-of-a-friend in New York has been
working on this material too. Apparently these characters only started appearing in the last two years, along
coastlines bordering the North Sea. And she has having
a crack at translation. I can't wait! (We are getting on
VERY well!)

The b&b is amazing! It's a proper time capsule. The two dudes who run it are totally from the past! There's some serious psychogeography to be done on this whole place. It feels so oppressive.

Seriously mate, thank you for putting me on to this. This is the only channelled, structured magickal practise we've seen in the last century. There aren't people reading books and re-enacting what a bunch of Victorians were doing. This is living magick. They are in touch with sentient beings and the sentient beings are directing their practise. This is like Cefalu and the Secret Chiefs and Dee and Kelly's angels all rolled into one and it's happening NOW!

Oh, and I found a quarry where they filmed loads of Doctor Who! I can hear the blasting from my room! Going to go and have a look tomorrow!

Clearly the place was getting into Alex's imagination too. I had managed to forget his actual belief in magic (or magicK as he always wrote it). My loose interest in the subject was always at odds with what I always felt was a credulity on his part. Sure enough, the next email had a completely different tone.

I did a working in the church. Something happened. I can't really explain it. Ever since, it has been with me. Clawing at my insides and waking me from terrible dreams. I have had sleep paralysis three times in as many days and the strain is getting to me.

Sending him this stuff has been a mistake. Now I was worried. I offered to join him.

> No. Don't. And whatever happens, I want you to know that it's not your fault. It won't be your fault.

After that I didn't hear from him for a few days and I was sick with worry. I had feverish dreams about the church, and woke up deeply troubled. His phone was going straight to voice-mail. I rang the bed and breakfast, but they denied he was ever there.

The last email from him was desperate and terrifying.

> From: Alex Cummins (bell_weather@mailserve.co.uk)
> Sent: 05 November 2008
> To: Andrew O'Neill (destructo9000@netmail.co.uk)
>
> Andrew
>
> I don't know if this will even get to you. My email has been hacked and all my messages to you have been deleted. I had to use the computer in the B&B and I think they somehow got my password. They are in on it. Everyone here is in on it. And I think it goes deeper. I can't go to the police. I think it might even go up as far as government. I dunno. I know I sound paranoid. I feel paranoid.
>
> They are preparing for something. Something is coming up from the sea. Through the church somehow. They

are opening up a gateway to let something through.
Something ancient. I have to stop them. FUCK. This is
a bad idea even emailing you.

The graffiti is a warning and a calendar, and it is happening TONIGHT. I don't know if there's anything
I can do to stop it but I am going to try. You will
hear some fucked up shit. They will spin this as the
act of a lunatic. But I know you felt something in that
church. It's been growing ever since I got here. Demons
and Satan and Hell are all REAL but they are so much
more huge and terrifying than any anthropomorphised
version. They are nothing like us. They exist at a different scale. We are ants. We are nothing. They are glorious and they are beyond good or evil and they are inside
all of us. They are inside me. My skin crackles with electricity and my eyesight is keen. I now know that human
life is a distraction. The skulls crack and the bones rot
and yet it all continues. We will all die, Andrew. I will
die.

There is nothing more. Nothing but the blackness and
the glory of death.

⁂

The first thing I saw on the news was the explosion. The
church was destroyed by dynamite stolen from the local
quarry. In the rubble were five bodies. The rector had suffered a massive head injury. It is unclear whether it happened
in the explosion or before. Four teenagers from a local care

home were dug out of the vault. They were wearing robes and seemed to have been in the middle of a rite.

The father and son from the bed and breakfast were found brutally murdered, their heads severed virtually from their shoulders.

A full excavation on the destroyed building some months later found that a long tunnel had been dug from the crypt floor down to the cliff face, leading directly beneath the sea.

I helped the police as much as I could. I was initially under suspicioun, but let go after I turned over my communications to the police.

Alex's body washed up three weeks after his last email, three miles down the coast. His eyes were missing and elaborate symbols had been carved into his skin.

Whether something really was to happen on that stretch of coastline I will never know. Did Alex really prevent something terrible by killing those men, or was he simply sent mad through the delusions brought about by that cold, dark vault?

All I know is that I can't walk along a cliff face without shivering, looking into the sea without feeling a cold dread.

And I no longer visit village churches.

KIRI PRITCHARD-MCLEAN

THE MAN MADE
OF WORMS

HARLEY HAD BEEN scared of the dark for years. He'd try his hardest to fall asleep as quickly as possible, humming lullabies to himself, counting sheep, holding his breath till he passed out; he'd tried it all. Eventually he'd drop off but things weren't much better in the land of nod because he'd dream of his dad and when he woke up, he'd remember that his dad had been gone for years now. So, Harley would be left in the dark. Just him and his thoughts. Well, nearly just him. You see, things hide in the dark. All sorts of things hide in the shadows and creaks of a dark room, but some things don't bother hiding in the dark at all. The man made of worms never hid. The man made of worms would just stand in the corner of the room, mumbling like a drunk uncle at a wedding. Harley could hear the worms moving under his tatty jacket, squeaking against each other and throbbing their wet bodies into a human shape. Lots of people would think that would be scary, but when it's just you and your mum, you get tough, and Harley was especially tough. What's a little bed wetting between you and your mum anyway? Harley learned pretty quickly that if you gave the man made of worms what we

73

wanted he'd do the same for you. Harley didn't quite crack it straight away; in the beginning he'd spent a whole day collecting really nice dark, moist soil to offer to the man made of worms. He managed to fill a whole pillowcase full of the stuff and dragged it into his bedroom while his mum had locked herself inside the bathroom again. He hated the smell. Harley thought that's what it would smell like if you were buried alive and that, next to popping candy, was one of Harley's biggest fears. Popping candy might seem like a weird one, but think it through, why does it need to fight back if it's not a living animal? It's definitely alive and Harley wouldn't be a part of that. Harley thought that soil was a great offering, especially as all he wanted was a bit for his remote control car that had broken. But, the man made of worms didn't want soil, particular that which had been gathered indiscriminately from next door's garden. There was a bare minimum of two cat shits in there. The man made of worms told Harley what he really wanted: he wanted something the boy owned: "Not just anything either," he wheezed. It had to be something that was valuable to Harley. That night he left his biggest conker in the corner of the room the man made of worms appeared in. He'd had that conker for three autumns now and his dad had helped him bake it in vinegar, but he just wanted his car to work again. There's no point having a conker to play with when no one at school will play with you anymore. Harley told himself it's because he always beat them, but he knew that wasn't the truth. He knew that since his dad left, Mum had fallen behind on the washing and Harley could smell his own jumper, even when it was shut inside his cupboard. The other kids called Harley smelly and they were right.

Harley didn't see the man made of worms or even hear him the night he came for the conker, but when he woke in the morning not only was the broken part gone, the whole car had been upgraded and was now better than everyone else's at school. If they came near him they'd have known that.

Soon Harley learnt that the more something meant to you, the better the thing you got back was. He wasn't a greedy boy though, he'd only ask when he really needed or wanted something. He knew that his friend, the man made of worms, could be very useful indeed so it was best not to take advantage of his good nature. Nobody's perfect though and there was that one time that Harley had asked for a Kinder Egg: that wasn't a need or a really want; at best that was a whim.

Sometimes you just crave one though, don't you? Probably not worth giving up his best Batman for, but he didn't know the toy would be one of those pre-made ones, did he?

The air got colder, Harley's days were shorter but just as lonely and the man made of worms hadn't visited for a while now. The worms always slowed down in the colder weather so he found it difficult to speak; the worms that pushed his face and mouth into the right positions to form words were too slow and it made very hard to understand. Harley thinks he was embarrassed about this so hid away. Christmas was coming and Harley wanted to give his mum a present. She hadn't smiled without Dad and he couldn't remember what her eyes looked like without red edges around them. He knew that his mum had got him a good present because he had seen her sneaking into the spare room to check on it. It was in a dark green box on top of the wardrobe and Harley just knew it was going to be great, she was brilliant at getting presents. Except the year he got that Cher costume; he'd asked for a "Thor costume". Harley learnt a valuable lesson about handwriting there. Silver lining, he won the school talent contest with his rendition of 'Believe'. So, one night when Harley was lying awake thinking about what he could get his mum, the man made of worms turned up. "You've been awfully good this year," he slurred, in his voice that sounded like air escaping from a tight space. "If you could have anything from me, what would you wish for?"

Harley didn't even pause, "I'd have my dad back and he could bring Mum's smile with him." The man made of worms was quiet; Harley couldn't even hear those squidgy earthworms pressing against one another. It went so quiet in his room that Harley slipped into a deep sleep and dreamt that he and his mum were able to fly and they visited France. No one could understand them and they went hungry and had to sleep in a barn. Harley learnt a valuable lesson about languages there. Harley woke up, he'd slept in. Well, sort of. It was 7.21am but it was Christmas Eve and it was rare Harley made it past 5am in previous years. Mum wasn't up yet so he decided to head downstairs and finish the card he'd secretly been making for her; if he bumped into Santa Claus, no problem. He would pretend he hadn't seen him and just get on with it. Just like he had when his mum had taken all those pills and made herself sick. Push it down, get on with your day. That's how you do it.

Harley wished he had a better present for his mum, he'd love to see her smile again. She had one wonky tooth you could only see when she really smiled and Harley missed it. Just as he was adding the last cotton wool ball he heard a voice behind him: "What, no glitter? Your Mum loves anything sparkly." Harley turned around and there was his dad, sat in his chair, just as he remembered him. A baggy T-shirt, even baggier boxers, complete with errant testicle protruding. He flung his arms around him and couldn't wait to show his mum. She was going to shout and then laugh and then cry and then they'd all laugh and all cry together and he'd sit between them on the sofa all day watching cartoons or whatever; he'd be happy that they're both here.

"It's Christmas Eve, you get to open one present, what's it going to be, Harl?" asked his dad. Harley knew exactly what he wanted to open: the dark green box. He ran upstairs, three at a time, shouting for his mum. She loved having a lie-in, she'd be in bed when Harley got himself ready for school and sometimes he'd get home and she'd still be having a lie-in! She had to see this though! What a brilliant present he'd got her, "Well done, Harley," he thought to himself. He pushed a chair against the cupboard in the spare room and jumped up. On tiptoes he slid the dark green box down from its dusty perch and plonked himself down with the box on his lap. He wanted to wait till Mum was up, but something made him open the lid of the heavy box anyway. His dad was standing in the doorway with the kind of smile you have when you know something no one else does. Harley saw the same smile in his own reflection in a lift mirror as he sneaked out a fart two weeks ago while shopping. The lid popped off and inside, staring back was nothing but gritty, grey ash. He looked at his dad, he must have got the wrong box. "Muuuuuum, I've opened the wrong box, I'm sorry. I don't know what this is."

'Your mum isn't here." His Dad smiled. "You didn't think I'd let you make a wish without taking anything for myself, did you?" Harley didn't understand, he just stared at his dad's stretched smile. As a worm wriggled out of his dad's T-shirt and plopped onto the carpet below he realised what was in the box: it was Dad. Now it's just Harley and the man made of worms and Harley is too scared to wish for a way out.

TO DO

ON AUGUST 5TH 2015 *Edgar P. Frampton brutally murdered Charles Weaver at his luxurious home in Gumley, Northamptonshire. The night prior to the murder both men coincidentally made a To Do list for the following day. What follows are those To Do lists.*

1. Morning prayer

one. Meditate. Focus on him. Visualise Mr Weaver's face as it looks now and as it will look when you have finished this list. Step into his soul, feel what he feels and what he will feel the moment he accepts and embraces The End. Breathe. Then watch an episode of Malcolm in the Middle.

2. Shower

two. Bathe. Use lavender bath salts so you will smell like Mr Weaver. This will mask your scent once inside his home and it will aid you in becoming him. View this bath as a baptism, you are reborn in his likeness. Remember to wipe the sides of the bath as the water drains to avoid leaving dirty waterline marks.

3. Breakfast (bircher muesli and sliced apple)

three. Eat bircher muesli with an apple (sliced). Dissect the apple with the knife you took from Mrs Gibson's home. Remember Mrs Gibson and how she felt which in turn is how you felt also, how you shared the same heart, the same eyes, the same euphoria as The End engulfed her. Drink something that goes well with bircher muesli, perhaps grapefruit juice, perhaps Irn Bru.

4. Feed Flapjack

four. Watch from the study window as Mr Weaver feeds his beloved cat. Remember sneaking into his house the night before and poisoning the cat meat with hemlock, enabling Mr Weaver to also push a life into Nothingness, bringing the two of you closer than he realises, at least for now. Watch as he delights in his cat's demise, as he experiences the glee of witnessing the final breaths of another. Then feed your own cat and make sure the food is not poisoned.

5. Get dressed (the suit you wore to the UK Excellence Awards)

five. Put on Bumblebee Onsie. Wear nothing underneath. Pretend to be a busy bumble making love to flowers that impersonate lady bumbles in order to trick the bumbles into helping the flowers breed. Put on mask of Bo-Jo. Bo-Jo stands for Boris Johnson. Alexander Boris de Pfeffel Johnson. The Mayor of all London. Be the Mayor. Bee the Mayor. The Bee Mayor. Mayor Bee. Mayor of the bumbles. Fuck the flowers of London. You are a Tory Bumble. Bo-Jo and the Boris Bikes.

Eton and Oxford and The Bullingdon Club. The BEEingdon Club. The Tory Bumble killed waspy Ken Livingston with his stinger in the elections, stung by the Tory Bumble. In his student years he smoked the Mary Jane, puffed the cheeb, blazed jays, toked blunts. Sleepy, fat Tory Bumble. The munchies.

6. Watch video of Matthew's wedding

six. Allow yourself into Mr Weaver's house via the backdoor using the keys he gave you when you housesat for him that time. Buzz into his kitchen like a little Tory bumble. Help yourself to a handful of cutlery from his cutlery drawer. If there is honey in his cupboards then smear it over the Bo-Jo mask, sticky bumble honey all over. Buzz into the ironing board cupboard and close the door after you. Be alone with the ironing board.

Wank(?)

7. Do the ironing

seven. Make whimpering sounds from within the ironing board cupboard. The same sounds Mr Singh made. The whimpers will attract Mr Weaver. As soon as he opens the cupboard, lunge at him with the handful of cutlery, penetrating his gloopy stomach. Maybe shout "Tory Bumble" as he collapses onto his back and jump up and down like a happy bee. Do not let him go to The End just yet, leave cutlery in stomach, carry him upstairs, take pleasure in his moans and groans. Tell him how beautiful he sounds.

8. Phone dad. Make things right.

eight. Lay Mr Weaver on his massive bed. Take photos of him using his own camera phone. The passcode is 1982, the year of his son Matthew's birth. Click! Click! You don't need to wind it on because it's a clever computer. Post photos on his social media, be Mr Weaver, tell people how much fun this is, what a great time you're having now your friend is here. Unblock yourself from his facebook and twitter. Read any comments posted on the new photos out loud to Mr Weaver, do funny voices for all the different people. Maybe a funny walk for each character too. Become them all. Show him that you are everybody. Update him on any 'likes' or 'favourites' or 'retweets' or 'shares'. Jump up and down on the bed and tell him "it's all about online presence baby" over and over again and slap him across the face a lot. Think of a hashtag.

9. Donate £10,000 to Unicef

nine. Tell Mr Weaver not to move, don't shout, whisper. Buzz over to his study and grab the shiny flask of whiskey from his big desk. Buzz back to the bedroom. Ask Mr Weaver if he missed you. Open the whiskey and offer him "a tipple" then throw the contents all over the cutlery in his belly. Shake it out until it's empty. Then put on a Scottish accent and sing "You take the high road and I'll take the low road" while he dances with glee on the bed. Check social media to see how the new pics are getting on, block any haters, don't get involved in arguments they're only trying to get a rise out of you. Read out comments to Mr Weaver in a funny voice again.

10. Pop in on Mrs Simm, help with anything you can (housework, medication etc)

ten. Flip Mr Weaver over onto his front, climb onto his back, straddling his form. Push his head into the mattress with both hands. Deep, deep, deep into bed. Feel his skull in your bumble paws. Ride him as he squirms as he becomes a marvellous bucking bronco. Feel the panic flow through him and into you where it is recycled and leaves your body as joy. Tell him not to say thank you, tell him that it's your pleasure. Tell Mr Weaver how much you loved housesitting for him that time. How you would sit naked in each room and picture this moment, how when he returned and gave you some fudge to say thanks you ate all the fudge as soon as you got home then made yourself sick into the toilet and didn't flush the toilet for a week so you could look at the sick every day and remember how much you loved housesitting for him and how you couldn't wait to push his head into the mattress. Feel Mr Weaver's body slow down as the life within him begins to retire, try to imagine what his thoughts are as he accepts his gorgeous death. He is a flower and you are the Tory Bumble, his pollen covers you and he is covered in your love. As he gives in and finally slips into The End lay on top of him, matching his positioning, limb for limb, digit for digit, close your eyes and become one. Hold your breath, think of nothing, be Mr Weaver.

11. Give talk at St Barnabas Sixth Form about business ethics

eleven. Get completely naked. Shed the fuzzy wuzzy skin of the Tory Bumble. The sweet Tory Bumble must rest after all the good work it has done. Mayor of the Bumbles, Mayor of the buzzy Bees, you have served your fuzzy buzzy people well. Once naked, look at your tiny penis in the wardrobe mirror, study the birthmark on your balls, observe your concave chest, examine your spotty thighs. Notice that you are perfect. Take a photo of your tiny penis (called a dick pic) and post it on Mr Weaver's facebook. 'Like' the photo yourself to get the ball rolling. Stare at your reflection some more. Take five. Talk to Mr Weaver about the day so far, what he's enjoyed, what could've been better. Don't take his responses personally. Look at your naked body in the mirror again and shave your armpits in Mr Weaver's bedroom using his aqua marine razor from the bathroom. Stare at your naked body again this time with your arms raised in the air and see if you look like a different person. Talk like Marilyn Monroe in the mirror, put on a voice. Sing "Happy Birthday Mr Weaver" even though it's not Mr Weaver's birthday, it'll be a funny joke. Pretend to be Marilyn Monroe getting murdered by the mafia sent by Frank Sinatra, Old Blue Eyes, Marilyn Monroe begging the Godfather, begging Al Pacino. Pretend to be Al Pacino and sing "Happy Birthday Mr Weaver" in his voice, you are Al Pacino standing over an air vent with his skirt blowing up and showing his vagina. Check facebook to see how people are responding to the dick pic. Block the haters.

12. Offer to help St Barnabas rebuild their library with a generous financial contribution

twelve. Wank again(?)

13. Help paint the local youth centre

thirteen. Allow yourself into the garden shed using the keys Mr Weaver gave you when you housesat for him that time. Help yourself to the really cool hacksaw, the red one that he keeps in a plantpot. Tidy the shed. Kill at the cobwebs. Padlock the door behind you and spit in the ugly garden. Walk round the entire garden spitting. Ugly, ugly, ugly, stupid garden of shit. Then try and kick one of the fish while it's still in the pond. Fuck you, fish.

14. Have lunch at youth centre cafe

fourteen. Eat a lunch in Mr Weaver's dining room. Don't know what to eat yet, depends on what he's got in. If the fridge is bare then order a pizza. Frank's Pizza, best pizza in town, all the toppings your heart could ever desire, stone baked, proper stone bake oven, proper Italian pizza chefs, when it's your birthday they put pizza dough on your head and everyone has a laugh and you're meant to take it off but i left the restaurant with it on my head still and my parents made fun of me but I didn't care because I had been to Frank's Pizza for my birthday. Order Frank's Seafood Special Pizza and when you eat it shout "mama mia!" sometimes in an Italian voice. Maybe Mr Weaver will have duck pate in the fridge and you can eat the duck pate. When you eat the duck pate shout "mama mia!" in an Italian voice. Drink a peppermint tea with your lunch, leave the bag in, notice how the flavour changes as you drink like you've got a different drink every time. Remember when Mr Weaver told you never to leave the bag in. His pudgy little face when he told you never to leave the bag in. His bushy eyebrows and his long ears telling you that 'one' must remove the bag. Telling another person how to drink their peppermint tea. It's no way to conduct yourself. He didn't understand personal preference but that is what life's about is different people being different and being the same as each other at the same time and I knew, I knew I had to teach him about how we are all different by showing him that we are the same, we all get the pizza dough on our head for our birthday but we don't have to wear it the same Mr Weaver.

I ALWAYS LEAVE THE BAG IN.

I ALWAYS LEAVE THE BAG IN.

YOU DRINK YOUR TEA AND I DRINK MY TEA.

MY BAG IS IN.

ALWAYS.

BAG OF PEPPERMINT TEA IN THE CUP.

PEPPER TEA.

MINT TEA.

PEPPERMINT TEA.

IN.

THANK YOU.

Sit there in Mr Weaver's dining room drink your peppermint tea with the bag in different drink every time and gargle with it as it cools down and shout "mama mia!" sometimes and then he will learn, he will learn once and for all. Then stop being naked and put the onesie back on.

15. Go for a long walk along the canal and think of mum

fifteen. Hacksaw Mr Weaver's head off. Time it and try and beat your PB which was Mr Fitzgerald in just 05:12:44 (great going!) Once the head is off, rinse it in the shower so Mr

Weaver looks sparkly clean! Put the Bo-Jo (Boris Johnson, Alexander Boris de Pfeffel Johnson, Mayor of London, born in New York City) mask on Mr Weaver's dead severed head and carry it outside into the garden then walk into the house and take the new Bo-Jo Head on the exact route you took when you entered the house so Mr Weaver knows how it felt. Find a fun way of saying "Bo-Jo Head" out loud, maybe with a bassy voice or a froggy voice. Take Bo-Jo Head into the living room and turn on the home entertainment system. Play "Hey Ya!" by Outkast track 9 on the 2003 album "The Love Below", part of double album "Speakerboxxx/The Love Below" when Big Boi aka Sir Lucious Leftfoot and Andre 3000 aka Benjamin Andre did two separate albums and then released them together as a double album. The album is in Mr Weaver's CD collection, you left it there when housesitting especially for this moment. Play it at a loud volume (23-27) Dance with Bo-Jo Head.

My baby goat mex surround because she
loves miso and this I know fo sho
But does she really wanna widda emphysema wok owl dart doe.
Don't try to fight the feeling coz the fought alone is killing
me right now (sing into the eyes of the Bo-Jo Head.)
Thank GOD foam I'm undead foster ting too
together cause weed own note howl.
(Do hand claps with your right hand
and the Bo-Jo Head's face).
HE-EY YA! HEEEEEY YA!
Hey Fellas!
Yeah?
What's cooler than being cool?
I scold!

I can't hear ya ice head what's school urban bee ink coo?
I scold!
Oh white oh white oh white oh white oh white ok no ladies!
Yeah?
I'm gonna harvest thinned downing just a fuse second
Now dote halve me brake dick thinned down fawn huffing.
Eye wanna sea Ewan orb adders beehive yeah
Lens me sun sugar
I AM YOUR NEIGHBOUR.
Shake it like her pole or old pitcher.

Fuck Coldplay.

16. Visit mum's grave. Pay respects.

sixteen. Get off with the Bo-Jo Head, really go for it.

17. Watch the sunset from on top of the old hill

seventeen. Place the Bo-Jo Head on the window sill looking out at the passers-by so everyone can see Mr Weaver. Walk into the ugly garden and shout at the sun as it sets. Call it a quitter, tell it to get stuffed, tell it to swivel. Try and kick one of the fish in the pond.

18. Make your way home via your childhood home, think about how far you've come

eighteen. Take the long way home in bumble bee onesie in the dark. Go and look at the house where you helped Mr Robinson find The End and think about how far you've come.

19. Get home. Lock up. Whisky.

nineteen. Get home. Watch Malcolm in the Middle. Frankie Muniz, Bryan Cranston, Jane Kaczmarek. Laugh at the situations they are in and how none of them realise that one day they'll slip into The End. Eat dry cereal with your hands. Make a prank phone call to Radio Northampton Psychic Simon Show claiming you are a listener with a ghoul in your butt.

20. Run bath with lavender bath salts

twenty. Brush teeth. Floss. Check the house for murderers. Sleep under the bed . . .

21. Climb into hot bath with a razor. End it all. Sleep.

On August 6th 2015 at approximately 10:23am the body of Charles Weaver was found face down on his bed, a selection of kitchen cutlery embedded in his stomach. The cause of death was suffocation.

The body of Edgar P. Frampton was discovered in the garden, also face down, this time in the pond, totally naked, with a hacksaw embedded in his throat, it would appear he slipped while attempting to assault one of Charles Weaver's koi and fell on said hacksaw which, we believe, he was holding at the time. How the neighbours failed to notice a dead, nude stranger with a hacksaw in his throat until the following morning is beyond me.

It is believed that Edgar P. Frampton killed 17 people and is the infamous "Killer Bee." Before his To Do list was unearthed we had all mistaken the Boris Johnson mask for a Barney Rubble mask.

It is believed that the two men met when Edgar P. Frampton used to work at Charles Weaver's hugely successful restaurant Frank's Pizza as a supervisor. The pair began to socialise but fell out over a "bag in/bag out" argument that resulted in Frampton handing in his notice and vowing never to set foot in any branch of Frank's Pizza ever again. The restaurant chain has recently been in the news when it was revealed that they do not cook the pizzas in stone baked ovens and the "skilled Italian pizza chefs" are in fact underpaid teenagers. Charles Weaver put out a statement saying he was "utterly ashamed" and his behaviour was "virtually unforgivable."

In his will he divided his fortune up between his son, various youth organisations in the Borough, his cat Flapjack and an ex Frank's Pizza customer named Rita Simm who was once taken by surprise at the restaurant when an employee threw pizza dough onto her head, resulting in her attempting to flee but, blinded by the dough, fell down a steep flight of stairs. It was her birthday.

'Hey Ya!' was Number One on the Hot 100 for 9 weeks, reached Number One on the Rhythmic Top 40, and was Number One on the Norwegian Singles Chart for 7 weeks. It was nominated for Record of the Year at the 46th Grammy Awards but was beaten by Coldplay's 'Clocks'.

HIDE AND SEEK

HE WASN'T TRYING to kill himself, he was just putting far less effort into staying alive. He paid little attention to traffic or sell-by dates on dairy products. He paid even less attention to personal hygiene or any other forms of cleanliness. It had reached the point where even flies were deterred from vomiting on him. As with so many broken, stinking, vestiges of a human being, this was not how it had always been.

Martin had been distracted while shouting "27!"

The weather was too delightful. It was a summer's day that creates instant nostalgia. Every colour of nature, every ruffled picnic blanket, every sound of children playing felt so perfect that it was like a warm memory even as it happened. It had no frayed edges, no flies in the tonic or dog poo on the sole of the shoe, it was as delightful as tourist board sanctioned postcard.

Nevertheless, he was perturbed. The delight was fractured. The dog shit on his shoe was a game of hide and seek. It was the fifth game of the day, the final round. There was only the two of them. He didn't like letting his son out of his sight, but in such circumstances, it was a necessity. He was as paranoid as you were meant to be in the twenty-first century.

You can't let your children out of your sight anymore.

"22 . . . 23 . . . 24 . . . 25 . . . 26 . . ."

"Are you playing hide and seek?"

He was disturbed by a stranger.

"No. I am a grown man who comes to public areas to cover his eyes and count out loud. I'm surprised you haven't read about us in the tabloid newspapers. Lurid men in park lure children with their sightless counting by swings."

These were none of the things he said to the elderly man covered in corduroy and broken veins who felt it necessary to break his concentration from counting and peeking. He was not peeking because he needed to beat his child at games. He was not that sort of parent. He was happy enough in himself to allow his boy rein victorious at Monopoly, Cluedo or Sardines. Of course, that rarely happened: he was a child and so lacked the acumen to stockpile London streets and utilities wisely, but if his son somehow ended up with a hotel on Mayfair, he took his boy's victory with good grace. He preferred board games to things in the outside: easier to control the environment.

Hide and seek was making him nervous.

He had just enough imagination to imagine the worst. His mind had conjured up the image of his beaming son, squatting and believing himself victorious, but then tripping and sliding and ending up face down in the moat of this castle.

His ginger hair being nibbled by fish, the smiley face on his yellow T -hirt transmogrified into a howling mask of agony.

Fish probably don't nibble on hair, but that didn't get in the way of the grotesque dreamscape.

"Lovely day for games." A vague mist of unkempt gums projected from the old man's mouth.

"Yes, it is." He didn't want to reply; he wanted to concentrate and peek.

The man's wife was probably dead, he just wanted a conversation. This was very annoying, but he was English. He'd offer pleasantries and once the old man was out of earshot, he'd calm himself with a volley of muttered swearing and hate.

Could he start counting again?

The old man looked like he was expecting more.

"It's two-all at the moment, so this is the decider."

The old man had no ear for false jollity. He'd probably never get as far as a second sentence with anyone. He had approached that age where almost all conversations would be of false jollity or faux concern.

He went back to counting and peeking, but this distraction had left him at a loss.

"29 . . . 30 . . . 31 . . ."

"You've got to let them win . . . I remember with my boy . . . god rest his soul . . ."

Oh no, the old man had thrown a curveball. This wasn't fair.

Only the second sentence and he's tossed in the death of his son, what a devious bastard. He knew what he was doing.

"So much fun, hiding in the dunes of Studland."

Studland. Wasn't that where there was a naturist beach? Was the old man still on about hide and seek or had some urinary infection played with his mind leading to an awkward jolt of memory that had time shifted to his kiss-me-quick days of peeping from the Marram grass?

"Some days Rory would be hiding for hours. But I'd always

93

find him in the end. Innocent days, before it all turned to . . ."
The old man sniffled or sniffed, was it a cold or an emotion?

He had to say something. "I'm sorry to be so distracted,
but we have to be home soon, and I did promise him this one
last game."

A sniff . . . "probably lost at sea, we'll never know, if . . ."
Silence.

He went back to counting.

Through the crack between fingers he couldn't spy his son
anymore. He saw a woman in the distance wave at the old boy.

The old boy remained motionless, maybe hurt by the lack
of concern for his dead child.

Perhaps he should say one more thing, it was getting uneasy.
This was worse than the time Martin bumped into an old
school bully who insisted on telling him about his latest cancer.
He was already late for the cinema and his only memories of
this man were of schoolboy brutality and pinched skin. He was
waylaid by tumour stories long enough to miss the trailers. He
hated to miss the trailers. Once he got home, he hastily blocked
the dying bully on all the social media he could think of. As
he did so, the forced niceties and empty interest he had been
made to show on the pavement was converted into swearing
so voluble that he disturbed his wife's TV viewing.

"43 . . . 44 . . ."

The old man was still staring out him with rheumy eyes.
Damn, he was cornered into further conversation

"I suppose those memories of the dunes help through the
harder times of loss"

Oh Christ, he was being driven towards sentimentality.

This was not a good idea, the old man would open up and then he'd never get away.

"What helps what?" the old man replied curtly, as if no one had said anything until now.

"Hiding in the dunes . . . those sort of memories of your son must . . ."

The old man stood staring, the creases of confusion turning to anger.

"Whose son? What are you talking about? You could be reported, this is public property. I know people at the Forestry Commission! I can have you banned from woodland!"

He strode off in the direction of the woman who had been cawing for him. He could now see her face; it looked like a face that had spent the last few years apologising to strangers.

"48 . . . 49 . . . 50."

The old man was now being led away into the distance. Some children were playing boules while a picnicking parent used an empty bottle of rosé as a pillow.

As for traces of Alfie, there were none. Martin was surrounded by the last remnants of castle walls at the base of a motte and bailey. The motte, or was it the bailey, was out of bounds. That had been agreed. There was a well at the top and the steep and degraded sides were too hazardous for hijinks.

He turned towards the moat, hoping that might lure Alfie's eyes to peep over the wall and, if he spun around quickly enough, he'd catch a flash of copper hair and nail down his whereabouts.

He pretended to focus on the water, moved as if to suggest he was going in the opposite direction.

Three seconds, four seconds, then spin and . . . nothing, not a flint disturbed.

Would it be best to start at the nearest or furthest wall. Had Alfie double-backed and was he right now just metres away from him behind the hawthorns or that hollow, dead oak?

He was a merciless giggler, if he'd stayed stock still Alfie would give himself away with a helium chuckle. He must be further away: to tiptoe or to sprint around the moat?

He chose sprint, occasionally zigzagging through collapsed arches in case Alfie was still moving around; he rarely acknowledged the unwritten rule that you should stay in your first chosen cubby hole.

There he was! The back of Alfie's head was sighted in the tall grass. He slowed and drew breath, how he would surprise Alfie as he moved silently as a commando, carefully avoiding grit that would growl under his plimsolls. Would Alfie look around in time or did he have him in his grasp, he ducked down, the tiny hint of orange almost motionless. How thankful he was that Alfie had inherited his mother's hair, just exuberant enough to be a giveaway on a sunny day. Stifling his breath, he crouched. His legs were coiled and ready for release. On the cusp of cramp, and then he leapt. How disappointed Alfie would be.

He loudly booed a supermarket carrier bag. This was the disadvantage of his vibrant red hair, unlike blonde or brunette, it was a colour chosen to brand a supermarket. He didn't prod or poke it, it seemed reasonably clear that the bag had had its grocery content swapped for a dog's evacuation. He left it rustling. He would have laughed, but his stomach was tightening. His brain was beginning to recede from the frontal lobes into lower mammalian paranoia. The little finger on his right hand was flicking like a metronome. It had only been a few minutes, if that, but long enough for increased flashing images of tragedy. There were two voices in him now: "Don't be so silly" and "But what if?"

He knew nothing had happened. What could happen? Accidents have to happen to someone.

"Alfie. We're going to have to go home now. You've won. Alfie . . ."

He hoped he didn't look daft, seeming to shout at nothing.

Silly parent panic.

If that stupid old duffer hadn't distracted him, senile old cunt. That was a word that didn't come to mind often. A sign of panic.

Don't be silly.

He went over to the boule children and their mum or aunt or whatever she was. He would have found her attractive on a different day.

He smiled and chuckled a question out.

"Sorry to bother you, you haven't seen my son have you? And don't worry, I'm not cheating on the hide and seek, we've got to go and I don't think he heard me, and he does take his hide and seek very seriously."

The aunt or mother or friend smiled back at him and lifted he head from her glass pillow. "I'll ask the kids. Have you seen anyone hiding?"

"He's got ginger hair"

"That boy with ginger hair, have you seen him. His dad needs to get home."

The older boy, freckled and nine-ish, like Alfie, replied, "I think I saw him going up the motte."

So it was a motte.

"Thank you. Can I ask a favour? If you do see him pop up, can you ask him just to come over where you are here?"

"Sure."

He should have known he wouldn't follow the all the rules, he wanted to win, he'd be behind the bracken around the well. He lightly jogged around the motte; he could still surprise him. It was a relief to know he was up there, now the games could begin again.

He took three steps at a time, up in no time, home for tea.

He was higher than the bushes and foliage, he'd soon see him.

His final step was a jump, ready to surprise Alfie, and admonish him a little too for breaking the rules. He had started to let out a "boo!" that faded into nothing because there was nothing.

Nobody behind the bracken or the fallen walls.

Enough is enough.

"ALFIE!"

He could view the whole moat from here, behind most of the walls and remnants of sculleries.

"Don't be so silly" was silent, "What if?" was turning into "Something has happened, oh god, something really has happened." The build-up of all those hourly imaginings of many deaths that haunt from the moment a child is born was real now. That stupid, asking-for-trouble seed that was sown from the moment you know a child is coming to you. All those imagined miscarriages, measles, car accidents and cliff falls, all those rehearsed, destroying departures, were real now, and all that time wasted imaging them didn't make a blind bit of difference to now.

His melodrama reawakened "Don't be silly." It probably

hadn't even been five minutes. Maybe he'd thoughtlessly wandered off, even at 9 years old they can be bloody stupid.

An ice-cream van.

That will be it.

The lure of a '99 makes sanity depart, and he had given him two pounds earlier today.

He stayed at his vantage point scanning the distance. No ice-cream vans, all he could see was that moronic old man still tottering to a Fiat.

By now, the old man was wholly to blame for this situation. Did he know the trouble he was causing? He wanted to grab that walking stick and thrust it down the old goat's throat.

He ran down the steps, three at a go, four, then he tried five. The back of his shoe clipped the concrete, and all pretense of co-ordination fell apart. Fortunately, he was near the foot of the motte, but he had built up so much momentum that every bone that could meet flint and cement did meet flint and cement. Knees and teeth cracked, a sluice of blood and saliva welled up in his mouth. It came out in a splutter on the cusp of a vomit.

He was helped up by the aunt or mother or friend, what a fool he must look.

He drooled out what might have been an apology.

"I'll get the kit, we've got one in the hamper."

"No. No." His words were lost in his hands as they frantically wiped his face. "I can't see him anywhere, please, I've got to find him."

She told him to stay where he was, they would look, and she asked his boy's name.

A semblance of Alfie came out of his mess of a mouth. She reassured him and handed him the green zipped bag that contained anti-histamines, antiseptic creams and plasters with anthropomorphic lions on. The tissue in his own pocket was probably the best start; it was soon bloody and soaked. The adrenaline provided just enough false promise to hobble to the moat. He shouted Alfie over and over again. Would a child even come to a father that looked like this, like Frankenstein's first draft. The endless wiping didn't stem the flow, and soon he stood dripping, his hands at at his sides, his desperation petrifying.

They found nothing.

Barely thirty minutes from this thing beginning, this thing that was once a game, the police were called. With a photo from his phone, he alerted social media, that his boy was possibly lost in the streets. He didn't want to think it was anything more than a mistake, a wandering off that they'd laugh at every Christmas as he playfully tugged Alfie's hair and called him "scamp".

His wife was told as the stitches went into Martin's knee, yet they were both silent. She was pragmatic.

He told the nurses he was allergic to all forms of anesthetic. They thought this unlikely and promised there was always something. He didn't want anything. He said any form of anesthetic, even if it did not have an adverse effect physically, would make him so paranoid and confused that it really would be better just to put the needle straight into his flesh with the nerve ends horribly active. He was begging to feel the threading through flesh, but they assured him they had something that was as safe as safe could be. He hated their compassion. He stared at their sewing, concentrated on his skin in a bid to outthink the pharmaceuticals. He jerked his leg, hoping a sudden tear would usurp the anesthetic.

His fragmented mouth almost explained what had happened, and yet nothing had happened. It was just a game of hide and seek, but it was his fault, or rather that old man. He started to aggressively recall the distraction, the details of a naturist in the dunes, he was becoming disorientated, but he fought against going into shock, fearful that this would mean he wouldn't feel each horrible realisation. He didn't want to sleep, sleep was for cowards; it was running away from it all. He worried that sleep would create hope, if he woke up to a new day, his mind would think that something magical may have happened while he slept. But he knew it wouldn't have.

He hankered for enforced insomnia, but his body was weaker than he was, and they cheated him by putting something in his bloodstream.

He didn't know what dreams he had, but he woke up as without hope as he had gone to sleep. There was solace in the hopelessness, but no solace in the thoughts of what had become of Alfie. He didn't know why, but he was without any optimism at all, he just wanted to know what had become of him.

Every few minutes, a new vision of Alfie appeared. They dragged the moat within 48 hours. Because of the certainty that something terrible had happened, he hoped his body was found trapped in the weed; at least that would mean he hadn't been kidnapped by snuff moviemakers or people with foul desires and no humanity.

However much empathy you possess, he knew one could imagine what he felt like it. He wasn't even there anymore. The rapidity of the change in circumstances. Everything that has gone before is deleted. Every experience that has made you who you are is now worth nothing. You have been rebooted into a new world that is just a thick, screaming fog.

He expressed sadness when the police gave him the good news that he was certainly not dead in the water; this was the beginning of the end of his marriage. She had not imagined what he had, so saw his sadness at the boy's failure to drown as a strange brutality that must always have lain within him. It wasn't and it hadn't, but he could never explain, if things left his mind it would only make it all worse. He could no longer communicate.

This led to his wife's suspicion that maybe he'd done something to Alfie. She would never have thought this, but all was different now, and so was he. She didn't blame him on the day, but he had become so strange that he soon disgusted her.

The investigation led to nothing but transparent clearing of his name, though not before the newspapers had ensured he would carry a mark with him for the rest of his life, not that he cared. A lawyer, a former friend as Martin decided he could have no friends anymore, suggested he could get him some money from the tabloids. Why would he do that? He needed money for nothing because he was nothing, all was nothing.

It was diagnosed as shock. It wasn't shock, it was the death of everything. He didn't know why he couldn't imagine any possibilities apart from bleakness and darkness and torture.

Friends had offered stories that gave hope for the missing, but they didn't know what he knew, even though he knew nothing.

On the day of his death, he had almost been run over twice.

Sadly for him, both drivers were methodical when it came to having their brake discs checked.

He had wandered through a building site, but no health and safety rules were being flouted, and even without a hard hat, he reached the other side dusty but unscathed.

It had taken a visit to the worst pub in town. Stinking and wretched, and reminding the boozers that he might represent their Christmas Yet to Come. From the moment he walked in, he was hated. Hairs bristled on necks. Finding the man with the broadest arms and eldest tattoos, he took to spilling his drink and others. He was pitied briefly, but not long enough to stop his skull meeting the edge of the urinal brutally and on more than one occasion. Piss damp and lost, he was not killed by another's hand. He left the pub bleeding, but pub-punished within the rules of the White Lion. Staggering and broken, he tripped, struck his head on metal post, and fell into the canal. There was no sign of a struggle, because he didn't. In the water, he breathed deeply for the first time in months, his lungs soon flooded. He battled against the sense of composure he had been told could assail you in your last drowning moments, but that didn't stop a sudden burst of copper hair breaking through the green fog of the water, as if his boy was coming floating back to him. Their hands did not quite touch. He was not really there.

They all stood around the coffin, each one surprised by how many were there. Since Alfie had vanished two years ago, he had changed. Most eventually avoided him, there was no point in doing anything else. In death, they came to mourn the man they had known, not the one that had been born after that day at the castle. His wife had mourned his death some time ago, but she came to stand by the hole with the others. An old man and his wife stood a little back from the family. They had not known him, except for that day that changed it all. He had had a urinary infection and apparently behaved rather strangely, but was better now and had been moved by the story of a father and his loss. They had lost a son too, probably drowned. They were as solemn as is fit for a funeral. The old man was quite unaware of how often he had been cursed by Martin, until Martin had shifted all the hate back on to himself.

The vicar began his final speech of the day, and all looked down at the earth.

There was rustling, but their focus remained on the hole in the soil as was right and proper.

It sounded like a thud. Maybe the gravedigger shifting stones while waiting to fill in.

No one moved, except for the old man. His wife tried to hold him by the elbow, but his spirit was freer now he was in his 90s, and he loosed himself from the grip and walked behind the north transept. There, below the pine tree, was a feral mess of a young man. He'd fallen with a branch. He looked startled, then beamed. His ginger hair was a messy mop, his yellow T-shirt torn and soiled.

"Shhh, don't tell him I'm here, I'm hiding."

He pulled himself up, giggled squeakily, and ran off over the wall.

CUNNING

PETER REYNOLDS AWOKE *with a start. His heart was beating fast, his tongue peeled slowly from the roof of his mouth like a plaster being pulled from a wound, and the tiny bit of moisture that went down his throat as he painfully swallowed did nothing to slake its harsh aridity.*

He was momentarily dumbfounded – that split second between sleep and wakefulness requiring his consciousness to kick in. And when it did, it immediately flashed open wide in panic and he shook his head in order to find some clarity. His subconscious sensed a need to be alert – he could sleep again in a moment but first he had to know that he was safe. For that split-second of alarm he had no idea where he was. It was dark but the musty, stifled air suggested he was inside. In the distance the noise that woke him sounded again. A horn. Of course – the hunt. Must be day. And the darkness, the warmth, the muffled nature of the faraway sounds – he was inside. Somewhere. Hidden.

His eyes blinked and darted around the room, on sentry duty as his thoughts gathered fast. He espied a chink of light glinting with the snow of dust particles punching through a – what – shuttered window? Must be. A hunt – posh people. Gentry adding pomp and circumstance to decorate their bloodlust. Of course: he was in a country house.

Flashes of the night before started to come back to him. Snatches of sound and image, less palpable than the fear they punched into his stomach. He heard Giuseppe screaming behind him somewhere. Then there was Horace looking at him, terror and a kind of pleading in his eyes, barking at him to run.

The room wasn't empty. He saw something move in the shadows. He felt around him, his hands touching something. The smooth, dry edges and coldness to the touch suggested stone. The room was quiet apart from a heavy panting which Reynolds soon realised was his own. He forced himself to breathe slower, easier now that moisture had sluiced his mouth: refreshing but with the fetid smell of the spittle brewed by an uncomfortable night's sleep. His breath smelt like he imagined algae tasted. Not that he'd ever considered licking algae . . . He stopped these peculiar thoughts. Shook his head. Concentrated. The slower breathing calmed him, and he made himself piece together the night before . . .

It had been a job, something to assuage the boredom. He didn't need the money – he never needed the money. Reynolds was happy with a full belly and a dry bed. He never understood acquisitiveness. Years of thievery taught you that stuff was just stuff. One man's valuable heirloom was another's shiny bauble. A priceless artwork to you was an ugly daub to someone else. For Reynolds the thrill was the activity – the blood coursing through the veins, the adrenal flush, the danger of being caught. To him the success was in outwitting his opponents, not gaining a trinket. His employers paid him well but once you've got money the novelty wears off pretty quick – he wasn't one of those people who knew the difference between Champagne and Prosecco so it was all rather wasted on him. He had been known to pull off jobs and throw away what he had stolen: there was the occasion when he breached one of the most complex security systems ever created in order to secure himself a stamp collection. Some arsehole had spent more on a book of stamps than some people live on in a year. He made his contempt known by scattering them to the wind - tearing out the pages and leaving them ripped and flung around their fortress. The wanton destruction had left him feeling as virile as the accomplishment of getting his hands on the stuff in the first place.

Last night's job had been similar. He'd been contacted by a man, a collector. "Do you know what a Mahog is?" came the query. No, but that wasn't really the point - where was it, how difficult would it be to steal, and how much was being offered to do it? The reply, indicating that it was a pagan spirit, came with some kind of ancient screed to add a bit of mystical provenance. The twisted calligraphy ensured that Reynolds got the message:

> *The Mahog is the link between beast*
> *and man, man and earth.*
> *The Mahog punishes the wicked.*
> *The Mahog takes the shape of beast*
> *and man and both at once.*
> *He can be fish or fowl, man or monster, wood or stone.*
> *He is of the land and of the elements.*
> *He is of all shapes and none and makes shapes of men.*
> *The Mahog is ancient and awful.*
> *The Mahog makes men what they are.*

Not very nice then, obviously. "Only one effigy of it is known to exist, a small wooden carving dating back thousands of years, stored away in a private collection," said the message. Oh and at the bottom, "Carfax Manor House, Sussex, stored on a sealed wing, 35 grand plus expenses – half up front, half on completion of the job." Thanks, that's what he had wanted to know. Next time leave out the spooky stuff. A picture was provided – the ancientness of this artefact made it rare and therefore valuable: it wasn't desired by his employer because it was eye candy that's for sure. So it probably didn't matter that it was hideous, its grisly visage contorted so that it looked like Ena Sharples's cum face.

He'd recruited two assistants – Giuseppe was fat and dopey, his warty face only marginally less attractive than his limp, clammy handshake, but he was loyal and strong and did what he was told without question. He didn't say much nor move very fast: the only thing akin to a personality that he had was a vivid streak of green hair from the front of his fringe all around to the back. A lustrous whirl of unnatural colour totally at odds with his slothful demeanour and monosyllabic conversation. Pete had used Horace before too: a pain in the arse who needed to learn that not everything that had happened since 1965 was shit but he was good with old fashioned locks and – as burglars go – something of an artist. And Pete appreciated this sort of artistry. Horace was a tedious old git who still thought that the handlebar moustache and earring combo would overcome his more obvious shortcomings (notably the fact that he was Horace) and make him a hit with the ladies. He had yet to be a hit with the ladies and time was running out. Horace was a baggy eyed, sunken cheeked chain-smoking complaint generator who would win gold if moaning ever became an Olympic sport. He couldn't be more stuck in his ways if he'd dipped his boots in glue and pressed the pause button thirty years ago. He was the sort who saw everything old as good and everything different as bad. Whatever Horace had experienced growing up was worthwhile and anything he hadn't, wasn't. He even managed to turn the fact that he only ate pies into some sort of virtue. His unfailingly repetitious diatribes against Pete's vegetable-filled lunchbox or decision to drink sparkling water gave Reynolds the distinct impression that Horace genuinely thought that not having an eclectic palette was the equivalent of working down a mine. Still, it meant he was at home amongst all these old relics, and his knowledge – which he wore lighter than he did the class and geography of his background – came in extremely useful as they snuck around the mausoleum. Horace also knew when to keep his mouth shut about the work (which was always).

The job had appealed to Reynolds because there was high security to conquer. The latest electronic systems beautifully augmented a few old fashioned thick wooden doors and heavy metal locks. It was a teasing symbiosis of ancient and modern. The artefact they were after resided in a sealed wing of this old country house. That was another appealing element for Pete – he was stealing from the sort of people he despised. The huntin', shootin', fishin' brigade with more money than sense. So much money that they had some of their relics in a wing of the house no-one ever used. You know someone's got too much money if the stuff they don't use is worth more than what some people live off all their lives.

Not much scared Pete Reynolds. He was cautious, yeah, but that was what made him good. Cautious? Cunning. He knew when to wait and he knew when to run. But lying there in the dark a gust of cold air arched the skin on his spine.

His eyes were getting used to the dark. The stone thing he had felt was clearly a statue, looming over him. That movement in the corner? It was definitely something alive. It was small and had a slightly lolling gait, and as it briefly groped its way past a shard of moonlight he fancied that it was a frog or ... no, a toad. Not quite so streamlined as a frog, and more carbuncled. He thought it had a stripe of colour down its back, but before he could blink the oily shadows from his eyes it was out of sight again, but he could sense it was still there. So he knew where he was, he was in the relic room. What he didn't know was what to do. And he remembered, he remembered the primal fear he had felt.

It had been fear that had come suddenly in that dusty, dank room of musty cadavers and ancient things. There was something unsettling about the real, organic hair and skin being displayed. An odd idea – an array of corpses as interior decoration. No wonder they were hidden away in this wing of the house. In the darkness these shapes loomed unsettlingly. It wasn't that he believed in Gods and monsters but here, amongst stuffed creatures and jars of preserved remains and Maasai spears and all sorts of eclectic relics with the stench of death about them, the sudden shock to his system had caused the pang of acid reflux to bubble volcanically in his throat. This wasn't the sort of fear related to the job – not a siren or a security guard or the prospect of incarceration. That stuff was an adrenaline rush anyway: he buzzed off that. This was something that lurked in the back of his mind, that reminded him of dark windy nights as a child where a rattling tree branch against a window during a power cut was enough to convince his younger self that the dead were stalking the night in search of an innocent young soul to devour. He'd put away such childish thoughts years ago yet here he was, discomfited. Discomfited for the first time in 25 years of thievery *by his quarry*. By a piece of wood.

The Mahog.

This effigy had stared back at him malevolently when he came to it: a horned creature of nightmares, its face contorted in fury by only a few deft slices from a primitive whittling implement. On its torso were the clues to its lycanthropic nature – a claw sticking out incongruously from its chest, one leg a cloven hoof, the other some sort of taloned paw. It was as if embryonic mammal and fowl were bursting from its frame, a menagerie of different limbs jostling for supremacy in a grotesque parody of nature.

It wasn't the imagery that disturbed him as much as the history he knew was etched in every splinter, every welt, and every scratch of the aged artefact. The hands that wrought it were long dead and he wondered about them, holding it all those centuries ago. Hands like his, belonging to a man who had subsequently lived and died and looked through eyes just like Pete's and whose life was as palpable and real and important as Pete's was to him. It was the same feeling he got watching silent movies, knowing that all of those spectral, black and white figures – flitting about at an unnatural speed, their gestures and facial expressions rendered eerie by the flickering quality of the murky film print – were still people. People like him, who since they had been captured on film had got on with their lives and aged and died and were now remembered by no-one except as two-dimensional images. That bloke in that crowd scene, that funny gesticulating figure – he laughed and

cried, was born and died: he would have had the news broken
to him of a terminal illness, or felt the sudden shock of colli-
sion in a fatal car crash, or endured a tearful farewell from his
children at his hospital bedside as his life ebbed away. Every
one of those extras would have had their own story to tell, and
each one of those stories – as all men's do – would have ended
in death. That this thing in his hand was thousands of years
old didn't stop Pete from pondering about the consciousness
of the person who had etched the carvings into the wood he
now eyeballed.

It wasn't the smell of death in the room that had got him
thinking like this, rather it was the *air* of death. The silence. An
empty room is silent, sure, but this room, this wasn't empty.
What this room was filled with was actually an *absence* of
life. A palpable vacuum which had sucked the mortality from
these rigid figures or hand-made artefacts. The darkness didn't
help. These dead things illuminated by torchlight threw up
gloomy shadows which did spectral dances as they bounced
off walls and corners as different light beams intersected and
pummeled them. Giuseppe gave a sharp intake of breath to his
left. Reynolds followed the beam and his stomach lurched and
then a cold shiver wafted across his exposed neck as he saw
dead, bulbous eyes staring out from tiny heads: the hair, he
noticed, tied up in a bunch on top of the crown. These weren't
artworks: carved trinkets or kneaded clay. They were – had
been – people. They were shrunken heads. He'd seen pictures
of these things before and they had been unnerving enough
but here ... it felt sacrilegious. These heads they were looking
at were what once contained the consciousness of these poor
souls. Actual people were now, post mortem, interfered with
in order to render them as trophies. It wasn't the fact that they

looked wizened or mummified that gave them their aura of spookiness, it was the grotesque idea that their life had been extinguished as part of the process that had got them here, to the neglected museum of someone who was clearly the most grotesque sort of person imaginable.

But that's all that everything here was - a trinket. Part of a collection. An acquisition. A victory. These things weren't here to be admired or cherished. They were the spoils of conquest: the conqueror here not victorious through strength or virtue, but through money. It was then that Reynolds knew what he was going to do. He was pretty sure the others wouldn't stop him.

He called out to Horace. Find something - anything - flammable. Where was Giuseppe? He smoked so he'd definitely have the raw materials and everything was dry in here anyway so it wouldn't take long to initiate an inferno. Give these dead things the cremation they'd probably have opted for however many years ago their spirits parted from their bodies. Horace was uncommitted and happy to oblige. He picked up the Mahog and tossed it to Pete, reminding him that it was what they had come for. Where was Giuseppe? Pete hissed an urgent whisper and played his torchlight over the silhouettes sporadically blocking his way. There he was. He shined the light in his fat factotum's face. Giuseppe was scared. He wanted to go. Pete reassured him. That was going to happen, but first they just need to start a little fire. As the word entered his thoughts he felt an intense sharpness rip through the flesh in his hand. Was it hot, was it scratching? He couldn't tell - it was a searing pain, that was for sure, and it made him flinch. He looked down a saw that face staring back at him, its eyes momentarily flashing with colour - red like fire, crimson like blood, scarlet like anger. His breath caught in his mouth and he blinked and looked again. Nothing. The redness was probably just a trick of the light – the torch somehow exacerbating the natural cherry hue in the wood. He gave the thing to Giuseppe, telling him to hold it while he gave Horace a hand. Perhaps having a job to do would take the Giuseppe's fear away. Pete wouldn't be long anyway.

He called out to Horace. Nothing. When he found him he was just another immobile silhouette. He said his name again, tentatively.

"I can't move," the old bugger had said, his voice an octave higher, light with a trembling timbre. He turned round to face Pete, slowly, his body contorting from the waist as if his feet were stuck in clay. His face was white, strings of spittle stretching from the top to bottom as his mouth tried to twist and form words. "Run," he seemed to be trying to say. Run. Pete heard a cry – it was Guiseppe. Pete had remembered turning but his legs wouldn't move – the inky blackness closed in on him in slow motion and as he felt his legs turn to marsh-mallow; the familiar feelings gave him a snatched moment of hope that this might all be a dream . . .

That was it. Had it been a dream? Was he pissed somewhere and he'd imagined doing the job and it going awry and all sorts of weird things happening. But then again, wasn't he still in the room? He felt something brush his face, something with a clammy, cold carapace. He lurched back instinctively, somehow becoming entangled in the legs of the statue. He flailed as his limbs and joints painfully collided with the stone and in his panic he fell. His motion took him sideways rather than forwards or backwards, which surprised him in the brief moments he was able to consider the strange nature of his collapse. The statue came crashing down around him, clearly breaking into pieces as it hit the ground.

He blinked and realised what had made him flinch, because now it was in front of him, staring at his face. The toad. The large, slow-moving toad. Had he imagined that stripe? No, that green stripe along its back. A fat, lazy toad with a green stripe.

He felt sick. In panic he patted his way along the statue. He had already realised that there hadn't been a statue when they had entered the room. He snaked his way along the shattered remnants: a dislodged arm here, a limbless torso there. And in the darkness he came face to face with the atrophied thing. An ancient looking stone visage, its rictus expression frozen – a snap shot of a moment of fear, hewn into permanent solidity. From the look on the statue's face Pete could practically feel the goosebumps erupting like napalm up the spine of the poor bastard. Pete looked closer. It was an old face, an old face with sunken eyes and a handlebar moustache, never to move again, resistant to progress, solid against the passing of time . . .

The Magog makes men what they are.

Pete's heart started beating, he found himself moving, quickly along the floor amongst the feet of the static cadavers. He could now smell death and formaldehyde – an ever more powerful musk that clogged his nasal passages. A movement in the darkness. Was it? He stopped. Nothing. Shadows. Or the toad.

Cunning Pete felt the sudden gorge rise in his throat, the follicles all over his body erupted as a wave of panic swept over him, adrenaline coursing through his veins and dragging panic and primal fear along with it. He knew he had to run, he had to *get out of this place, out of this building. His legs kicked in and he moved – this was no dream. His movement was faster, slicker, his legs pounding the floor and propelling him out through the half open door which he jerked around easily. His tongue was out now, panting, panting, and thoughts of being Peter receded into the background as the drive to escape, to survive, to run and run and run overtook him and he bounded out through the open window and onto the still dewy grass. He barely had time to register the blinding ray of sun that momentarily checked his progress before he launched himself again into his run, drawn by instinct, the instinct to survive, the incitement to run. And he ran as fast as his legs would carry him. His four legs.*

And the hunting horn sounded in the distance.

A GHOST STORY

I LIKE TO listen to my own music performed. I can sit, entirely unknown, and bathe in the richness of it. Each movement reminds me of sitting at my little desk and letting it fly around and fill my head. It was good then, but it's momentous now. They don't play it perfectly, they never do. I'm proud. I always have been. None of those wonks I knew in Paris could hold a candle to my writing and they knew it. They were my friends and I would indulge the froth they'd come up with, but the true astonishment, the true genius, the true worth was my own.

I digress. Each night I sit in my spot, summoned up by the divine wonder of my orchestration and I watch those around me and I mostly feel on a cloud. Of course, there is the occasional oaf rustling their damned sweets. The old men using the dark and the comfort of the auditorium to snore away and the red-faced drunks there only for appearances. People who arrive after the first movement and dart in during my well-deserved applause. Children. Monsters trying to take photographs and steal my music with their hand-held devices. They all warrant scorn. But mostly, I feel at peace. I finally feel raised up to the level I deserve.

When I lived it was by no means the same. My life now

seems like one miserable and bitter little day, lived out in a garret and ending in the cholera hospital. A life spent with paupers and only meagre flashes of what I deserved. My friends were kind, but as their stars rose mine sat and hid. My music was locked away on the page, my own talent withered on the vine. Standing at the back of the finest halls in Paris I would hear their nonsense bewitching people. Then the humiliation of the long walk home, turning into the alleyway and up the stairs in the pitch dark, no money for a candle to write down my own, superior, works.

After I died there was a long silence.

We'd been going out six or seven months. Now I think, oh god he was always so weird. Like Adam had to be right about trivial things. He wouldn't let anything go. And he had his own orders for everything, like he'd sorted his wardrobe by colour but the colours were in order best (light blue) to worst (yellow) and you weren't allowed to put them in the wrong place. And he took me to see his dad, who was lovely, a few times, but after we went he would be so angry. But I thought, fuck it, he's alright, I've got nothing else going on. So I let him take me out. It got my mum off my case about being single and he was good at getting tickets for things.

So that night - it's just weird that night is so important now - so that night I now see he was really not on it, he was shivery and really intense, like twitchy. And he started mumbling during the show. The performance, the music, whatever, so I whispered at him to shut up and he doesn't and really glares at me, which was fucking chilling. And that goes on back and forth for a bit, so I say to him "you're embarrassing me" and I get up and go out to the corridor and I don't see

him but he's obviously followed me out there and he kind
of bundles me into the gents' toilet and quite quickly I lose
consciousness and that's that and I'm back at the start of the
night again, meeting him outside the bar on the terrace and
him hugging me too tightly, knocking my bag off my shoulder.
Us going in, sitting down. Bickering. Going back out to get
him a pint to try and placate him. The lights going down. The
same night every night.

The first time I came back was a shock. Wholly disorient-
ing. Like being awoken by a bucket of cold water. All at once
I stood facing an upright piano while a boy of nine or ten
punched it to pieces. Only gradually did I recognise the notes
as mine. Mangled but mine all the same. A grandfather clock
told me he practised at the same time each day. A cheap calendar that wobbled with every note told me he practised for
the best part of February 1919. He played straight from my
manuscript, and he did not improve with practice. Not at all.
He was clumsy and impatient, with fat little hands and a dirty
face but to me he seemed an angel.

The first day lasted only a few minutes. I was there, I was
gone, I was fast asleep. Only on the next day did I start to
look around me. On the third day I realised I could move a
little around the house, but not out of it. I recognised it as my
sister's place, though she was long gone. It was much changed
but the same, itself so dreamlike as to make me queasy. A photograph of her, horrible with old age, sat on their poky dresser.
I was delighted to find one of myself as a youth, holding a
violin. An imitation violin, in fact. From one of those booths at
a travelling circus. The choice was with the violin or dressed as
a chef next to an exploding vat of casserole and I thought the

119

former more suited to my disposition. My little sister's image beamed under a chef's hat alongside it. The boy was so like her, grubby and feral and full of mischief. I reckoned him to be her grandson and I hoped to catch a glimpse of his parents, but nobody ever troubled him. And just as quickly, the light was snuffed out.

Ten years passed though I experienced none of them. The boy had grown up to be a man with fat little hands and a dirty face, awkward in a starched shirt, sat next to me at a student recital while another strangled a ballad of mine. I had seen him lose the fight to it in rehearsal rooms for a week before. I'd seen him hum it on a trolley bus and while chopping up carrots. Any time my music came into the world, so did I. The thrill of it wore off once I realised how rarely I was being awoken, and in such measly circumstances. Not once in the nineteen thirties. A couple of times again in the university in the decades after. I remembered a night-train I once caught through the Alps. Too poor for a decent carriage I slept on a chair, my scarf and the window as a pillow. I was woken with a jolt, and hurried to get my things together and disembark only to realise we were in the middle of nowhere, in the middle of the night and a gang of boys was mocking me. My sole revenge was that I had nothing for them to steal.

And then. And then! I was 'discovered'. I was a vinyl recording, I learned. I was part of *The Lesser Composers of The Late 19th Century, A Mail-Order Record Compendium.* I would venture the very best part. The title turned my stomach of course, but I saw so much of the nineteen seventies that it more than made up for it: dinner parties where I played in the background and was debated and discussed. Late-night school pupils scribbling away as my music focussed and soothed them. Amorous couples, even. But best of all I saw people who wept because of what I had written. My heart swelled. One evening as I watched over a middle-aged gentleman who was rightly tearing up while listening to my great sonata on large ear-speakers, I became aware of a kind of sound pollution in the room next door. I glided through and saw an awful-looking vagrant floating over a youth with a similar recording-player. He jumped to the ceiling when he saw me, and it was so long since anyone had been able to see me that I did the same. We tried to speak but his French was terrible and his Hungarian, non-existent. His get-up was far more gory than mine and we looked a strange pair to each other, but to see and be seen was overwhelming to us both and for thirty or so minutes we stood close. At one point I hugged him.

I wouldn't have chosen this place of course, but yeah, on balance I'm glad to be here. I can imagine if it happened to you in a churchyard or a warehouse or something it'd be worse. At least there's always people here. And music. For a while I was stuck replaying it, night after night. I knew that it wasn't that same night, but it was like I was sleepwalking through it and I couldn't stop. I don't know how long that went on. Then once, as I was pleading with Adam to be quiet, as I always did, as I was saying I would go to the bar, as I always did, I felt something grab my shoulder. It was so odd, like being wrenched out of my skin. And such a shock, like it felt freezing and I was gasping for air. And then in front of me, after all that, there's just this old German man, dressed like he works in a novelty Christmas shop. And he stank of drink.

And then for the first time I could see the night I had been stuck in, replaying without me, with the night it must have actually been going on around it regardless. Once I saw an advert where they sped up a motorway, they filmed it for a week or whatever, and all of the cars were just a long string of lights but the central reservation just sat there. That's what I seemed like, whizzing about while the rest of the world got on with it. It was quite something.

I thought he was having a go but he just had one of those stern faces. We went out into the corridor and we tried to have a conversation in both languages. I told him I had two sisters and he said he liked British food. It wasn't a great success but we kept trying. I think he'd woken people up like that before, so he was quite reassuring. I know his music so he must be about in lots of places a lot of the time. I do know he's famous but I call him Wingnut. I don't think anyone else takes the piss out of him like I do so it took him a while not to get the hump about it. I see him about quite often and he's really alright, although I wouldn't say it to his face cause he is the most arrogant man, you have no idea.

I look out for him now, when someone's looking through a programme I'm thrilled when I see him coming up. I count the nights and we have a laugh. Sometimes we sit in the members' bar upstairs while the show's on. I feel like if anyone's a member then we are. He says hearing his music's nothing new to him now so he doesn't mind hanging out. We get a good couple of hours before it ends and he disappears. He told me that in France there's a man about my age who was poisoned by the Russians as he watched the opera. He's wearing a cape, apparently. I didn't know that music made people come back. I thought it was just murder.

I do not understand the twenty-first century but it amuses me. I will tell you a good anecdote: I was summoned to a room, god knows where. It is good to see the world but a little like reading over a stranger's shoulder to do it in this fashion. I look around to see a gentleman sat at his office chair, my music on a digital box next to him. He turns on his office machine and for a few seconds a little tune plays. Five notes, no more. The instant it starts a fellow appears, scruffily dressed, a bald head, a look of tortured harassment across his desperate face. I nod to him. He huffs at me. The jingle ends, and so does he. A telephone rings, another little melody. A pained wreck of a woman appears to see it through. He shuts his machine to answer it. The woman goes. He opens the machine as he talks and it sings again. My old friend is back. I laugh. This happens some five times while my music gently fills the background. At one point the three of us stand facing each other and I am the only one of us who enjoys the joke. I am the only one who enjoys the joke until a refrain from one of my lesser-known songs is chosen to advertise food for cats. For six weeks I was shaken and prodded and forced to watch a kitten knocking a metal pouch from a glass table.

Tonight I arrived to this delight of a concert hall in London to find that I will be summoned here for two weeks. A full retrospective of my work, no less, I learned from a woman's programme. '[One of] The [many] lost great romantic composer[s] of the 19th century'. I can't stop smiling. A full two weeks to play it all! All except 'the [less successful] summer song cycle'. Whoever made that decision is a philistine. Nevertheless, I feel warmed through as I sit amongst the crowd. People seem enraptured, they really do.

I was starting to get bored, if I'm honest. I took to hanging around in the ladies', staring at people through the mirror in the hope that they'd notice me. For what? I don't even know. I just fell into a bit of a funk. I overheard the front of house manager, who is a fucking jobsworth anyway, training a new member of staff. As she was walking her through she pointed at the gents' where it happened: "Don't go in there! It's haunted!" and the lad is like: "What? No!" and then she's all "Oh yes this guy, his girlfriend was having an affair and he found out and took revenge on her!" Not even fucking anywhere near, mate. Honestly my blood was boiling and I tried so hard to do something, but nothing, not one hair on her head was ruffled.

Then things got worse. I didn't realise Adam was here too. I found him in the library upstairs and I wasn't prepared for it. I was just looking around for poetry books. I watched the siege replaying for a bit, terrified. So he'd taken a hostage and the police had had to shoot him. The prick. And then slowly his face turns and he looks straight at me. Like a painting coming to life. And that moment our eyes meet it's like being stabbed, and I'm dragged back into that night again. I had to wait for Wingnut to pull me back out.

So it was kind of wonderful to see him yesterday. I wasn't looking forward to meeting him from his programme notes. "An altogether arrogant, unpleasant and sickly young man, he was despised by his peers in Paris and largely spurned by his family in Hungary. After the composition of his sonata, widely regarded as his best work, he succumbed to the cholera epidemic around him and was buried in a pauper's grave." I thought, "Oh great, he sounds cheery!" but when he showed up, he seemed nothing like that. I watched him appear as the

music got going. He noticed the crowd, looked down at a programme and then just lit up. He was beaming. He has hazel
eyes and his hair is almost black, and his face, it's just lovely.
He's a bit skinny but that's ok, and he dresses like he works in
a microbrewery, but it's for real. And watching him smile, it
just made me so happy. I don't think he knows I'm here. He's
not noticed me walking past, or staring. I've been staring. I
can't explain it, it's like I understand something, like I've got
something now that I didn't know I didn't have before.

A woman is here. At first I was confused by her; there was no
other music playing and she seemed to be deranged: giggling
and nervous and eyeing me strangely. I'd been so naïve that I
had thought there could be no other way to come back. And
for that way to be far worse than even my sad circumstance
was almost too much to bear. She is very beautiful, although
she seems to be dressed like a German schoolboy. The future
is a country I will never understand.

So I spoke to him. His English isn't great but he spoke in
French and what must be Hungarian, I guess. He's funny. I
think I scared him and after that first time I just pegged it
into the toilets. But seriously, every night we've been hanging
out and it's been so nice. He's a dork. I really like him.

I am watching her watching the spot where she said it started.
I know it still troubles her and it hurts me. A couple sat there
are putting on coats and shivering. She's standing about them,
frowning as they play on a mobile telephone.

So this couple sat where I was sat, deliberately. Just because they're morbid fuckers. I saw them sat there on Wikipedia. They weren't even listening to the music, and I know I'm biased, but it's beautiful. And I felt so angry and frustrated that I started crying. And then as quick as anything he's next to me and I don't even know how he managed it, but he lifted the phone up, smashed the screen and broke it. There was such a commotion that the ushers ran over. It was brilliant.

I am going to tell her that I love her and I am going to propose marriage to her. I do not know how this will work, but I am going to do it and I do not know how I know this, but I am going to kiss her and I know that it will change things for both of us, for the better, forever.

So he shows up and he's looking at me really weirdly, and I don't know what he's doing but he takes me onto the roof terrace and we can see the city all lit up around us. Properly romantic, and he starts speaking really earnestly, but honestly his English is so bad I just start laughing. I didn't notice Adam showing up. That prick shouting like he's going to kill him, as if he can hurt anyone now. And I'm trying to calm them down, but it just gets worse and worse. Even some old guy who wrote the jazz in the bar shows up and tries to intervene. It takes so long the music stops. And he goes. I didn't realise it was the last night. He goes and it's the last time.

JASON MANFORD

JESSICA'S FRIEND

THE LONG DRIVE to Keswick in the Lake District was picturesque, Steve had always said so; and on this still, calm evening, with the burnt-orange sun setting behind tree-covered hills, the landscape was on full charm offensive. On the rare occasions he and the family made the long trip up North, Steve felt it was always worth the time it took. Just as the hours of monotonous grey motorway started to take their toll, the roads would turn into long, winding country lanes. On both sides the eye was treated to lush emerald grass carpeting the peaks or huge silent lakes with only their vastness equaling their beauty.

When his wife Claire drove them, she'd take the motorway all the way up to Penrith and drive across the top of the Lakes, missing most of their splendour. Steve felt this sacrilege, preferring the 'scenic route', taking in the beauty and history of Kendal, passing the scattered yachts of the mighty Windermere – framed by the hills like a Turner painting – and then up through the sleepy town of Ambleside into Wordsworth's Grasmere. Each time they visited the poet's favourite town, where many of the buildings and roads are now named after him and his poetry, Steve would note the cottages, the quaint flowerbed-filled roads and the traditional shopfronts and quote the great man himself (often to a rolling of eyes from his wife and young daughter, Lucy). "Of that magnificent temple which doth bound," he would start in as grand a voice as he could muster. "One side of our whole vale with grandeur rare; Sweet garden-orchard, eminently fair, the loveliest spot that man hath ever found," to which Claire in her deadpan way would answer drily, "Well he would say that wouldn't he? He's got his own hotel and spa here." She always timed it as the car pulled away from the Wordsworth Hotel and Spa, and the family would giggle at this long-running joke between two people, very much in love.

"Why are we staying here for the whole weekend?" moaned Lucy from the backseat of the battered Fiat Punto as it pulled into the driveway of Coleridge House, an imposing 19th century, detached country manor on the outskirts of Keswick. "Kelly in Year 6 has gone to Centerparcs!"

"There are several reasons we have come here, young Lucinda Robinson," Steve answered playfully. "Hmmm now, let's ask Mummy. Is it because Roger and Christine are our oldest friends?"

"No, Daddy," Claire replied.

"Is it because Lucy just loves playing with Jessica and sleeping in her room on the floor for three nights, even though they have nothing in common? Or that Daddy and Roger just adore being in each other's company?" Steve asked with mock inquisitiveness.

"Erm, nope and definitely nope," repeated Claire.

"Could it be because there is no way me and your dad could afford to stay in a house this big and this nice in the middle of the Lake District in the middle of July for nowt?"

"Oh *yessss*," said Steve with his best Churchill dog impression.

Claire turned to Lucy, ruffling her hair, "So little missy, we're all going to be on our best behaviour, enjoy our hosts' kindness and warm-heartedness and have a lovely super duper weekend, okay?"

"But Mum, Jessica is *sooooooo* weird, I really don't wanna stay in her room!" pleaded Lucy.

"Well, so is your dad, but I still stay in his room, don't I?" she said, giving Lucy a kiss on her head as they climbed out of the car.

"Hellooooo you gorgeous people, come on in!"

In a floaty white dress, long dark hair and push-up bra, Christine Jackson opened the door to the family Robinson. With real tits and a fake smile, her eyes attempted to focus on the threesome although they did everything but – the smell of gin evident even from back inside the car.

"Hello, Christine, you started drinking without us?" A kick in the shin from Claire did nothing to stop Steve enjoying his early evening quip.

"My dear friend, I started drinking in 1987, I'm hardly going to stop now, it's quite literally my only hobby," Christine laughed to herself, walking into the house, the presumption being that her guests would follow.

Entering the dark but impressive hallway, Claire whispered pointedly, "Why have you always got to be a smart-arse with my friends?"

"I'm sorry," Steve said, "I was just getting mine in before old red trousers Roger has a go . . ."

"Stop it, Steve," Claire warned. "I've been friends with him since uni, you know he's harmless enough."

"I'm just saying," Steve replied defiantly. "I'm yet to meet a bloke in red trousers who wasn't a massive bellen . . ."

"Claire! Lucy! What on earth are you doing with this homeless man in my house? I told you to bring Steve!" a pompously posh voice bellowed from the staircase and laughed raucously at its own joke.

"Too late," Steve muttered to himself.

Roger entered the room with a drink in one hand, a rolled up newspaper in the other and his loyal Weimaraner, Herbie, at his feet. He was, of course, wearing red trousers (Roger, not Herbie).

"Very funny as always, Roger. Nice trousers, by the way," Steve replied, winking at Claire. "What is it this time, my beard or my clothes?"

"Oh no, dear boy," guffawed Roger, "It's that odious odour of alcohol I can smell." Steve shared a knowing look with his daughter.

"How are you?" Claire asked Roger, warmly kissing him on both cheeks. Roger kissed back, before doing the same with Lucy and then with Steve, who squirmed in Roger's grasp.

"Oh Stephen, get with the times, how else do you think men greet each other in the 21st century?"

"A friend request on MySpace?" Steve replied, freeing himself.

He laughed another too-huge laugh, and with a slap on Steve's arm, he headed off in the same direction as Christine, "Come on, Herbie, let's find that ruddy cat."

In the silence, Claire looked at Steve with a raised eyebrow.

"What?" Steve asked. "That was a good reply, that."

"Myspace? 1996 just rang, they want their social media reference back," Claire said with mock disappointment.

"Yeah well, 1982 just rang too, they want their a-certain-year-rang-asking-for-something-old-fashioned-back joke back."

With an affectionate smirk, the couple made their way towards the large dining room for dinner with their old friends.

The Jacksons had ostentatiously provided far more food than the six of them could possibly eat; part of the couple's famous hospitality. In pride of place at the head of the table was Roger, hovering over a lavish spread of meats and cheeses, cakes and treats. Sat to his left was Christine, full of life and gin. In the middle of the table, offsetting her parents' over-exuberance, was Jessica - eight years old, dark hair sitting flatly across her pale face and sunken eyes. She seemed withdrawn and moody, much more like a puberty-laden fourteen-year-old when Zayn left One Direction than a breezy eight-year-old girl.

Steve and Claire sat down, Claire motioning to Lucy to sit on the spare chair next to Jessica. Approaching the chair, Lucy nervously offered a weak smile. Suddenly Jessica snapped her head in the direction of the happy-go-lucky little blonde, "Don't you dare sit there, that seat is for my friend."

Lucy froze. She had known Jessica all her life and whilst she'd always been, well, a little different, she'd never been mean-spirited. But something in the way she looked at Lucy made the hair on the back of the little girl's neck jump up like a tiny army suddenly standing to attention.

After a tense pause, a reassuring Roger intervened, attempting to laugh it off in a 'kids, eh?' kind of way.

Jessica glowered at her parents but then quickly softened, "Sorry, Lucy, but my friend sits there, you'll need to find another seat."

With quiet concentration, Christine gently poured another

unmeasured measure of Gordon's. Steve noticed her hand shaking as the liquid filled the well-worn glass, his eyes darting up to Claire's who'd noticed the same. Christine's usually smiley face had turned into a tired, worried scowl as she looked at her only child. "Jessie, you know you have no more friends coming today."

"But my friend . . ."

Slam. Christine hit her hand down hard on the table making Claire and Steve jump; Lucy let out a tiny yelp.

"Jessica!" Christine's raised voice emotional and staccato, "Let. Lucy. Sit. On. The. Chair."

Grudgingly, Jessica relented, staring hard at her mother. "Fine, but it'll be your fault."

Claire, staring wide-eyed at the little girl who she had once held in her arms at the hospital, looked at her husband, silently saying, 'What the fucking *fuck?*"

After a dessert that could've fed a third-world village (if, by chance, they were in the mood for tiramisu), the conversations about old times had thawed the atmosphere, and as Roger launched into yet another uni story, Steve leaned over to Lucy and Jessica and warmly suggested they go and play up in Jessica's bedroom.

Jessica didn't need asking twice and left immediately. Lucy was understandably reluctant. "You'll be fine, go see what Wednesday Adams' room's like," her dad said with a wink. With a half-smile, Lucy, the ever trusting future 'people person', got down from the table and, uncharacteristically, sulked out of the room.

As the girls left the table, Steve looked over to Christine. He noticed her watching the girls closely; her hand gripped the glass and her once pretty face was sunken with worry. She noticed him noticing and swiftly beamed a huge smile right back. "They're growing up so quickly." Steve nodded.

"Hey, Claire," a well-oiled Roger reverberated, "do you remember that fucking fancy dress party we had in second year when the police were called? What an absolute ruddy riot . . ." Claire laughed, and for a moment Steve allowed himself to zone out, lost in thought. He stared at his wife's precious smile and found himself relaxing. ". . . next thing I've got Colonel Sanders in a fucking headlock . . ." Roger continued to entertain loudly, but to Steve it was a mere whisper as he gazed lovingly at the way the corners of Claire's eyes creased and how she ruffled her nose when she laughed, how the hell had he deserved . . .

A piercing cry filled the house. Christine leapt up shrieking, knocking three empty bottles of Prosecco to the floor, smashing every one. "Lucy!"

Steve knew the scream like any father would.

The fast feet of two little girls echoed as they came rapidly down the wooden staircase and into the kitchen. Jessica's black hair stuck to her face with sweat as she fell into her drunken mother's arms. Lucy grabbed for Claire and held her closely; her young body shivering, quaking.

"What happened Lucy, tell me!" Claire asked worriedly, "What's going on?"

As her daughter peeled away from her chest, Steve noticed red spots on his wife's white blouse. He knelt down, took Lucy's face into his hands and looked. From the edge of her right tear-filled eye to the middle of her cheek was a deep, red and bloody scratch. Steve's stomach lurched as his little girl sobbed in his arms.

Lucy wept, "I was just reading, just reading."

Steve looked to his wife for answers, but her eyes were somewhere else.

"Steve. Look." Steve followed his wife's gaze. In Christine's arms lay Jessica: no tears, no noise, only stillness, but across her face, from her right eye to the middle of her cheek, the same, deep, red and bloody scratch.

In the comfort and warmth of the lounge, after both pretty faces had been treated and covered, the girls had fallen asleep in their respective mothers' arms. In the corner, poking the fire, stood Roger, deep in his own thoughts as Steve, fresh from investigating upstairs, approached.

"Anything?" enquired Roger.

"Not a thing. Have the girls said anything, anything at all?" Steve asked, looking at Lucy and Claire, both fast asleep on the Victorian-style sofa.

"Nothing," a newly-sober Roger replied. "We'll have to wait till morning to get an answer out of them."

"Lucy said something about Jessica's friend, but, I mean, who? Has there been someone in the house? An animal?" A confused Steve was trying to put the pieces together and was coming up with diddly squat.

"I don't know, Steve," Roger slurred, looking at his dozing wife. "I can't keep up with their friends, I mean . . . her imagination runs . . . it can't . . . then there's this fucking cat that keeps getting in, so maybe, oh fucking hell, I don't know, I'm drunk, don't listen to me dear boy." And with that, Roger took himself off to bed.

Other than the unanswered questions, Roger had left the stench of alcohol in the room; it reminded Steve that he needed a drink. Leaving his girls asleep on the couch, he crept out of the living room and towards the kitchen.

He was not normally a big drinker, certainly not compared to Roger and Christine, but tonight, Steve felt, was an exception. He just couldn't shift that knot of anxiety in the pit of his stomach.

Her face. Her precious face. Had Jessica done it? But then, how had it happened to her too? She was strange, and with alcoholic parents who knows what goes on, but violent? At the kitchen door he clenched his eyes shut to try and rid his mind of that shocking image. Not the cut itself, that would heal in time, but that look: terror mixed with pleading in eyes so young, he just couldn't shift it. He steadied himself against the door frame and took a moment.

A scratch and a scurry across the tiled kitchen surface snapped him out of his shadowy thoughts. "What the fuck was *that?*" he thought to himself. He gently pushed the door, which creaked every year of its age, and crept into the gloomy kitchen. The only light source was from behind him in the hallway and the only sound was the sedating hum of the oven's extractor fan.

That scurry again. This time it was right by his feet. He leapt and squealed. Steve hated mice. He scrambled for the light switch.

The bare bulb gently swung left to right as it was brought to life. A horrifying chill entered Steve's body and ran right up his spine. Every single one of the cupboard doors and kitchen drawers had been pulled open. Not just open – wide open. As far as they would go. Steve's eyes darted around the room at speed as he took it all in, his head pinned against the cold, tiled wall. All the chairs, the chairs they'd sat on all evening, were piled upside down on the table. All except for one chair which stayed in its place at the table. Waiting? For whom?

Steve's heart pounded hard in his chest, like a man buried alive pounding against the coffin lid. He clenched his eyes shut again in the hope he'd imagined it. He opened his eyes again, but nothing had changed. The light bulb had stopped swinging and there was silence. Not comforting silence. Not, 'everything's alright' silence. Dreadful silence. To his left, Steve heard a sudden scurry again, but could still see nothing. Then a loud smash to his right grabbed his attention. Two plates hit the tiled floor and shattered all over. "Fuck off!" Steve heard himself say in a moment of primeval honesty, "Little *bastard*."

On the shelf next to the other plates and kitchenware was a cat. The one Roger had been hunting all night no doubt, but here he was, knocking stuff off shelves and shitting Steve right up. Relief washed over him, a soothing thought entering his brain. Logic spilled into his mind like water breaking its dam. As he chucked the cat out of the back door, he smiled to himself, a sardonic smile. Why were all the drawers and cupboard doors open in the kitchen? How had it happened whilst he'd been upstairs and the girls were asleep on their mothers? Roger. Of course. Pissed, plastered, cat-chasing, red-trousered Roger had obviously been searching for a bottle opener, or a corkscrew or some Febreze, anything to quench his drunken thirst, and search he did. "Every bleeding drawer, Roger, you old pisshead," Steve chuckled to himself.

Lying next to Claire on the couch, Steve stroked Lucy's hair lovingly and closed his drowsy eyes.

"Are we going first thing?" murmured Claire wearily.

"Too fucking right." Steve grinned to himself as Claire snuggled into his shoulder and promptly fell asleep.

An inaudible whisper disturbed Claire's family slumber. She opened one eye. In the darkness she could just make out the shape of Herbie the dog, breathing heavily, fast asleep. She drowsily looked around the room, trying to source the noise. Sat opposite the dying embers of the fire she saw Jessica. With the sharp sting of premature opening, Claire managed to open her other eye. She struggled to focus on the little girl so tried to tune her ear into what she was saying.

"No, I don't want to," Jessica said a little louder but still in a hushed tone . . . "they're my friends."

This woke Claire up. Watching this creepy little girl who may or may not have cut her daughter's and her own face whisper to the final, glowing embers of a fire in the middle of a Victorian house at 4am made Claire think one thing. That child was a fucking fruitcake.

"I don't want to."

Claire got up, and against all her better judgment, walked over to her. "Jessica?" she said, invoking her most motherly voice, but plagued by the fact she was sure she'd seen this scene in about a million horror films that Steve had made her watch. Claire was sure this was the bit where, when she reached out to touch the girl's shoulder, she would turn round rapidly with a face and/or voice of the devil and threaten to, or possibly actually, kill her. Claire did it anyway. Her hand reached to touch Jessica's shoulder, "Jess? Jessie. Are you okay?"

Jessica did turn round, but gently, tears in her eyes, finally looking like the little girl that Claire remembered. "I don't want to hurt anyone, Auntie Claire," and with that she burst into tears and flung her arms around Claire's neck and sobbed.

"Oh baby, I know, you're a good girl, shhhh, it's okay." Claire stroked Jessica's head and held her tight as the young girl wept in her arms.

"But my friend," Jessica blubbed.

"Who darling, who's your friend?" Claire enquired.

Jessica leaned back so that her soft lips were right next to Claire's ear. She whispered in the tiniest of voices, "My friend wants you to die."

Claire shivered to herself and struggled for a reply. "Well that doesn't sound like a very good friend, Jessica."

"He's not, he makes me naughty," Jessica said, pulling away from Claire and looking her in the eye.

"Okay," Claire said, even though this was the furthest she'd been from 'okay' in her entire life. "Where's your friend now?"

Jessica stretched out her hand and extended her finger, pointing just behind Claire's head.

"Behind me?" Claire asked. "Brilliant, course he is," she said to herself, turning gradually to look.

"Can't you see him?" Jessica asked.

Claire looked round. There was nothing. Relief. "No darling, I can't see him, there's nobody there."

"He's dancing around, he's always dancing, look!" Jessica started following some invisible nothingness around the room, as it 'danced'.

"Sweetie, there's nothing there, it's your imagination," Claire reassured her.

"It's not, Aunty Claire, Herbie sees him too," Jessica said with a giggle.

Claire looked in the direction of Herbie. The old grey dog was sat up and his steely blue eyes were engaged, looking at something. Claire looked back to Jessica, then back at the dog.

A wave of fear swept across her body, the reassuring smile fell from her face and she suddenly felt debilitated. Herbie and Jessica's eyes were looking in the same place, at the same time . . . at the same thing.

"Jessica," Claire murmured through cold tight lips, "what does your friend look like?"

"He's a tiny clown, about this big." In the light of the dying fire, Jessica implied her friend was around three feet high.

Claire smiled a little with relief. "A three-foot high clown? Well that doesn't sound too bad, what does he say?"

Jessica leant in again. "He doesn't say anything, he's never spoken."

"Why's he never spoken?" enquired Claire.

Rubbing her eyes, Jessica yawned, "I'm tired now Aunty Claire, can I go to sleep?"

Ignoring Claire's question, Jessica stood up and walked over to her mum on the sofa, cuddling into Christine and closing her eyes. Claire walked over and pulled the blanket over the young girl's shoulder and stroked her tear-soaked hair. She looked back at Herbie. His eyes were still darting around the room; Claire shook her head and put the incident down to coincidence.

A bony hand grabbed Claire's wrist tightly, "You don't want to know why." She lurched back; Christine's raspy voice had sobered somewhat.

"What? Why? Who is he?" replied Claire nervously, still trying to free herself from Christine's grip.

"I don't know," Christine whispered, "but her friend doesn't talk because his mouth is all sewn up," and with that she released Claire's wrist and fell into as deep a sleep as her daughter.

Claire slipped away from the sleeping pair and back to her sofa, desperate to go upstairs and sleep in a proper bed, but her attempts to rouse Steve and Lucy came to nothing. Reluctantly she closed her eyes.

A breath in her ear woke her up suddenly. "Steve?" But Steve was on Claire's other side, holding onto Lucy, snoring and dreaming. She could see the shape of the shadows of Christine and Jessica on the opposite sofa so she put it down to a draught and attempted slumber one more time.

What felt like rough, wet lips slid slowly across her ear. Claire froze.

A guttural, forced voice directed its venom into her. "Get. Out."

The last of the dark liquid slipped out of the Nespresso machine and into Steve's cup, "So let me get this straight – a three-foot clown poltergeist with its mouth sewn up wants a little girl to kill us all?"

Claire, sat at the kitchen table, on her third cup, nodded her head, "Yeah basically."

"And it can't talk?" Steve asked.

"So Jessica said, yeah," Claire answered.

"But it told you to get out?" Steve added.

"Yeah, okay Steve, that's the implausible bit, is it? Why do you keep asking me the same questions like a Ghostbuster Columbo? Let's just go," a clearly scared Claire pleaded.

"Firstly," Steve said, "that's a fucking great idea for a film. Secondly, I am not sneaking out of your friends' house in the middle of the morning because a midget, mute clown told us to."

"Well, firstly," Claire retorted, "you can't say 'midget'

anymore, let's not upset this thing anymore than we have done, and secondly, you don't even like my friends."

Steve grabbed a bottle of whisky and poured some into his coffee.

"Are you drinking? It's 5am," Claire said.

"What is it they say, it's 5am somewhere," Steve replied without looking up.

"I think they say 5pm," Claire suggested. "I just think we need our wits . . ."

Two plates flew off the shelf and onto the floor. The couple looked at each other, confused. Steve's mouth opened, but the explanation escaped before he could reason it. He reached out to touch the shelf, but before his fingers hit the wood, a child's deafening scream stopped him in his tracks.

"Lucy!" they both cried in unison, and rushed out of the kitchen.

The lights in the hallway flickered on and off aggressively, momentarily causing Steve to stumble backwards into Claire. He was breathless. Another scream came from inside the lounge, this time from Christine. "Stop it, please, not again, we've done nothing wrong." The dog barked and growled furiously.

They rushed to the lounge door, but before they could get inside, it slammed hard in their faces. A group scream from inside prompted an instinctively violent response. "Lucy!" Steve cried, "Lucy, I'm coming." He banged and kicked the door as hard as he could, but the Victorian wood stood firm against his bloody flesh.

"Just kick it open."

Looking at her in a moment of incredulity, "I've got trainers on, Claire!"

"Just kick it in, for Christ's sake, Steve," Claire shrieked in his face.

"Alright, alright, I'll try!" Steve, stepping back away from the door, braved himself to take a run. By now the sound of screaming from the lounge was deafening, and with one huge kick his foot managed to penetrate the panelling. "Bloody hell, I did it." But his attempt to pull his foot out was unsuccessful, and as Steve attempted to free his size-nine Adidas, the door swung open with such great force that it pulled Steve in with it.

"Mummy!" Lucy yelled. She was cowering in the corner of the room by herself, looking every bit the little girl she was.

"Lucy!" Claire ran over to her and held her close. "I'm here baby, I've got you."

An earsplitting scream from the other side of the room pulled Claire's attention away from her daughter. The windows were open wide and banged ferociously; the wind loudly screeched and whipped through the room. Christine's once fashionable white evening dress was now flapping fiercely as an invisible, impenetrable energy was holding her against a wall, her face covered in bloody scratches.

Claire scanned the corners of the room for Jessica. "Where is she?" she cried over the noise, looking at Steve.

Steve was not looking back though. His eyes were staring upwards; a silent scream attempting to flee his mouth withered and died. Claire followed her husband's stare up to the ceiling where she saw Jessica, floating, detached from anything tangible, her black hair draped down towards the floor as Herbie hopelessly snarled and growled.

Claire stood up boldly. Every grain of her existence was

telling her this wasn't happening, that it was a terrible dream, a nightmare that she'd wake up from and tell Steve about at breakfast. A book hit the centre of her head and Claire fell down; blood poured from the gash.

"Claire," Steve cried out as his wife slumped to the floor, "Claire, are you okay?" He'd managed to free his foot but a hidden strength detained him on the floor.

Claire picked herself up; the sharp iron taste of blood in her mouth gave her a sudden anger from deep inside and she yelled at the top of her voice, "What do you want, you prick, just let her go!"

Jessica span round so her body was facing the floor. She looked directly at Claire, her eyes red with intensity, an ethereal voice full of wrath and fury spoke, "Get. Out."

Claire gestured at Steve, "See, it can speak!"

"*Really*, Claire?" an astounded Steve replied, "you're pulling an 'I told you so' right now?"

Suddenly two hands wrapped around Steve's throat. He yelped in terror as Christine spat in his face, "No one believed me, no one believed me, it's been here for months, please, help my little girl."

"What, how? Tell me how?" Steve said, managing to free himself from the distraught mother's grasp. "What do we do, Claire?"

"I don't know." Then a thought occurred to her: "Where's your phone, check the Internet."

"Eh? That's your plan, you want me to AskJeeves how to get rid of a poltergeist?" Steve exclaimed.

Claire exploded in anger at her husband, "For fuck sake Steve, will you please update your internet references! Right, I'll do it!"

"Do what?" asked Steve.

"I'm Googling it," Claire screamed back over the noise of the wind.

With thumbs like lightning, she typed 'poltergeist'.

She found something. "The name 'Poltergeist' is coined from the terms 'Poltern' which is German for 'to rumble or make noise' and 'Geist' which means 'ghost or spirit'," Claire muttered to herself.

"Alright, Stephen Fry," her husband shouted, "how do we get rid of it!?"

Claire scanned the page quickly. "It says you can ignore it and it should go away."

"Yeah, it's a bit fucking late for that, love. What else does it say?" Steve shouted in a panic.

"Salt, we need salt, and sage, we can burn sage, go, go!" Claire barked.

With all his strength, Steve got up, leaving Christine slumped on the floor. "Claire?" he shouted over the wind.

"Yeah?" she screamed back at her hero husband.

"What the fuck is sage?"

Steve got to the kitchen to find Roger sat at the table, nursing a whisky and a bloodied head, plates broken all around him. In a panic Steve started to go through every drawer and scour every surface for the poltergeist ingredients.

"Roger, I need sage," Steve demanded in distress.

"I can give you some sage advice, matey," Roger chuckled, sipping his drink.

"Great time for jokes, Roger, I'm trying to save your daughter, you dickhead." Steve grabbed what he needed and dashed back.

Bursting through the door, Steve heroically threw the sage on the fire and expectantly looked up.

Nothing happened.

He looked at Claire and Lucy cowering in the corner. "The salt, Steve, try the salt!"

He started to shake the salt into the air under Jessica's floating body.

After a moment, and realising the futility of his salt-throwing endeavors, Steve stopped. "Claire, this is how you get rid of slugs, not poltergeists. There must be something else on that page."

"There's a prayer, 'Saint Michael the Archangel', should I try that?"

But before Steve could answer, Lucy was pulled from her mother's arms and flung towards the fire. Steve dived towards her and managed to stop her entering the flames. "Do the prayer Claire, do the prayer."

"But we don't believe in God, will it still work?" Claire asked genuinely.

"We didn't believe in ghosts two hours ago, but now, you know, I'm thinking maybe there's something in it! Read the fucking prayer!"

"Okay, okay, I'll do it, hold on." Claire stared at the phone.

Steve and Lucy inched closer to the fireplace, Steve using every last bit of his strength to keep them both from being burned alive. "What is taking you so long, Claire? Just read it!"

"My 4G's gone off, I'm on E, it's taking ages to load!" Claire replied in a panic.

"Please, Mummy, do it," sobbed Lucy.

"Ah, got it." Claire standing directly under Jessica, started the prayer. "Saint Michael the Archangel, defend us in battle.

Be our protection against the wickedness and snares of the devil. May God rebuke him, we humbly pray. And do thou, O, Prince of the Heavenly Hosts, thrust into Hell Satan and all the evil spirits who prowl through the world seeking the ruin of souls. Amen."

Nothing.

A deep rumble under her feet.

Then forcing its way out of Jessica's mouth came a thunderous, otherworldly scream as the little girl fell from the ceiling and into Claire's arms, knocking them both to the ground.

The soundlessness of the room was the first thing that Steve noticed. The windows had stopped banging, the books had stopped falling and the fire had quietened to low growl.

Christine stood up and reached out for her daughter. "Jessica, darling girl, Mummy's here." Jessica ran to her mother and the two squeezed each other as if their lives depended on it. Herbie bounced up licking both their faces in excitement.

Steve and Lucy lay in a heap on the floor near the tamed fire as Claire knelt down beside them. "If there's one thing I've learned from this, it's not to depend on Vodafone in an emergency," she said, smiling and holding her family close.

Bustling into the room, and drunkenly surveying the ruin ,was Roger, drink in hand. The shattered windows, broken doors, smashed lamps and the burnt book-strewn carpet laid all around him.

"That fucking cat!"

The boot slammed shut. The gravel under Steve's feet crunched as he made his way to the driver's door. He got in and started the engine. Looking back, he saw the Jacksons stood at the front of the house waving. A totally normal scene if it wasn't for the fact all three family members had faces full of cuts and bruises. Still, they smiled as their friends took off, young Jessica looking much more like a little girl than when they had arrived.

Claire looked in the rear-view mirror to see Lucy waving out of the back window at her friend, and she smiled.

Steve held Claire's hand and gave her a warm, goofy grin. "Let's just do Centerparcs next year, eh?"

She chuckled, "You're such a dick."

"I know." He smiled.

"Daddy?"

"Yes, sweetheart?" answered Steve, turning slightly to see his little girl; his brave little girl.

Leaning forward, Lucy touched her dad's shoulder. "Can we just take the motorway home?"

Steve laughed, "Too right!"

DADDY'S GIRL

I DON'T REMEMBER the day she died, or at least I can't pin down any of the fleeting scenarios I have of her at the end to any specific day. I remember her strained smile whenever I was guided into that room, that reeked more and more of sweat, anesthetic and vomit, and how the brightly-coloured wallpaper seemed to mock the gut-churning grey truth that my mother was clearly fading into death. People I didn't know kept coming to our house: I remember being given a jigsaw with a picture of a little girl riding a pony; I don't know who by. I remember a huge bluebottle raging against the glass in our lounge window as muffled sobs rang out through the house. I remember silent meals with my father, watching fearfully as he rubbed his tired red-rimmed eyes. And I remember remembering, sitting on my own, willing her well, with the power of seeing her in my mind's eye laughing with me. I made up spells of repeating words in a certain order, throwing flower petals to the wind in the garden, whispering prayers into my teddies' ears. I failed. No matter how many times I made that jigsaw, I couldn't put her back together. She was gone. I never saw her dead body; I was given butterfly cakes and sandwiches at the wake.

The dreams didn't start straight away. I suppose in the same way that pus builds up around a splinter, it took time for my mind to poison. It would always start in the same way: I'd be at her graveside, it would be dusk, my father calling me from the car telling me it was time to go, I'd get up to leave and just as I was walking away I'd hear it. My name, a muffled scream breaking up through the ground, I'd call out to my father that she was still alive, that she needed help, but he'd just demand ever more aggressively for me to come now. Her voice would plead desperately and I'd start clawing at the ground with my hands, pulling clods of grass and soil away as tears of frustration and longing bit into my cheeks. It would seem to take an age, the soil getting ever more decrepit the further I got, my eyelashes and mouth would fill with grit and I could hardly breathe as I somehow managed to get deeper and deeper into the earth. Suddenly that vile, familiar stench of vomit and medical fluid would flood my nostrils heralding some horror to come, and there, finally I'd be at her coffin and I could hear her clearly choking, spluttering, crying out to me. My fists would pound at the wood with every fibre of my strength. This was the point in the dream that changed every time, as if my mind had to play out every conceivable ending. Once the coffin cracked and I fell into a mass of blood and internal organs, another time, she was there, a living dead corpse, screaming as I lay on top of her, maggots burrowing out from her eyeballs, bits of decaying flesh still hanging on to ivory bone as her skeletal hands refused to release me. Another time I broke through to find that she was as I remembered her: alive, healthy, but as she opened her mouth to speak, hundreds of worms came squirming out in an unending torrent. Of course the dream would end with me screaming, my heart pounding as adrenaline coursed its way through my veins. Sometimes my father would come. In the early days his face wore a mask of concern; it seemed to fall off as time went by, replaced by one of annoyance. Eventually he stopped coming in at all. I've heard many times that time is a healer, but I haven't found that really, I feel that time is a sculptor, moulding your thoughts and responses into different forms, layering them up so that you become some sort of living Russian doll, each part trapped inside another. And the outer one burdened with the weight of many.

I've often wondered if I'm a burden to my father. The truth is, I'm not sure what I am to him. He was always a serious man, an accountant by trade. He used to say that there was a great peace in numbers, that when you were dealing with definites, you knew where you were in the world and things made sense. He had an office at home, it was filled with heavy shelves bursting with folders, there were always piles of papers making little columns around the floor, it was his arena where he battled figures and conquered them into their rightful place. I wasn't allowed in and that suited me, that room was the embodiment of boredom: I hated maths; it seemed a cold and lifeless practice. His other passion however was a world away from equations and division. He liked to collect things. Fossils, rocks, stuffed animals, skulls and insects. If my father and I are two halves of a venn diagram, then collecting is where we meet. It was how he met my mother too, at a geology convention.

We go on collecting missions at the weekends and somehow when he's consumed by the beauty of a find, I can ask him questions about Mum. I've learned that if you catch him in the right mood, they can be gently slipped in, like swallowing a pill covered with butter. I would never ask him at any other time. I don't even know if I've learned that, it just feels instinctive.

He spends the vast majority of his life like a coiled spring, his responses are short and clipped, and when we are watching television or eating a meal I'll catch him staring off into the distance, and see the bones at the side of his face move as he clenches his jaw, and I know he's thinking of her. One time we'd travelled all the way to the border as he knew a really good spot for butterflies: he was after a Comma, they're not easy to find. The sun was shining and the clouds looked like a sheet of crisp white lace stretching off into the distance. As we gathered our nets from the back of the car we exchanged a rare smile, and before we started he instigated a game where we each had one foot in Wales the other in England. I couldn't remember a time when he seemed happier. After a while he called me over; I hadn't managed to catch anything of interest. "Come here, Lucy, I've got something you'll like." I skipped over, eager to see what it was. He held up the jar and there inside was the biggest moth I'd ever seen. "It's an Elephant Hawk moth, I can't believe I spotted it, it's so rare to find one like this in the day, you usually have to lure them at night with beer and the smell of tobacco." I gave him a quizzical look. "No, really, they're drawn to it, rather like how your Aunty Sue lured Uncle Dave." We both laughed. It was a stunning creature: tawny beige velvet with strokes of blush pink across its body and wings. I seized my moment. "So how did Mum lure you, Dad?" He blinked in surprise a few times, but didn't take his eyes of the moth. "She didn't have to Lucy, I was completely captivated straight away, it took me weeks to pluck up the courage to go and speak to her. Believe it or not, I actually deliberately dropped something near her in the end, a geode, it tumbled across the floor and she bent to retrieve it for me, and that was that, we spoke and I could hardly look at her, she had the most incredible face, perfect symmetry, rather like this fellow here, she always joked that it was rock and roll that brought us together, I still can't believe she fell in love with someone like me . . . .and then . . ." His voice cracked slightly and he looked down, he took a deep breath, then looked up at me with the most intense stare. "You look just like her, Lucy Willow, your eyes, your mouth. I'd break if you ever left me." He reached out a hand and put it on my shoulder, squeezed his fingers so that the grip was on the edge of pain. "Alright, Dad, I won't leave you, I promise." He held that stare long enough for a knot of anxiety to clench itself into being in my stomach and it sat there like one of his rocks for the rest of that day. We drove home in near silence. I couldn't help but imagine her still being here, how different things might be, but I was supposed to just carry on. I'd always felt sorry for him, nervous of him, but that day I felt the first tinges of anger.

When we got home I was instructed to get the cotton wool balls. I knew what this meant. He lined up all the collection jars, one creature in each: the moth, several butterflies, a large stag beetle, we never did catch a Comma. When I came down he was standing there holding the bottle of chloroform, with a face mask on and white gloves. Even though we'd done this many times before, I did suddenly feel something akin to doubt: why couldn't we just be a normal family. I was twelve years old and I hadn't brought a single person home from school since going up to secondary. I'd had a birthday party when I was ten, my Aunty Sue had come over, we played pass the parcel, I had a hedgehog cake and it was wonderful, until Layla Browning had wandered off to explore, went into one of the collection rooms and wouldn't stop screaming after seeing an adder in a jar of formaldehyde. The next day at school her and some other girls crowded round me by the coat hangers: "You and your dad are freaks," and then she spat at me, the other girls laughed and they all ran off. After that I was taunted regularly. I handed my father the bag of cotton wool balls. "Put your mask on, Lucy." I did without question. He carefully unscrewed the lid of the bottle, took a single ball out the bag, lifted it to the bottle mouth and tipped the clear innocent-looking liquid onto it. "You can do the honours." I nodded and quickly pulled the latex gloves that were waiting for me on the table onto my hands, took the ball from him, and deftly dropped it into the first jar, quickly replacing the lid before the poor creature had the chance to escape. There is a sickly fascination involved in watching something die like this, to have the power to bring about something's demise so swiftly. The moth fluttered its wings a few times, perhaps a little frantically, and then with all the grace of a leaf falling in Autumn it simply dropped to the bottom of the jar, utterly still. "Makes you wonder exactly what happens at the moment of death, doesn't it?" His voice mumbled from behind the mask. "I suppose it does, Dad, yes." I pondered it for a moment, he continued: "Some creatures can slow their heartbeats down to just a few beats per hour, and there are even frogs whose blood can freeze and they stay alive. There is something else, a tangible intelligence separate from the physical: a soul, or whatever we want to call it, I'm convinced of it, and that has to be removed." We continued gently removing the souls of the small creatures we'd found, and then stuck their perfect bodies onto black velvet-covered pads with long, delicate pins.

Two years have passed since that day. My school life has become a living hell. Layla Browning is still the main ringleader, with her vile band of minions who'll do anything she says. I've mostly learned avoidance tactics: I spend break and lunch times in the school library, it feels like I'm in a prison, but instead of bars there's books. I've found a type of freedom within them though, so there is some solace. I've started writing myself too, mostly ghost stories, I'm sure they're rubbish and I wouldn't let anyone read them, but I enjoy the process; in fact they've started consuming my imagination. I can sit through a whole lesson and not take in a single word, as in my mind I'm wandering down some horrific dusty corridor. They all seem to be about vengeful ghosts, souls with unfinished business.

I don't always manage to avoid my bullies. Last week I ran into them whilst heading for the bus at the end of the day. It's usually a quick-fire round of name-calling, threats, sometimes I'll get pushed, but this went further, much further. There is a small clump of trees, the vaguest attempt at a woodland with some greenery beneath it, just alongside the main school gates, right next to where all the buses park. They are course a magnet for smokers, kissers and those generally not wanting to be seen. My bus parks right next to them. They were waiting for me, it was a swift and subtle ambush. They grabbed my bag from the back, my arms flailed at the air, reaching for some invisible saviour that wasn't there. My whole body was yanked backwards and I stumbled, tripping over. I ended up sitting in the middle of an eclipse of loathing. The names and insults rained down: "freak", of course, "fat, ugly cunt", "why don't you just kill yourself?" I tried to get up, instinctively to run, I could see the bus door open, others getting on, I knew there was no point at all calling out for help, no one would come, they'd be more likely to take pictures of me in this pathetic state, print them out and stick them all over school. I closed my eyes and just waited for it to end. Suddenly I felt hands on my hair, pulling, yanking my head about, this way then that. I desperately tried to get up, but two hands pinned me by my shoulders. I dug my nails into their soft flesh: "Right you little bitch, you've asked for it now." Layla's voice was a symphony of rage, and a flurry of kicks battered my back as if I was a piece of steak. I heard a strange metallic rushing sound, panic exploded from my stomach as I thought I was about to be stabbed, and I started to writhe like a wounded animal: "Stay still or we'll fucking kill you!" I tried to scream, but it felt like my throat was blocked with cotton wool. I froze. "Right, let's make you look like the freak you really are." I felt my hair tugged at again, and I realised the metallic noise had been several pairs of scissors drawn open. And so I sat there like a woman accused of witchcraft in Salem and had my long auburn hair hacked off in chunks. They ran off after that, leaving me in a state of utter trauma. The pain in my back was excruciating, and my hands began to tremble uncontrollably. The bus engine chugged itself into action, my vision was blurred with tears, and my legs were numb. I looked up just as the bus pulled away and that was the first time that I saw her with my waking eyes. There was no denying it, it wasn't a trick of the light: my mother was on that bus, wearing the nightgown that she'd worn in her bed-ridden state. She looked right at me, and put her hand up on the glass as if she was reaching out. I suddenly couldn't breathe properly, and my heart started to hammer so hard I thought I was going to die. I simply couldn't believe what I'd just seen: 'I've gone mad." I shook my head and my stomach lurched, sick pushed its way into my mouth, everything I could see suddenly spiralled off as if sucked into a vortex, leaving blackness and merciful oblivion.

When I opened my eyes I could see my hair on the ground

in front of me and it all came rushing back like a smashed picture reversing into solidity at speed. The taste in my mouth was vile, and I realised that a persistent buzzing was coming from my bag. It would be my father, he'd be beside himself with worry: I was never late home and he always insisted on knowing exactly where I was. He wouldn't allow me a proper phone like everyone else. I had this device that looked like a ladybird, it was a type of pager, designed for very young children so that parents could keep tabs and make contact. I was a freak, and so was he. I collected myself together, took it out and paged him back, explaining that I'd just missed the bus. There was no way I was going to tell him what had just happened, he wouldn't help the situation, he'd only make it worse. I looked at my hair on the ground and instinctively gathered it up, as if it was somehow salvageable. It looked so helpless. As I gathered it up my tears fell in its stead.

Nothing could have prepared me for his reaction when I finally walked in. Luckily my coat had a hood and I was able to disguise the state of my hair. As I entered the house, he was pacing like a mad bear in captivity, wringing his hands and mumbling. "Hi, Dad, I'm really sorry, I had to go to the toilet at the end of the day and I just missed it." He looked up at me with that stare, that horrendous stare that seemed to bore right into me. "You little LIAR!" He barked it out like a frenzied dog, his teeth were bared as he literally pounced at me from across the room. "Who is he, Lucy Willow? I will find out one way or another." I was so taken aback, I didn't know how to respond, no boy would ever find me remotely fanciable. I'd hardly allowed myself the indulgence of a fantasy. "No, Dad, you've got it completely wrong." I was so scared and angry and in shock, I thought I might actually pass out again. He had come right up to me, his breath in my face was pungent and bitter and he was hurting my arms as he clutched me. "I'll shake it out of you if I have to," and with that he made a rag doll of me as he shook me hard. The hood of my coat fell back revealing the travesty of what they'd done. He gasped, and stood statue-still, glaring at my head. I felt totally exposed, ashamed, and suddenly furious with it all, him, the bullies, I even hated my mother for being dead in that instance. "There!" I screamed, "are you happy now, I wasn't with some non-existent boy, I was being fucking beaten up and tortured, because they hate me, because I'm a total weirdo, just like you are!" I yanked myself away and ran to my room, torrents of tears finally un-damned after so many years of silence.

As I lay on my bed, my whole being racked with pain, it all fell down like a house of cards around me. My whole perception of reality just gave way, I could almost sense some relief amidst all the grief. I'd been living in total denial, avoiding the blinding truth: my father was mad. The house had been getting ever more filthy, dust building up like life's sediment on every surface, paperwork everywhere, stacks of unopened mail, and his silences had become unbearable. We still went collecting at weekends, only ever for insects and small creatures now, and it seemed that this was now his only pleasure; his only joy in life was to kill things, and maybe it was mine too. Our only connection was through death, and he would speak ever more philosophically about the movement of molecules matching the patterns of the stars, how the universe without matched the universe within, and where once this kind of conversation had filled me with wonder, I was finally admitting to myself that it filled me with total dread, as if I'd known all along that he was deeply unwell and I just couldn't face it, as he was all

I had. The pain of that isolation was entirely encompassing, and I howled and gasped for breath as it seemed I'd tapped into a well of never ending sadness. And to think he thought I might have had someone else who cared about me. My aunt and uncle had stopped visiting ages ago; I don't think they knew how to handle him, nor me, for that matter. We had no friends. We were alone.

I dreamed about my mother again this week and I saw her again in the daytime too, just once. I don't know if she's really there reaching out, trying to tell me something. Or if I am going insane. I don't know if I'm more scared than comforted by that thought, but I'm struggling to make sense of it all. The dreams have changed too, they're getting longer, more intricate. That first night after my hair was cut, I must have fallen asleep crying. My dream started as it always does, at her graveside. This time though, I reached her coffin and found it was a closed door and that I was standing in front of it. The scene was utterly familiar and as I turned the handle and walked in I realised it was my mother's room and that she was on her deathbed. I was carrying a cup of tea in my young hands, I was a child again. There was an eerie stillness in the room, fragments of dust danced like tiny fairies in the sunbeams breaking through the gap in the curtains. My footsteps fell in time with her just-audible breaths and as I approached the bedside, I could see the sheets were marked with yellow-brown stains around the top. She was lying on her back fast asleep. I reached her side and started to lift the tea to the little cabinet beside her. Suddenly her head jerked around, almost mechanically, and she stared at me wide-eyed and shocked. Startled, I fumbled the tea cup and it unbalanced in my hands.

Time slowed down and in perfect coordination as the tea cup and its contents fell towards the floor, she pushed the sheets back, revealing a single massive blunt-headed spear pushed deep into her chest, pinning her to the bed. As the cup crashed down, blood gushed up from the entry wound blooming deep crimson into the white bedding. I looked up at her face, her mouth opened wide as if to speak, she gasped deeply but no words would come, her arm reached out for me as more and more blood came, now spilling onto the carpet and running down her arm on to me. I tried to run but my feet were fixed, I could taste the blood as it splashed up into my face. She drew me closer and I saw that her other hand was pulling at the spear, trying to get it out. I just wanted to run, but I knew she needed help, and against all my instinct I climbed onto the bed, which was now utterly awash with gore. I sat on top of her and pulled; it was almost impossible to get a grip, but I persevered and finally it started to move. Once it had shifted a little it seemed to just come. I had to stand to pull it right out and as the sharp point ceased its contact, a mass of fluttering poured out from the wound as hundreds of Elephant Hawk moths filled the room. They formed a cloud around my head. I looked down through them at her face: she looked utterly at peace, a gentle smile on her face as she closed her eyes. The fluttering of the moths became unbearably claustrophobic, I batted at them with my hands, and suddenly realised I was awake under my sheets, my hands flailing at the fabric as it brushed against my face. I sat up and saw that it was morning. It was the first time I had ever seen her in a state of peace in a dream and although it was horrendous, I hadn't woken screaming, something had shifted.

I had to face my father, and deal with my hair. Fortunately

it was a Saturday. I grabbed a hat from my room and put it on, I couldn't bring myself to even look in the mirror. As I went down stairs it occurred to me that he hadn't even come to my room, no attempt had been made to communicate, to comfort me, and there's no way that he hadn't heard me crying. He was sitting at the breakfast table which had been set for two. "Good morning, Lucy." He glanced at me with slightly sad eyes but didn't hold the look. "I trust you're feeling better." It was said as a statement, not a question. He wasn't interested in my feelings, or maybe he just couldn't handle them. I suppose he's never known how to deal with difficult situations. Why was I even thinking about him!? He's not the one who's getting bullied. We ate in virtual silence, my head a tumbling mass of difficulty. I was going to have to ask him for money, to go and get my hair sorted out. I wasn't even given pocket money, ever. Even for chores, not that he set any these days. He controlled all income and outgoings. I even used to save up my dinner money, going without food, just so I might be able to get myself something, but we didn't really go shopping anyway, he ordered food and household goods over the internet and if I needed new uniform or shoes, he took me, picked things out and I would just agree. I spent all my saved money on sweets from the vending machine in the school leisure centre. At least it felt like my choice. I used to eat them on my own in the toilets.

"Dad, I'm going to need some money to go to the hair-dresser's." I hated having to ask for anything. "Oh yes, alright, well, I'll have to phone one and ask exactly how much it'll cost. I can drive you into town as well."

As I walked into the hairdresser's I realised I'd never been in one before. My Aunty Sue had cut my hair once years ago when she was babysitting me and Dad had hit the roof. All the girls in there were wearing slick black outfits, they all seemed impossibly pretty with cool hair and beautiful make-up. I hadn't even thought about what I was going to ask for and the realisation that I was going to have to show them my hair was almost too much. I was about to turn and walk out when a lady came over. "Hiya, I'm Sarah, have you got an appointment?" I nodded quickly. "Can I take your coat, love?" Without even answering I took off my coat and handed it to her. She must have sensed that I was worried: "Do you want me to take your hat as well, sweetheart?" I clutched it to my head without thinking. "No, that's fine, umm, thanks, I'll keep it on." She laughed a little. "Alright, but we'll have to get it off at some point!" I couldn't even respond. "Come on over to the desk, and we'll get you sorted, what was the name?" She lead me over to another smiling girl. I looked at her and must have seemed like a rabbit in the headlights. "Lucy Willow Thompson." She looked at the book in front of her. "Yes, here you are, 11 o'clock, you've got Sarah." I was relieved, I liked Sarah calling me love and sweetheart. "Right, well looks like I'm going to get so see under that hat after all!" I was offered a cup of tea, and shown to a chair. "So what sort of thing are you after, Lucy Willow? Lovely name, by the way." There was a slightly uncomfortable pause. "My hair has been ruined." As I spoke my chin started to flinch and I could feel an uncomfortable lump in my throat. I desperately didn't want to cry, but it was no good, the tears started. "Oh, sweetheart, it's alright, look we've all had hair disasters, did your mum do it for you? Or worse, did you have a go yourself?" She was trying to make light of it, but of course there was no point. I took the hat off. I don't know what I expected, from the mirror or from the hairdresser. This was the first time either of us had seen it. Sarah was calm. It looked awful, and I just broke down entirely. "Right, come on my love, pop your hat back on, we're going to go for a little walk." She lead me through the building to the staff room at the back. I could feel other customers staring at me. She closed the door and just hugged me tight. Gently tapping the back of my head against her chest and I cried and cried. "It's alright, Lucy, just let it out, love." I wanted her to never let me go. After I'd calmed down and had another cup of tea, she set me up in another chair in front of a big mirror. "This is where we do each other's hair, so you get to be an honorary member of staff today, and I'll tell you what, you have got such a pretty face, I know how to totally sort you out." She ran her fingers through my remaining hair. "So, do you want to tell me what happened? You don't have to, but I'm not going anywhere for a bit, eh!?" She was the nicest person I'd ever met and once I started talking, I couldn't stop, the pain in my back was a persistent throb and I kept having to shift in my seat, but I told her all about the bullying and about how my dad just wouldn't talk. "I've got a daughter not too much younger than you, and I'll tell you what, there's no sugar coating it, girls can be right little bitches. She had trouble a couple of years ago with a group, oh I could have walloped the bloody lot of them. Look down to the side for me, love. You've got to tell someone, a teacher; your dad sounds like he's in a world of his own, but he loves you, of course he does, I'm sure, if you really let him in on it, and what about your mum, sweetheart, does she know?" "She passed away when I was little." "Oh I'm so sorry, petal, that was thoughtless of me." She put her hands on my shoulders. I looked up at her, she'd closed her eyes and was taking a deep breath. "It's okay," I said, "it happened a long time ago." "You're a little trooper you are, and I'll tell you what, you're going to need a stick to keep the boys off by the time I've finished with you!" My cheeks went slightly hot and I couldn't help but smile. "Now, don't be scared, I'm getting the clippers out, lots and lots of girls are going for this look, you're lucky, none of the cuts have gone down to the scalp so we can actually make a clean go of it." We chatted on about lots of things, I even told her about my ghost stories, she called me Creepy Karen. When she'd finished, I didn't recognise myself. I couldn't believe what she'd done, for the first time in my life I looked *cool*. She'd shaved around one side, left it slightly longer on the other and left a floppy fringe at the front and wooshed it over to one side. "So, what do you think?" She held up a mirror at the back and it looked immaculate. "I really love it, Sarah, I can't believe it." "Told you I could sort you out! And look at how pretty you are; no, not just pretty, you're beautiful, Lucy. Your cheekbones and eyes, and not a scrap of make-up, all natural, what a stunner! I'd say you were a bit hidden behind all that hair you must have had." It was true, I had always hidden behind my hair. "I feel like a different person, it's weird!" I gave her another hug before paying and leaving, and left feeling better than I had for ages.

My father was waiting in the car outside for me and I suddenly didn't care what he thought of my hair; I sort of hoped he disapproved. He didn't say a word as I got in. We drove off towards home in total silence. As we neared our house, his voice broke the quiet, "I'd like to know exactly who did that to your hair, Lucy." "What? Her name was Sarah, she was really nice, Dad." "No, I mean who has been bullying you." I looked over at his hands, his knuckles had gone white as he was gripping the steering wheel hard. I thought about what Sarah had said about reaching out, maybe I should just let him in. "Do you remember Layla Browning, she came to my birthday party and started . . ." He interrupted me. "Yes, I remember her, I assume she's not alone?" I sighed, this felt anything but caring. I felt interrogated. But at least he was asking. "Yes, there's three others: Emily Chapman, Jo Banks and Grace Armitage, but Layla's the worst, but you musn't say anything, please Dad, it'll just make it worse." He didn't say anything after that, he just mumbled to himself under his breath and clenched his jaw.

I couldn't stop staring at myself in my bedroom mirror when I got home. My Aunty Sue had bought me a make-up kit for Christmas a few years before, it was just one for little girls to play dressing up. My father had hated it, of course, he'd said no daughter of his was going to look like a cheap tart and he forbade me to use it. I still had the box though, and felt like trying some on just for fun. I didn't really have a clue what to do, and I thought maybe I'd end up looking a bit like a clown. The colours looked bright, but when you put them on you could hardly see them really. I used some blue shadow on my eyes and painted some red shiny lipstick on, it was virtually translucent anyway. I put some mascara on my lashes, it felt heavy and annoying at first, but it really made my eyes look different, bigger and more obvious. Was I a beauty? I let myself imagine it was true for a second. The bruising in my back let itself be known and I wondered for the first time what might be lying in store for me next time from Layla. I looked down as I rubbed my back, and when I looked up she was there, my mother, behind me. I drew breath. She was clear and solid. I felt the hairs on my arms and neck prickle as I held her stare. Slowly she drew her index finger to her lips and placed it there, she held it for a second and then pointed to the ceiling.

I spun around, terrified, exhilarated, to find an empty room. I looked back at the mirror but she'd gone. I was breathing fast, slightly dizzy and feeling sick. "What do you want with me, Mum? Please, you're scaring me. I love you, but please." And for the fourth time in two days I cried, heavy, exhausted tears.

I didn't dream about her again until last night, and I haven't seen her again, thank god; this week in school has been intense enough. Everyone stared at me as I got on the school bus, and a whole wave of people started telling me my hair looked good; I don't know how many times I heard "You look totally different"; even my Form Tutor, Miss Daniels, looked shocked when I walked into class: "Well, Lucy! I hardly recognised you, your hair looks fantastic." I sat down and glanced across at Layla: she looked furious. Dean Bradshaw, one of the most popular boys in our year wouldn't stop looking over at me. I couldn't hardly believe it was happening. He and Layla had been an item once, but he'd finished with her and it had been this major fuss, Layla had cried in the toilets all day and refused to come out, everyone had talked about it and the teachers had to get involved. I couldn't help it, my mind ran away with itself: imagine if I went out with Dean, it would be the ultimate revenge. At first break, he came over to me at the lockers, my mouth went dry, he was with his mates and I thought for a minute he was going to say something nasty, but he didn't. "Nice job, Lucy, really suits you." It was like a gilded hook slipped itself into my skin. I couldn't stop thinking about him. I managed to avoid Layla and her gang all day, but I still had to get to the bus. I sat through the last lesson in a state of increasing worry; when the bell rang it marked panic. I decided there was safety in numbers, I just needed to absorb myself into a group and they wouldn't be able to get me. I was trying to work out who and how, when I looked up at the school gates and saw a familiar car. My dad was there, I felt totally relieved for a second, but this was quickly obliterated as mortification took its place when I saw him standing and talking to Layla and Grace. I couldn't see Jo or Emily. I stood stock still, I didn't know what to do: I couldn't just breeze up and act as if nothing had happened, but before I could make a decision I watched as they walked off, leaving my dad to get back into the car. To my amazement he drove off. So he'd actually just come to talk to them? He clearly didn't want me to know. I wasn't sure how to feel and I desperately wanted to know what he'd said. I couldn't see that this was going to help things in any way: now I was a grass as well as a freak. But he'd done something for me. Just then Dean walked past, "Come on, you'll miss your bus." I looked down and started walking, totally self-conscious. "So what are you up to later?" "Oh, um nothing really, just watching TV probably." "Well some of us are hanging out down at the skate park at St Marks if you wanna come." I couldn't think what to say. "Thanks, I'll try and get away!" Why did that come out of my mouth, I made it sound like I live in a prison. I needed to at least pretend I'm normal.

I spent the rest of the journey home working out how I could get to the skate park. Should I lie? Should I just be honest and see what happened? Should I try and sneak out after dinner? He never checked on me once I was in my room. Did I even want to go to the skate park? I'd probably just be standing there on my own trying to be invisible. What was the point? *Dean Bradshaw.*

He was in his office when I got home, barely glancing up as I came in. I went straight to my room and only came down for dinner. A few basic pleasantries were exchanged and other than that it was the usual silence. I was desperate to know what he'd said to Layla and Grace, and I knew I just had to come out with it, "Dad, I saw you at the school gate today." I hesitated. "Please, what did you say to . . ." "What did I say to those vile little bitches?" He carefully put a forkful of chicken into his mouth, and as he quietly chewed a look of disgust came over his face. He dabbed at the corner of his slightly snarling mouth and placed the napkin down gently. "I gave them the short, sharp warning they deserved, for . . ." his breath quickened, and his voice grew ever so slightly louder, "for violating your body." He spat the words out; speaking them seemed to unleash this temper, his whole head began to tremble with rage, the muscles around his mouth and on his brow contorted until he looked truly terrifying. He slowly raised himself off his chair, and leaned forward on the table staring right through me. "You are my daughter, even though you're now unrecognisable, you are still mine, do you hear me? Mine! No one has the right to touch you!" His teeth were so clenched the words were distorted, and the pure unadulterated anger was beyond reasoning with. Then it passed, was just wrapped back up and put somewhere within him He sat back down, calmly shook open his napkin, placed it carefully on his lap and carried on eating his meal as if nothing had happened. It took me a moment to realise my mouth was hanging open. I didn't broach the subject of the skate park.

The next few days at school were the best I'd ever known. They were suddenly a stark contrast to home life. Whatever my father had said to Layla and Grace, it worked, they wouldn't even look at me. Surely he couldn't have threatened anything too heinous or someone would have been alerted? It remained a mystery.¿ I wasn't about to ask so I decided I'd deal with it if anything came up, and if I heard nothing, I could just notch it up as one of the very few occasions my dad had done something useful for me. Dean Bradshaw has wanted to actually hang out with me, I think he's going to officially ask me out, I don't know what to do. How the hell can I invite him to stay at my house? And how the hell can I spend time with him outside of school? I am in a prison and something's going to have to give. I've been feeling scared of showing Dean the real me, but every time he asks me something and I just answer honestly; he seems to think I'm cute. I'm not sure how cute he'd find my blood-soaked dreams or my dead mother's spirit stalking me, but one step at a time. He asked me what my phone number was, and at first I was so embarrassed to admit I didn't have one I tried to lie and say that I couldn't remember my own number, then he said I could text him and he'd get my number that way. The next day he seemed genuinely hurt that I hadn't messaged him and eventually I had to admit the truth, which led to a wider set of truths about my dad being revealed. I really thought he'd just think "freak" but he thought my dad sounded eccentric and interesting. It made me feel really sad as I'd once seen him as fascinating, but not any longer. Being around Dean reminds me of looking at photos that have been taken with a soft-focus filter over the lens. Everything feels warm and comfortable. It's the most delicious feeling I've ever had. He brought a phone into school yesterday and gave it to me. "It's my dad's old work phone, he gets them on a contract, but they get upgraded every six months, so this is yesterday's news. You can use it to message me; if you don't over use it to go online and stuff it won't be a problem." I admitted that I had no idea how to use it; he just seemed to think that was funny, and showed me how to send and receive texts. It now feels like the single most important item I've ever owned. After school, I basically spent hours texting him back and forth. I actually felt a veneer of normality had been skimmed over my life, but dinner time shattered that faint illusion. I think I might actually have to run away from home. I came down early, he was muttering around in the kitchen before walking in and putting our plates down. "We're going collecting this weekend, Lucy, it's about time." Needless to say, I could have listed any number of things that I'd rather do. "Is that because you want to spend time with me, or you just want me to spend time with you?" It just fell out of my mouth and I felt amazed by my own assertiveness. "What on earth do you mean by that? Are you attempting to imply that I am not interested in you?" He seemed in one of his mild-mannered, bumbling moods, but I knew that like flicking a light on, he could switch in an instant, so I chose my retort carefully. "I mean, what if I had other plans? I'd tell you about them obviously, but what if I didn't want to go . . . with . . . you?" He'd started breathing heavily again at the mention of other plans, the fight or flight instinct in me almost prevented me finishing my sentence. "Well Lucy Willow, I just thought it was about time we bonded again. I've sensed a distance and I don't like it very much. I assume you would tell me if, for example, you had a texting buddy or something?" Those words felt like an ice-cold hand gripping my heart: he knew, somehow he fucking knew. "Oh, so I'm right am I, I can tell by your face, Lucy Willow, you're not such a clever girl. Little pings, little pings, didn't think to switch the ringer off?" He furiously tapped the side of his head. "I think you'd better bring me the phone, don't you?" I couldn't speak, there was no denying it, why had I been so stupid? I was so scared, I started to cry. "Oh water works won't help, it's a boy, isn't it, admit it, admit it!!" I just nodded, feeling sure I was dooming myself somehow, but I'd already done that. "You're just like her, a fucking slut!" With that a plate inexplicably flew off the side in the kitchen. As it violently shattered so too did my childish impression of my parent's love. If you've ever experienced finding that the whole foundation of your life was a lie then you understand what happened to me in that moment. It wasn't so much that the rug was pulled from under me, the earth that held the floor that held the rug disintegrated leaving a bottomless void into which I fell and there was nothing to catch me. I felt numb, utterly numb, as I went to get the phone. He shadowed me to my room, and I realised he'd shadowed me my whole life, that's what he was, a dark space where no light could penetrate. I had to get away from him, I had no idea what form and by what means that would take, but my mind was pinned to that notion. Freedom.

I couldn't even cry. I lay in my bed as the full horrifying truth washed over me in waves, realisation upon realisation. He'd made her ill with his control, his jealousy. He had always been mad, it had simply taken me years to really see it. My mind was racing and I assumed I wouldn't fall asleep, but eventually I did. Although it wasn't a peaceful one. They say that dreams are the subconscious mind working things out that it hasn't been able to solve in the day and that it has a language of its own, one of metaphor and symbolism. I think that maybe dreams are potentially something more, that they are a door, a means for those outside of our space and time to communicate with us, and perhaps in order to converse they have to learn the language of the subconscious to be heard.

Maybe that's utter, utter nonsense and I am simply tortured
by some kind of guilt mixed with grief that I cannot seem to
be absolved from, but I am compelled right now to believe
the former as I had the strangest dream yet and I'm not sure
I've actually woken up from it. It started as expected with
all the labour of excavating a grave single-handedly. I again
found myself at a door, and I opened it to find that it was
my own bedroom door, and I was sleeping soundly in my
bed. She was there, my mother, standing at the bottom of the
bed looking over me. She placed her finger to her lip again to
denote silence. I nodded and she walked towards me, she took
my hand and led me upstairs. Our house is on three floors,
my room is on the second, as is my father's. The very top
floor contains two collection rooms and the processing room,
which I've always been banned from. My father has always
told me that it was full of dangerous chemicals, and things
that would upset me; this was where he stuffed creatures. I
would have gone and sneaked a look, but it was always locked
anyway. Tonight though in this parallel world of dream, my
dead mother had the key. She placed it in the lock and turned,
the sense of foreboding was overwhelming as was the stench
that bombarded my senses. I gagged and drew a hand up to my
mouth. A single glowing bulb swung gently in the middle of
the ceiling which was alive with masses and masses of winged
creatures; they crawled and fluttered over each other, clicking
and whirring. I suddenly realised my mother was no longer
by my side: she was still in the room, but was standing on a
chair in the corner, both hands completely obscuring her face.
A gentle sobbing sound coming from her. There was a bath
on one side of the room filled with blood and what looked like
intestines and other organs; a dark crust was forming as flies

buzzed around it. And in the centre of the room with his back to me, was my father. His arm hinged at the elbow, was methodically swinging up and down as he worked on something I couldn't see. A vile sawing noise rang through the room. I couldn't bear to look, but knew I had to see: this was what she was trying to tell me about, this scene was the pinnacle of truth that had to be exposed. I crept forward, desperate to remain unseen to him. As I approached I could see a tumbling mass of hair juddering over his moving arm as the full horror of his actions became clear. He was sawing off the face from the severed head of an unknown woman. A scream attempted to leave my body, but was stifled by fear. I couldn't bear to look any longer, so I wrenched my gaze away and as it fell onto my mother she lowered her hands revealing a black hole of nothing where her own face should have been. I could just make out the back of the inside of her skull as she gently shook her head from side to side as if somehow trying to apologize for what I had just witnessed, was indeed still witnessing.

I suddenly sat up in bed, panting, bathed in sweat. I felt utterly, utterly appalled and terrified beyond belief. Were these dreams distorted reflections of past realities? If so then my father wasn't just a mad control freak with jealousy issues, he was a completely insane psychopathic murderer, who had killed and dismembered perhaps several women, one of whom happened to be my mother. I shook my head, refusing to accept it. "I'm just highly stressed," I whispered words of comfort to myself in the darkness. And so I'm sitting here in the early hours of the morning going over and over events leading up to now. I'm shaking uncontrollably and for some reason freezing cold. A strange tinkling noise just came from my dressing table. I'm going to put the light on. Oh my God, the key, the fucking key from the dream is sitting on my table. Oh Christ, I'm still asleep, it's one of those lucid dreams where one leads into another, please, I just want this to be over. My bedroom door is starting to open, oh no it's him, no it isn't, there's no one there. I can't go back into that room, please I can't bear it. It's no use, I can feel a tugging sensation pulling at my arms. Why? Why the hell do I have to go again, I've seen enough, I just want to get out, why are you putting me through this? Alright, I'm fucking going.

So I'm in here and it's just like it was, except for the bath of blood and all the people. What am I supposed to find? Go on then, drag me somewhere, no?

"Lucy Willow, how many times have I told you, you're banned from this room." "Dad, I didn't hear you, I'm sleep-walking, or maybe we're sleepwalking? I don't really know what's going on anymore." "No, I'm not really sure anymore, Lucy, the only thing I'm ever really sure about these days are numbers, when things add up, and I don't think you can add people up. You know, it's funny, it was numbers that revealed the truth." "What do you mean, Dad? What truth?" "Well you've always wanted to know about your mother, and I suppose you have the right. I've always just tried to protect you from it, Lucy." "Just tell me, Dad, you killed her, didn't you?" "She really did bring it on herself, Lucy. Like I said, it was numbers, you can't hide behind them. Little bits of money going out here, little bits there, it wasn't difficult to track; she thought she was being so clever, so careful. But I knew. I only had to follow her once and I saw them together with my own eyes. The filthy slut. Do you know I still haven't really forgiven her, even after all this time, it still eats me up, like maggots in my stomach that I just can't get at. But oh, she was such a beauty your mother, just like you are, my Lucy Willow. I couldn't bear to let that face of hers go. So I didn't. Look, it's here in this cupboard, no don't try to pull away from me, look it's perfect, isn't it, like it could still be alive, I was so careful, no don't scream, Lucy, it's a homage to her. It wasn't too hard to do in the end, I just brought her up here after she'd died, after everyone had said their goodbyes and before we buried her. I'm proud of how well I did, she got the face she deserved in the end, I had one waiting, no-one was going to miss a cheap two-bit whore off the street. She had no idea what was coming to her. You know the real irony of it all, she adored you, worshipped you, more than she'd ever loved me, I used to give you poisoned tea to take in to her. No don't cry, she deserved it, Lucy, it's what you get if you cheat. And it seems that you've followed in her footsteps. Honestly, planning on meeting up with some boy without my consent? No stop struggling, stop or I'll have to . . . stop . . . or you're going to make it worse for yourself, Lucy"

The Daily Chronicle June 12th

House of Horror Reveals Dark Secrets

Police tape is still sealing off 22 Crowbridge Street as forensic teams continue to work around the clock piecing together the morbid events that have taken place in what is already being dubbed "The House of Horror." One male, 52 year old Roy Thompson, has been taken into custody and charged with the murder of one female, and accused of the murder of two more. The alarm was raised when 14-year-old Lucy Willow Thompson failed to turn up at school for over two weeks. Officers were finally called to the address after Social sSrvices failed to raise a response. "I've been working as a police officer for over 10 years and I've never seen anything like it," said PC Simon Morris. "It was like something from a horror movie, a bath full of blood, and severed body parts." It seems that Mr Thompson was an amateur taxidermist and had added his own daughter to his collection. The face of the late Mrs Thompson was also discovered, sparking a fresh murder investigation. "We are in the process of exhuming Mrs Thompson's body in order to perform tests to see if we can establish the exact cause of death, which had been registered as natural causes," said PC Morris, who also informed us that DNA tests carried out on tiny fragments of bone found at the property have been linked to missing prostitute, Joanne Wilmslow, last seen around the time of Mrs Thompson's death. Excavations on the garden are continuing. "They were such a quiet family, who kept themselves to themselves. We all felt sorry for them really after the mum died, but you just don't expect anything like this, the whole community is in shock," said close neighbour Margaret Green.

HARRY

If there's one thing I regret
it's the pregnancy and the marriage

Monday has arrived late and overripe and all its seeds look like
arseholes and every arsehole has a voice and my life is a giant
shit-filled peach stuffed with seeds that you bury just to kill
them but they grow into forests of faeces their great brown
branches drip in the wind and excrement in the elements
means they all go white in the morning sun and scrape off
your shoe okay I'm sorry it's just my little dog's been sick and
it'll come off anyway you don't bury seeds to kill them you
idiot don't you know how plants work they don't work idiot
they're plants plants are just animals on the permanent dole
now clean your shoes my brown carpet doesn't need a more
authentic shade of brown

The child killed the dog it carries the skull around in its
mouth

I wouldn't eat that peach if I were you it's filled with shit

I woke up the bed is broken again the bed was always broken

we broke the bed with the same intercourse that broke our minds and polluted our bodies and gave you the child that gobbled up my life I cannot wait for it to die it is too large and wants too much it isn't normal for its eyes to be so many and everywhere and its skin is too shiny and hard like a crab's and it ripped you apart when it slid out

there
were
spines

We called it Harry like the prince and the wizard and agreed that was its name til it found something it identified as at the moment I think it wants to be a doctor but it hasn't figured out the back-together part yet

Harry presses against the television won't touch a computer only likes static I've seen it lick the screen and black-and-white snowflakes come off on its tongue they crackle before they sizzle in its mouth and its backful of black eyes all go white for a moment like tiny pools of milk criss-crossed with ridges of shiny blackened bone

it likes the static and needs the volume turned up and its colossal body becomes a shadow with just the edges lit by the TV and it is too much of a spider and a beast to be my son of course I don't look like a spider I guess the condom broke of course it broke the sperm that built him must've been barbed I hate it

I hate Harry it killed the dog

the dog was asleep and Harry scuttled onto it and chomped it with his underside mouth the dog didn't die we heard it scratching inside and barking for days then Harry pulled his legs in and shuddered and sprayed a red mist over the lounge

your priest was visiting and said we had to love the child as our own because it was God's will that a cannonball mollusc slide out of your vagina and eat the dog

but he really shut up when Harry came in the room and he shouldn't have screamed when the blood spurted out and a dog's foot hit him in the lip and I shouldn't have laughed back when that was something we could do

you rammed your wheelchair into Harry to make him apologise but he just lay there with all those eyes staring at us with no explanation of why he killed the dog and your priest said he'd pray for us but mostly said buggerfuckshitfuckfuckfuck and spat out fur I don't know where he went I guess wherever priests go

I can't feel my legs

Harry took them during a dream

There's an old man who lives on my street. A fat old man who is jolly to everyone. Once a year, we have a Christmas parade and the old man plays Santa, sitting on top of his red Mini Minor, which is pulled along by eight local boys dressed as reindeer. He laughs and whips them a bit and there's nothing suspect or sexual in what he's doing because it's Christmas and at worst

his motives are as neutral as the car. The parade goes beautifully,
he hands out chocolates and toys to the smaller children and
when the parade is over none of us notice he hasn't unharnessed
the reindeer, who stand around speaking teenage slang to each
other and generally being insufferable in their harnesses and
bells. Drunk and laughing, Santa climbs into his car, slams his
foot on the pedal and eight reindeer boys get torn into venison
as they're dragged along the asphalt, thrashing and jingling all
the way . . .

Harry had scuttled to the bed and got my ankle in its mouth
made noises like a duck's foot stamping on wet plastic
it snapped my leg my marrow boiled he cut me clean at the knee
the dog's skull has been sharpened and is good for tendons
our kid is clever I felt a jaw within a jaw and the tag from
the dog's collar and we should've bought a cat their heads
are smaller and would do less damage or a guinea pig or a
goldfish or maybe we should never had sex or ever met and
you could've become a nun and I could've been chemically
castrated he took the other leg the room flashed blocks of
static and when I screamed the static was solid and filled my
throat like a humming rush of burning sand I saw a glow
behind my own eyes
when he stopped I was stumps
HOWZAT

I said Harry get off the bed
you said he could sleep with us
I said he just ate my legs
you said I never had any legs
a meowing sound came from somewhere inside Harry

and for one brief moment we had a cat

I think sometimes I'm having a phantom limb interlude but I think Harry can eat concepts too so I tell myself there's no invisible legs or he'll take them away I know he can eat emotions you wanted to leave and then you didn't want to leave he slept near your head some nights didn't bite just slept near you and suddenly you didn't want to go and you ran me over with your wheelchair when I was crawling across the floor because I wanted to go and Harry did that horrible squatting thing he does and the bathroom was sprayed with the juice that was my legs

I don't know when I sleep I just know I come back from somewhere else

There is no rest the many-eyed bastard is too big and too arbitrary it doesn't blink the eyes could be watching or they could be dead there is no thought inside that shell or if there is it means its father naught but harm

there's not much in common between dogs and legs except meat and that I liked all of them and I took them all for walks ha ha ha ha ha ha My child is cruel and loves its mother

Your mother gave us a set of steak knives for our wedding and I'm sure they weren't meant to be used to stab a disabled woman and her mutant child but a gift is a gift and the gift I give myself is all of us dead and ground into muddy pulp near the family tree a smudge on the records and a footnote in local gossip this house gets sold and bought by a couple who listen

to the neighbors talk about the crippled girl and her amputee
husband and the child they maybe had

*Never saw the husband or child only ever saw the mother she
was so brave people are animals if I ever find the thugs who
slashed their throats I'll kill them*
*There was a huge creature there too look I saw it I look I look
I look*
*I just never felt so satisfied to see anything dead not sure I
entirely understand why but I just felt so relieved when I knew
whatever it was couldn't hurt us*
*I think the police said it was ambergris which comes from whales
and they use it to make perfume but why would ambergris be so far
inland that's what I want to know how did the ambergris get here*

You banned me from the kitchen and the front door and the
backyard and the computer and my phone but I can turn on
the television for Harry and I can come to bed and when I'm
in the wrong place you run me over and you punch me in the
face and Harry looks at me when I flail and crawl to where
I'm meant to go I think you like that part of your day I think
you like it considerably

In the bathroom I vomit black

rubbery particles like scraps of bin-bag pour out of my face
and onto the floor
some bits wriggle on the porcelain like licorice sperms
Harry clicks in his skinny legs clack off the tiles click-clack-
clack I loathe that clacking it sounds like cockroaches backs
breaking

Harry's tongue flops out on the floor and he drags it across
the wrigglers
he licked them up and laughed I think he laughed he rumbled
somewhere in his husk
I puked directly onto his back and slapped him with my palms
and punched and punched and punched his goddamn rocky
sides curled my fingers into his eyes and pushed into the dark
jelly my fingerbones went cold and I pulled them back I was
defeated and my child unhurt Harry showed me his mouth
where a dog and cat skull danced with each other inside a
cylinder of curved teeth like a washing machine for flesh
I'm getting through to you son
I spat black at him
I am getting through to you
he came forward and slowly lowered his open mouth onto my
head
I don't know if it was a warning or love but I felt the words in
my brain start to skitter out through the top of my skull and
my forehead is a mess of fine tooth marks dotted in perfectly
straight lines and the indent of a cat I hate him

I hate the fucking child I hate its freezing eyes I hate the tongue
that flops I hate the pricks of blood on my forehead fine as
measles I hate you I hate that you don't talk you mutter and get
confused by anything that isn't Harry and your eyes lose focus
when you gibber about anything and you don't talk until you
gibber because you know everything that's happening is wrong
but it's happening to us so it can't be and our son is jagged bone
and eyes sunk like black coral whatever happened to Coral she
was old and lived down the road whatever happened to the road
whatever happened to us we built a relationship based on lies

I know there were lies

lies are just trust with extra fun bits and someone somewhere
must've had something extra fun our son is a fucking crab but
nobody minds hallelujah

Harry has learned to get by
everybody's thoughts get fugged when he's around your sister
was here for hours she's had a lifetime of trauma
we had no real explanation for how my legs had been hacked
off
but she seemed to understand something had happened
which isn't much just a thin slip of comprehension that I had
no legs anymore but no alarm about it like I always had no
legs anymore
you both drank tea and ignored me while I puked and had
no legs

I am always puking now I try to get it in your tea sometimes
but you stabbed me why did you stab me I'm sick you stupid
bitch I'm vomiting up wet shadows

The TV fried the walls with electric snow the rush of noise
has a drumbeat it's Harry humping the plasma with his mouth
he never makes a sound you just hear hard shell tapping
against TV like a crab claw against glass it is so slow a tch
tch tch tch tch tch spread over half an hour

you sat in your chair and looked at nothing your mouth down-
turned but no mood alive I was on the carpet with the remote
you don't like it when I get too tall I changed the channel and

Harry's tongue caught the colours off a deodorant commercial he humped in a frenzy finally a teenager an insect jangled by hideous lights and the sound told us we'd have freshness for twenty four hours while our child burned

its legs got tangled and jets of white steam shot out its eyes and bleached them red I laughed and yowled at the boiled bastard and threw the remote at the TV which shattered a nasty streak behind I know the static makes him happy and yes dammit he's a boy he's our freakish horrible son and I hate him with the depth that comes from love and the TV was off and the room was dark and all I heard was him bumping the table in what I hope was pain

you wheeled yourself into the kitchen while Harry jittered and brought the kitchen knife over and stabbed me in the lips it spread the middle of my front teeth and I stopped laughing and started bleeding and screaming and spat blood and wrigglers on the lounge room carpet you cried and clambered on top of Harry and the steam scalded you but the tears from your eyes went into its eyes and you both lay still until its eyes went completely black again and you murmured and twitched and Harry carried you to the bedroom and I knew we'd never buy any deodorant

The bed is lopsided I lay on the edge closer to the ground

You are beside me Harry rests on us I don't know if Harry can sleep or knows what sleep is I don't know that it could do anything if it dreamt I just know it likes to eat the dust of television signals and the occasional limb and pet

I love you but you've maimed me and there's nothing but vagueness in my voice when it comes out there is no tone just a numb mumble and my arms don't feel a strength my skin bubbles as if burnt and each blister has a wriggling thing I have two arms made of embryos or herpes and a voice that drones nobody would listen to me if they could and the wind whistles where my front teeth used to be
pheep   ifyoucouldhelpmethatdbegreat   *pheep*
yeahjustadollarpheep
I am the most invisible thing in a house of invisible people and a monster that everyone can see if I asked you for money you wouldn't give me the money thank God I have a home and a God I suppose I have a God I did capitalise the G

Harry is moving now and I can see you are crying but your face will not move and he's curled his legs around us and I see the dog and cat and we are together again you and I

Our arms hang limp from the underside of our son I can feel the air outside but our heads are pulled back along the ribs of a thick tube and I think I am staring upwards but at what this world is smaller than the world and our house and our bed this is a world that ends with Harry and I am surrounded my torso is belly-down and we are here for the child that we built tears don't drip on my face they leak into the new skin he is much softer on the inside than I thought he'd be but always cold we are freezing I cannot hear you and my teeth would grind but this is not my mouth, my mouth is filled with jelly and that jelly was my tongue
my teeth I think are in the dog the sharpened skull

I try to hold your hand but you swat me it's good to know you still care baby

I can feel the grass of our front yard overgrown and tangled and pavement scrapes my knuckles and now there is a fabric and beneath the fabric bone and breathing and whoever it was will die

And my brain dissolves into Harry

we dragged the bastard forward together through life,

then he squatted
and we rained.

THE BASEMENT CONVERSION

THE DRILLING WAS so loud it made Lucy want to bite down on a piece of wood. She thought that if her husband had chosen a project specifically to make her unhappy, he could scarcely have picked something more effective than a basement conversion. The noise vibrated through the whole house, through every wall and every floor. The dust lay on every surface in a thin sheen. When she made herself a sandwich at lunchtime, it tasted granular, like a picnic on the beach.

All of which she could live with, if the end result was worth having. She had survived the refitting of the kitchen, which had been just as loud, just as dirty, and had robbed her of a place where she could make herself a cup of tea for consolation. And she had managed when the bathroom was knocked out and replaced, with only a vile chemical toilet in the back garden for a week, and having to shower at the local pool. But the basement conversion was less tolerable than either of those more disruptive events, because she had no idea why they were doing it. She understood the numbers, the increase in value per square foot which they were adding to the property. James barely articulated his annoyance that she couldn't see what a good deal it was, to add a whole extra floor beneath the ground, and increase their living space so considerably. She couldn't explain to him that some things were more valuable than money: peace, and cleanness, and not having to apologise to her neighbours for the noise and the mess as the trundling conveyor-belt poured thick clay into the skip outside their home.

He behaved as though she didn't understand money, disregarding the fact that they had met as undergraduates, decades earlier, in the same economics class. She thought back to her student days in Birmingham, wishing she could just take a train one more time to New Street, and then the 61 bus out to the university, and wander around a campus which had probably changed beyond recognition. She had always understood money; she had no memory of a time when she couldn't convert currencies in her head, or calculate interest rates, or analyse the risks of competing investment funds. She was a born accountant, her father had always said, meaning it as a compliment. That was how she had taken it too. She had never claimed to be anything special, but she had always been good with numbers.

She had graduated and stayed in the city to train as an accountant. She took her first full-time job at a firm on Colmore Row, continuing her relationship with James long-distance, or intercity, to be more precise. They used to meet at Euston or New Street (the latter more frequently at first, as he came back to visit their friends and relive his student life, a welcome release from the tension of his first job, working in the City of London). Gradually, it became Euston every weekend: after five mornings of being in the office before dawn, he could no longer face the train journey to see her, falling asleep before the train reached Watford Junction, shaken awake by a cleaner in

Wolverhampton, his stop missed. Soon after that he stopped meeting her at Euston, but told her to make her own way to his flat in Angel (a fashionable area now, she acknowledged, but different then, in the 1980s). She didn't fear for her safety – it was only two stops on the Northern Line, after all – but she missed him waiting for her as she stepped off the train and into the capital, where everyone walked so much faster than they did back home, so relentless in pursuing even their most trivial goals. She would look down at the ring which sparkled on her left hand, and wonder if he knew that she would have preferred something less sparkly if it meant he would come and meet her at the station, his face lighting up when he saw her, as it once did.

She couldn't now remember when he had persuaded her to give up her job and move to London. There were accountancy jobs in abundance here, he had promised. And he was right. She was employed within a week or two: the City had an unquenchable appetite for people like her. But she never warmed to her new office, built moments before she started working there, scarcely finished. She remembered everything being grey and cheap, plastic wall panels coming unstuck from the wall above her desk, a thin slick of hardened yellow glue beneath them.

That was why she hadn't minded giving it up, when he was transferred to Singapore, or was it Hong Kong first? She no longer found it worrying that she couldn't remember: their lives had been so similar no matter where they lived: James wore the same suits, they ate in the same restaurants with the same financiers and their same wives. Lucy had never fitted in, as soon as they discovered she had no children. We've been trying, she would say, but no-one wanted to be tainted by her failure. These people saw themselves as golden, however pedestrian they seemed to everyone else. They treated any admission of non-achievement as toxic, a miasma which might infect them too, even as they sent their two perfect offspring to the International School in whichever city they currently inhabited.

By the time Lucy and James moved back to the UK, to London, it had changed more than she could have ever imagined. Gone were the taxi drivers who had once been her neighbours. Now it was all people like James. People called the process 'gentrification', though Lucy kept thinking that the gentry (at least in Jane Austen novels) had rather better manners than her new neighbours. Even these she would miss, however, when the houses were knocked through into three or four tiny flats, and their multiple tenants – younger versions of the landlords who they viewed hungrily as role-models – began arguing in the street about parking places and bins.

Lucy was forty-five years old, childless, and married to a man who no longer loved her. She couldn't quite see this as a tragedy, since she had only a vague memory of the man she had agreed to marry: the James who had been young and cautious but kind, and capable of easy delight. She felt as though a doppelganger had replaced him, one who saw virtue only in the price of things. She needed to do something to make herself less unhappy, though she had no idea what. The idea only presented itself when she received a leaflet through the letterbox, promoting classes at the local college (she kept this information to herself when asked to tick a box explaining where she had heard about the course. She didn't want them to believe that junk mail worked).

She signed up for Fine Art and Art History, because although she knew nothing about either, she felt vaguely as though she might want to know more. She had lived next door to a girl reading Art History at university, and her room had always been filled with handsome young men, their teeth stained from smoking roll-up cigarettes and drinking coffee black. Lucy's tutor was an exuberant woman in her fifties – grey hair escaping from an ugly plastic clip – who announced that they couldn't possibly understand frescoes unless they attempted the process themselves: she taught them to apply plaster to a surface and level it off, so they could experience the difficulty of applying paint to it before it dried, and the impossibility of applying paint to it unless it was perfectly even. If you want to understand Florentine painters, her tutor declared, you must imitate them, even on the smallest scale. Lucy spent days picking small flecks of plaster off the skin around her fingernails, but she still enjoyed the beginners' course and signed up for the intermediate one.

In the moments when the drill went silent, she could hear the occasional ping, which irritated her beyond measure, an added insult to the headache which already plagued her. She wondered which of his electronic devices James had left at home. But then the drilling began again and she realised that the cessation and resumption was worse than a constant barrage of sound. Every time it stopped it reminded her of how she loved the quiet, and every time it began again it seemed louder and more insistent than before.

James had no interest in her new-found enthusiasm for art. He didn't want to go to a gallery or visit a museum. She thought about reminding him how many men in his position were patrons of galleries, but she realised she would prefer to go alone. To attend an exhibition among all the other visitors and tourists meant queuing and jostling, but she didn't mind that as much as the sterility of after-hours openings, where the only people present were ones who preferred to clink glasses with their fellow guests rather than look at the paintings on the walls. Even if you liked numbers as much as Lucy (who had long thought of the number four as another woman might think of an old school-friend: a trusted companion through the years), there was nothing delightful in an evening spent measuring net worth amid beauty.

At the end of the college term, she was expected to bring home the pieces she had worked on in college: the line draw-ings of wooden mannequins, the still lives of fruit, the land-scape watercolours and the experimental miniature fresco. They had an open evening first, for all the friends and family of the artists to come and admire their work in the studio where it had been made, and where it was all on display. Lucy mentioned it to James, but he showed no interest in attending. When she asked about it a second time, he snapped that he had an important dinner with clients that evening. So she had gone alone, and drunk a small glass of warm white wine with her classmates, telling them that James was away on business. She took her work home in the back of a taxi and put it up in the loft, where it would be in no-one's way.

The pinging sound interrupted her thoughts again, and she realised it was coming from the office. When they converted the room – buying a large oak desk and a chair more heavily engineered than most early spacecraft – it had been on the pretext that James would work more from home, and would be able to spend less time in the City. But he spent longer hours at his company than he ever had. She waited, teeth gritted, for the drilling to begin again, but a different noise had begun now. Perhaps the drilling was completed. The builders were supposed to finish today, she knew. Perhaps this had been one last flurry of disturbance before they left. She walked through to the office, and saw that James had left his computer turned on. It was whirring away angrily, and as she approached it, she could feel the heat radiating from the monitor. She reached over and flicked the mouse, to bring the screen to life so she could switch it off. Another infuriating ping accompanied her movement. As the screen lit up, she saw the message which had prompted the sound.

When are you going to kill her?

James arrived home a little earlier than usual. He was carrying a bottle of wine and a bunch of flowers which looked as though his secretary had spent several minutes choosing them.

"For you," he said, and she took them and went to the kitchen to find a vase. "I'll go and see how it looks'" he said, skirting past her to the stairs which used to lead to the cellar, but now led to the basement they didn't need. He picked up his torch – a large, heavy, metal one – from where it hung on a hook behind the door. After a few minutes, she heard him call her. "Come and see," he said. "It's looking great."

She had no energy for tears. She walked carefully down the stairs, one hand in her pocket, the other holding the rail so she didn't trip. There was no need to make things easier for him.

He turned as she reached the bottom step, and she felt panic rise in her chest. The light was dim in the basement, but it still glinted off the blade he was holding in his left hand.

"What on earth's the matter with you?" he asked. She couldn't speak. Was this how she would die? Her throat cut in the basement of a house she had never considered her home?

"Bloody builders have left half their tools behind." And he threw the Stanley knife into a small toolbox with a clatter.

Lucy took a breath. She wanted to gasp her gratitude, but she couldn't without giving herself away. She should never have read the messages: it made no difference that she hadn't meant to. What on earth was she thinking, believing her husband to be a murderer? The idea was ludicrous. Of course, it was a conclusion that most people would draw, if they had seen what she had seen. But it was obviously a mistake. They were playing out a silly fantasy, like lovers sometimes did. She felt a small twinge thinking of her husband as another woman's lover.

But it was only a twinge. She wouldn't die of it.

The basement looked better than she could have imagined. The new walls were beautifully finished, and she was astonished by the size of the space.

"What will we put down here?" she asked.

"I'm still deciding" he said. "I thought a home cinema, but I don't watch many films nowadays, do I? They're all the same."

She forbore to reply that this was not the case.

"Or perhaps a gym," he said, patting his paunch. "That might be a good idea. And I thought we'd use this bit for a wine cellar."

Lucy followed his gaze to a small door, set into the wall. Now her eyes were accustomed to the dingy light from the two bare bulbs snaking overhead, she could see that the builders had indeed built a small room with thick walls, directly beneath the kitchen

"Open it," he said. "Look inside."

Lucy wished she could just tell him what had happened. That she had read the messages by mistake. That she knew about his mistress. That he could leave her, and she wouldn't make a fuss. She didn't want half of his money, half of his home, half of his life. She only wanted what she had always wanted: a life of her own. And she didn't need anything of his for that. But she couldn't quite bring herself to say it: something about the messages had seared themselves into her mind. The woman was vicious, that was plain enough. And determined to marry a rich man. But Lucy would not fall into the trap of believing her husband an innocent stooge. She had seen his replies. Was he leading the woman on? Making promises of marriage he had no intention to fulfil? She was almost incensed on the woman's behalf.

She reached for the door handle, trying not to flinch as she felt him step close beside her. She pulled back her fingers as though the handle were burning hot.

"Ow," she said. "Splinter." She put her hand to her mouth, as if she could bite the wooden shard out of her skin.

James rolled his eyes – of course his wife would find a splinter in a newly-sanded door. He reached around her and opened it himself, flicking on his torch and pointing it into the gloom. The cellar room was everything she feared: small, dark, unlit.

Soundproof.

"Yes," she said, stepping backwards. "That'll work well as a wine-cellar."

He raised the torch suddenly, and without thinking she lifted her right arm to protect her skull, feeling the bone crack as he slammed the hard metal into it. She twisted her body to see him lift it a second time, his mouth drawn back in a snarl. Only then did she remember that she had known this was coming, even if she had tried to disbelieve it. She took the tiny can from her left pocket, and depressed the lid.

The noise was deafening. James stepped back from her, dropping the torch so he could cover his ears with his hands. Lucy saw it roll beneath him (she could not hear it hit the ground: the rape alarm was far too loud for either of them to hear anything else) and tangle itself in his feet. He tripped and fell into the wine cellar, and she slammed the door, hearing the catch click shut before wondering if she could race up the stairs before he pushed his way out and tried to kill her again.

She let go of the alarm, but still it hollered on the floor. She felt the handle rattle beneath her hands as she pushed all her weight against the door.

"Let me out, you crazy witch," said her husband, though the voice no longer sounded like his. The door handle suddenly fell at her feet, and she thought stupidly of the smirking builder who looked - to Lucy's eyes - like a man who would cut corners. The alarm was finally quiet, and she heard James curse as the handle on the inside of the door - now it had nothing to support it - fell off too. She kept her weight pressed against the door just in case, but moved her hands carefully downwards, so she could look through the tiny hole at the furious eye of the man who had once loved her and who had just tried to kill her. She turned away from him in disgust and walked back up to the kitchen, shutting the door behind her.

Two weeks later, Lucy stood back and admired her handiwork. The artisans of Renaissance Florence would doubtless have made a better job of things than she had. Plaster should be smooth, her tutor had taught her, like the surface of a lake on a calm day. Still, she was pleased with the result.

The police hadn't even imagined there might be a door behind her wall, let alone a room. They were not really looking for her husband in his home, of course. It had been the most cursory inspection. In fact, she suspected they weren't looking for him anywhere: middle-aged men left their wives all the time. And his colleagues must have testified to the mistresses, because the police had asked her so tactfully about other women, as they sat drinking tea from her favourite cups, directly above the entombed body of her husband.

The first thing she would do, she decided, was go to Italy.

ABOVE AND BEYOND

PETER'S BREATHING WAS heavy as he carried the dead fox back to the car. "This will do for a dog," he thought to himself. "Aren't they practically the same species?" He wrapped the fox in a bin bag, careful not to ruin the upholstery of the car, and inwardly congratulated himself for being so observant. "Not many people would spot roadkill at this time of night," he thought. "Being a great dad is hard." He smiled, before looking in the glove box for some wet wipes to clean his hands.

It had all started so innocently. Peter lived for Saturday night, the one night of the week he could read his daughter Abigail a bedtime story. Burgeoning her love of literature was a source of great pride to him, and he was suspicious that his ex read to their daughter in a dull monotone, so he was eager to make these nights count. The routine was simple. Abigail was dropped off after lunch, they both enjoyed a weather-dependent outdoor activity followed by drive-thru McDonalds for a treat, then back to his house. Peter marvelled at how cynicism for Saturday-night television evaporated as he watched his daughter enjoy programmes he usually loathed, but in reality he was just gearing up to bedtime, when he could read to her and pretend that he saw her every day. The first time he'd gone 'above and beyond' had been during a story about a bird who was too nervous to fly south for winter, and had treated itself to a big meal of worms to assuage its nerves. During one of his vigorous act-outs, where he flapped his arms and pretended to fly round the room, it suddenly struck Peter how much his daughter would enjoy seeing him eat a worm. A little girl of her age, what could be better than that! So he got Abigail out of bed, and sat her in the kitchen whilst he scrabbled around the garden on his hands and knees, looking for a worm to put in his mouth. Eventually he found one, and served it up on a plate with some garnish, like they do in restaurants. His daughter already thought this was hilarious. Peter then draped a 'Visit Great Yarmouth' tea towel over his forearm like waiters do in films, before adopting a cod French accent and asking 'madame to inspect the dish.' Abigail was now beside herself with glee as he reached for a knife and fork, although Peter was beginning to have second thoughts. He stared at the worm wriggling around on the plate, and tried to remember from when he was a kid if chopping a bit off the back would kill it. Abigail covered her mouth with both hands, such was the ferocity of her laughter, as Peter ate the first bit of salty worm. "Christ," he thought, as he forced himself to swallow. "Don't the French eat worms?" His whole body was shuddering as he tried to commentate on the meal in a cod-French accent, before remembering that he should be acting like a nervous bird, as opposed to a French waiter – the French waiter was something he had improvised, and nothing to do with the story. After a couple of mouthfuls he started to gag, and cursed his naivety for thinking it would become easier as he got used to it. Eventually he finished eating, and the tears of laughter dripping down his daughter's cheeks offered all of the justification he needed, as he bent over a toilet bowl to vomit.

"I wonder how much people pay for colonic irrigations," Peter thought to himself as he winced at the violence of his diarrhoea. "I'm sure I read about Native Indians purging their bodies by being sick, or was it Aborigines?" Peter couldn't remember. What he could remember was the look of delight on his daughter's face as he drank a cup of pond water, just like the main character had done in the book he was reading her. The plot revolved around a meek little girl of about Abigail's age, who exacted revenge on the school bully by making her drink pond water. Peter hoped empathy with the main character wasn't the reason Abigail liked the story so much, as his daughter being bullied was a constant in the anxiety dreams he suffered. How do you even deal with bullying as a parent? He had no idea, but he did know that he should make the one night of the week he saw her worthwhile. The water looked ominously murky as he filled his glass from the pond. As he lifted the pond water to his mouth he regretted not using the brown Smarties mug he had lurking at the back of the cupboard, at least the cloudiness of what he was about to drink would be disguised. His lips thinned as he took a taste, trying not to think about what was in that stagnant old pond of his. Abigail was giggling by now, rocking back and forth with her hands on her knees. "God, she's adorable," Peter thought to himself, before remembering that he should be acting the part of the bully. "Er, what have you put in this drink?" he said, in a stupidly high voice. "It's delicious." Abigail was really laughing now, so he continued to improvise. "Mmmm," he said, inwardly chastising himself for being so unconvincing. "How would they film this if it were a Hollywood movie?" he wondered, as he downed the last of it – bits of soil and sediment bouncing against his teeth. "I suppose they'd have millions of pounds to spend on special effects." He sent his ecstatic daughter to the bathroom to brush her teeth as he swilled his mouth out with Ribena Toothkind.

Abigail flicked efficiently through the children's book section of her local library. She was looking for clues on each cover, whether it was blood, the author's name being written in a 'scary' font, or even a parental warning. They were the best ones. Any book with a parental warning was perfect, as that meant Mum wouldn't like it, and Dad would be stupid enough to act something out from it. She hadn't told any of her friends at school about her father's enthusiastic storytelling, as if word got back to her mum, she'd step in and try to stop it. Her mum didn't even like her to eat icing at birthday parties; if she knew that Dad had pretended to be an anteater and scrabbled round the park looking for something to eat amongst the dogshit and crushed cans of lager, she'd claim he was a bad influence and stop her from going round. Abigail smiled as she remembered how bad Dad's anteater voice had been. "What an idiot," she thought. "What a stupid, stupid idiot."

Peter couldn't help but realise that the things he was having to eat were becoming more and more grotesque. But his daughter chose all of the stories, and as she grew older, her tastes would naturally mature and darken. She had undoubtedly developed a taste for the macabre though. "That's pretty natural," he thought to himself, as he stared at the dead fox on his kitchen table. It could have been beautiful, but it stank, and its stomach had been messily cut open by the car that had killed it. If he were more of a *millennium man* he could apply make-up to the rotting carcass he'd picked up on the side of the road to make it look like a lady fox from a cartoon, or at the very least clean up its wounds, but he'd only recently discovered that younger men trimmed their pubic hair before nights out, so he made do by draping his Great Yarmouth tea towel over the fox's spilling intestines and liberally spraying the kitchen with Glade. Abigail would arrive soon. He'd have to ensure his ex didn't come in to the house without appearing weird or arousing suspicion, as the sight of a dead fox next to the microwave would imply he'd gone mad. "What a reason to lose custody," he thought, allowing himself an incredulous smile. "There's not a court in the land that wouldn't think it was strange, and if you ask me – that's the problem with this country."

Peter picked up the book he was reading to Abigail. A morality tale about how loyal dogs were to their masters. The book took a bizarre twist when the owner (a medieval Prince) ate his dog to show the knights in his army how battle had hardened him. To make everything appear medieval, Peter had bought some satin from a local draper to hang around the flat, lit candles, and bought himself some mead online (Abigail would drink squash). He secretly hoped that if he was a bit drunk, the taste of fox flesh would be more palatable. He'd already lit the barbecue in his back garden, as he was attempting a hog-roast sort of arrangement. As the doorbell rang he gladdened, realising as he walked through the house that fox meat wouldn't compromise his new low-carb diet.

"Why have you lit so many candles?" Peter's ex asked, as she hung round the door. "Are you seeing someone new?"

"No? Er, what makes you say that?" Peter was totally blindsided by the bluntness of the question.

"I just remember you having fairy lights when we started

going out, and you thought it turned you into Rudolph Valentino," she snorted. Abigail made a face at this, she found any talk of how her parents had once been together very weird. "Come on, Daddy, story time!"

"Just remember, no refined sugar," his ex said as Peter closed the door. "And if you look at the ingredients that means tomato soup and all sorts of things."

Peter nodded subserviently as she walked back to the car. Abigail was visibly enthralled by all of the satin, and the effect the candles had on his quite dingy flat. "Story time! Story time!" she pleaded. Just like Peter, she'd read on from where they'd left the story last week, and she knew he'd have to eat a dog at some point that evening. This was going to be even better than the other stuff. Peter made Abigail a glass of squash, and poured himself a generous glass of mead. He tried not to think of the diseases wild animal's harbour, as he went out to check on the barbecue's process.

Abigail closed the book and looked up at him expectantly. She could see from the nervous look on his face that he had something planned. Had he killed a dog? Can you buy dog meat from a shop? She'd know if he tried to fob her off with a bit of pork that he'd bought from Tesco, but that wasn't Dad's style. After all, she'd seen him eat worms with her own eyes, and she'd heard him spend all night on the toilet after drinking pond water, so he must have something up his sleeve. She thought her father was pathetic. Her mum fussed, and her step-dad was a bit scary, but her real dad was a pathological fucking loser. She even called him Peter in her mind. He reminded her of the teachers who couldn't cope with naughty kids at school, but he didn't have the option of asking Mrs Pearce the head to step in. "Hahaha," she thought. "Poor Dad." She couldn't believe some people sympathised when her parents divorced. Absolute suckers.

"Come through to the garden," said Peter, snapping her out of her daydream. "I've got a surprise."

It had started to drizzle, and the apple Peter had put in the fox's mouth to make it 'look medieval' had burnt. All in all, it was a sorry state. Taking out the bookmark from that week's story, Peter put on his 'medieval' voice. "After losing a thousand men in battle, I declare to the court that I am no longer a man, but a warrior, and I offer to them the meat of my loyal and faithful hound." As he bent over to pick up his knife and fork, Abigail peered at the fox. She immediately recognised that it was a fox and not a dog, and stifled a giggle. Was there nothing he wouldn't do to impress her? Her mind raced as to how he'd killed it. Had he done it with his bare hands? Her mother hated the foxes that went through their bins, and her step-dad used to throw stones at them when they were in the back garden. Had her dad stoned a fox to death? If so, her respect for him increased somewhat. What a nutcase. None of the other dads she knew would do that. Peter continued with his bad medieval-Prince impression, procrastinating badly, as tucking into the slightly burned roadkill he had on his barbecue was becoming unavoidable. His procrastination was so transparent, that both father and daughter became engaged in an intimate dance – she forced laughter as he pranced around, as he vainly bided for the time he knew she wouldn't give him. Buoyed by Dutch courage, he cut into the fox's leg. He immediately regretted not skinning the fox, but he wanted Abigail to think it was a dog, and thought a skinned mammal lying on a barbecue would look too vague. As he hacked at the charred flesh he chastised himself for not buying a steak knife from Tesco, and started muttering about "doing a job properly." It dawned on him that skinning the poor thing might have disguised that it was a fox, although she didn't seem to have noticed it wasn't a dog anyway. All these thoughts swimming round his head made him realise that he was actually quite pissed. He put some fox meat in his mouth, some stray fox hair caught on his tonsils, and he watched his daughter laugh through his tears as he vomited onto the grass of his back garden.

Peter lifted a spoonful of soup to his mouth. He felt absolutely terrible. As it turned out, fox meat didn't agree with him. Despite burning the meat for hours on a barbecue, he caught some horrendous bacterial infection from eating roadkill and was off work for weeks. His GP had raised an eyebrow when Peter lied badly about staying on a campsite that had been "really, really dirty," but a bacterial infection caught from eating fox meat to impress your daughter who thinks it's a dog is not a conclusion you immediately spring to, so the GP merely dismissed Peter as one of his oddball patients. His illness hadn't been contagious of course, so apart from one week when he had to make do with Skype, too weak to leave his bed, Abigail had still come round every Saturday. Unable to muster the strength to jump around and act out characters from her favourite books, Peter had really seen the limitations of a weak croak during their bedtime story sessions. Suddenly he was rum without the coke, cheese without the onion, McGowan without the impressions. His daughter had become frustrated at this, even resorting to a foot-stomping tantrum that had been the talk of the cul-de-sac. Peter had never seen Abigail like that before, and he realised how much their story time must mean to her. He resolved to do something really, *really* special, as soon as he was back on his feet.

It was quite difficult, making enquiries about 'the dark web,' It's not really something you google. Peter wondered how the IRA had done it in the 80s. Didn't they have links with Libya, or was that the other ones? He wished he'd taken more notice of the news. Although maintaining an interest in current affairs throughout the 80s and 90s, merely to source semtex more easily for when you're trying to impress your daughter after you split up from her mum, would have involved a prophet's vision and the kind of discipline that would make Peter a very different prospect in today's competitive job market. In the end, he procured some illegal fireworks from a man in Soho, and was going to make do with good-old-fashioned petrol. He'd bought a couple of fire extinguishers from his local Halfords (he wasn't an idiot), so as long as the cake he'd ordered arrived on time, this was going to be the best birthday any little girl had ever had.

As usual, Abigail had read to the end of the story, and was hoping that her dad had something special planned. She'd feigned interest throughout a fairly boring sci-fi book about a child army, knowing that the space station explosion at the end would at least push her father out of his comfort zone. But she had never expected this. He had covered her treehouse in tin foil, and supersoakers and nerf guns (also covered in tin foil) were liberally scattered around the back garden, clumsily replicating the book's final battle. Peter was trembling as they began the final chapter – "Shall we read the last ten pages outside?" he suggested.

Abigail looked at him. "Whatever you say, Daddy," she said coyly. He sat her down in the middle of the garden, and looked to make sure the fire extinguishers were close at hand. He lit the small bonfire he'd prepared before beckoning Abigail up to the treehouse. As she made her way up to where Peter had left party food and paper plates, he noticed the petrol had given his little bonfire a ferocity that made him slightly nervous, but the fire extinguishers from Halfords calmed his nerves enough to carry on. He read from the book, as Abigail ate Party Rings and Chocolate Fingers. "Sector 5 is ablaze!" he shouted, turning the pages. "I think the Valdron Engines have been struck by a stray Cosmo-Charge!" This was his cue to light the first firework. Abigail watched as he lit a mini Catherine Wheel, which started spinning and throwing sparks onto the food and paper plates. As the paper plates started to burn, Abigail screamed in surprise. Dad had really done it this time. "Fuck," Peter muttered under his breath. He was out of his depth. He hadn't even been to the fireworks night his local Rotary Club organised for a decade. Oh bollocks. The Catherine Wheel was burning far more viciously than he'd expected, and sparks were starting to burn his skin.

"Peter! PETER! WHAT THE FUCK IS GOING ON UP THERE?"

Oh Christ, this was all he needed. Sean next door was in his garden, looking justifiably perturbed. Plumes of black smoke were affecting his vision, and the crackle of the bonfire was making Peter very, very nervous.

"PETER, I'M CALLING THE FIRE BRIGADE, HANG ON."

"I'm fine, Sean," Peter shouted back, trying to sound in control. "Just reading Abigail a bedtime story." Abigail had stopped laughing now, she was fascinated by how frightened her dad looked.

"Read some more, Dad,' she shouted. "How does it finish?"

"Erm . . . bear with me, darling," Peter muttered, fumbling for the pages. Those Halfords fire extinguishers were there if he needed them. There was nothing those Halfords fire extinguishers couldn't handle. After another thirty seconds or so, the Catherine Wheel started to burn out. It took him by surprise, and Peter breathed a huge sigh of relief. He smiled at Abigail, and the way she looked at him broke his heart. "She knew Dad was panicking a bit there," he thought. "We'll probably laugh about this one day." But Peter hadn't noticed that the bonfire in the garden had grown, and was edging towards the other fireworks. "Now where were we?" he asked Abigail, buoyed by their shared moment. Now that the Catherine Wheel in the treehouse had calmed down, he'd imparted this question with what he thought was a Bernard Cribbins-esque homeliness. He started the story again. "I think the Valdron Engines have been struck by a stray Cosmo-Charge!" At this point flames from the bonfire reached the fireworks he'd casually placed on the ground. A rocket flew up into the treehouse and hit Abigail square in the stomach, bright colours shooting out of the wound. As Peter looked on, open-mouthed, she lurched forward, fell, and cracked her skull on the side of the garage before landing on the bonfire below. Peter stared in disbelief at his daughter's burning, broken body, utterly unable to move.

Fresh from his call to 999, Sean ran back into the garden, and saw the burnt-out, smoking Catherine Wheel. Relieved, he shouted up at the treehouse.

"Bloody close shave! I'll go and tell them not to come, Peter. I should have known you'd have it under control."

STEWART LEE

TEST PRESSING

I AM NOT a superstitious man. I fear neither ghosts nor gods. It was just that the events of the previous day had shaken me, and I woke in the small hours with a start. My cowardly and credulous subconscious, formed from the race memories of our cave-dwelling ancestors huddling around a comforting fire in a great black world, meant I half expected something.

But the same white walls surrounded me. The same red velvet curtain, made many years ago by my late mother for her and her first husband's first home, hung heavily at the same window. Outside the same night buses rolled by towards Highgate or Abney Park, a cemetery I now avoided walking through. And the same magnolia tree branch scratched gently at the sill. And I could hear the same street-girls at our gate arguing with the same pimps as usual. And I was alone, as I had been for some years now. Yesterday seemed far away.

Yesterday, Sid was still fifteen years older than me, as he had always been. I had met him tape-trading True West bootlegs via small ads in the inky pages of the weekly music press, back in the pre-internet dark age of the late Eighties. As a teenage record collector, I found it reassuring, inspiring even, that a grown man of all of thirty-two years old was still crate-digging in charity shops daily for ancient acid-rock nuggets.

Even then, Sid dreamed of quitting at the council to retire and run a record store, calling his longed-for rat-race escape plan, rather tastelessly, 'the vinyl solution.'

But now, at sixty-two, Sid, it seemed, had it all. I considered him one of life's winners, the dope-smoking tortoise that quietly trounced all the coke-head hares and got to shack up with the caramel bunny. A south-coast sea breeze buffeted the back window of Sid's comfortable covered market unit, The Sound Hole. A patient and loving acid-folk wife, still in near mint/excellent condition despite decades of repeated play, brought sandwiches and soup at lunchtime. Regulars dropped by to retell record-collector anecdotes, impenetrable to the uninitiated, aging acolytes of the secret clubhouse of their boyhood imaginings. And wide-eyed hipster kids came in to bathe in the glow of Sid's arcane knowledge, in the hum of his unseen powers. Of course, nowadays, were I to go back to London with plastic bags of luxurious old records, ashamed of what I had spent, there is no-one I need to hide them from. But I don't buy stuff anymore. It's all just grave goods that someone else will, eventually, have to deal with.

Rumors of the death of vinyl, it turned out, had been greatly exaggerated, and weekends still drew scores of pilgrims to Sid's psychedelic shrine, racks of authenticated fragments ready to be rifled through beneath walls adorned with original San Francisco sixties posters and austere seventies punk flyers. There were few places I was ever happier, and I didn't visit my old friend enough, though now I was alone I took the train south more often than I used to. And this was something I think, sensing my sadness, Sid quietly encouraged me to do, regaling me with excitable telephone calls about his latest vinyl arrivals that I really had to hear.

My seasonal Sundays at Sid's Sound Hole followed a set pattern. Having left London early I'd disembark at the little railway station before ten, buy two strong coffees from some tax-avoiding chain in the pedestrianised city centre, and then wander down with them to Sid's stall in the seafront market through the gabled remnants of the old town. The old quarter was now home to dozens of arts and media refugees from the same corner of London I'd managed to cling to, displaced by unwashed oligarch money and rising rents.

Sid's customer base had, it seemed, followed him south, hugging second-hand vinyl to their heaving bosoms, because it smelt of memories of youth and possibility. Tony Tone was there now too, the customized-guitar maker, plugging jacks into hollowed-out turtle shells, strung with telegraph wire, in a workshop by the beach; and Polly Screech the antiquarian book-dealer, once our long-term London-coffee-shop confidante, now doing business entirely online from a barge moored in the creek, freed in her own words, from the "ball and chain of analogue premises"; and Lhasa, the occultist musician, still recording shamanistic folk-trance epics, destined for instantly-collectable limited-edition pressings, that he mailed out to Japan from the post office in the old square.

One time when I was here last year, I ran into Lhasa on the seafront, his cape billowing behind him in the breeze that blew in off the brine. "You're down, man," he said, but I knew he'd been in the Hebrides the last year or so, and couldn't have known what had happened, "and that's when you are vulnerable to the psychic vampires." He rolled his bright blue eyes and sucked his cheeks back into his hollow white face. "Come back to my place, drink a bowl of mushroom tea, and I will place you under the protection of serpents." But I told Lhasa

I hadn't joined the National Secular Society as a pissed-off teenager only to start worshipping snake gods as a miserable middle-aged man, and we agreed, good-naturedly, to differ.

On the promenade, the wind blew police tape around the doorway of the old Quaker meeting house, abandoned in the Eighties, and earmarked for as yet unrealized development into luxury flats for the big city incomers. The builders' job had been made just a little bit easier. Somehow the door had been left open, a bystander explained, and someone had got in, stripped out the last remaining period fixtures and fittings, and then started a small fire that had now fizzled out.

"They look for opportunities, any signs of vulnerability or weakness," a policeman pronounced to some bystanders. "They can slip in through the tiniest gaps in your defences and before you know it, it's too late. They might have been sizing the place up for ages, years even, waiting for the right moment to get through the door." The tape flapped around. Onlookers made appropriate noises and dispersed.

Inside the shop, Sid and I would sit and talk about mutual musical acquaintances, news and politics. I was always worried about the war and when it would go global and what that would mean. Eventually a polite disagreement – Sid had moved a little to the right of me since his relocation – would close down the conversation and bring us to the real business of the day. I would take my usual place in an engulfing armchair near the counter, and Sid would unsleeve and sniff his latest rarities, before placing them on the turntable and asking me to identify each artist before the needle hit the run-out groove. I never did.

Who knew The Pretty Things recorded library music as The Electric Banana? Was this really a quasi-legitimate live album released by the post-Lou Reed Velvet Underground?

Did Mountain's Felix Pappalardi honestly make a record with the Japanese psychedelic free festival favourites Blues Creation? Where did Sid find this stuff? Even before the internet created a vast on-line resource of once forgotten knowledge, Sid seemed omnipotent in his musical all-knowingness.

But today, like me, he was puzzled. An unmarked, white-label seven-inch single spun to a close, near mint, all but unplayed, but definitely four or five decades old. Its doomy organ drones and arhythmical electric bass faded, utterly unresolved and quietly appalling in their oddness, unadorned by trebly guitar or even a hint of vocal harmony, but the record's disquieting aura hung in the aisle of the Sound Hole as if something had died and been left to decay beneath the floor boards.

"I give up, Sid," I conceded, "and I'm not sure I even want to know what it is." At this stage in our negotiations, Sid usually glowed with inner pride, teasing me for my ignorance, barely able to conceal his delight in his own superiority. I wondered if he had sought out this impossible curve ball of a record to stimulate me. Like a lot of my acquaintances, Sid sometimes seemed to think he was duty bound to distract me from my memories. But Sid was genuinely perplexed.

"Go on," he said, encouragingly, "what do you make of it?"

"Really? Well, it's got the feel of late Sixties, early Seventies proto-metal. I wondered if it was Earth, the pre-Black Sabbath band, but they had no keyboards. It's got that bad vibes, black magic feel, but it's not kitsch like Black Widow, and it doesn't feel insincere, like when Zior spent a weekend trying to cash in on the craze and recorded that album as Monument . . ."

"Yes," said Sid, looking almost ashen, "I wondered about all that, but there's no info, a paper sleeve, and nothing even scratched into the run-out groove."

"I tell you what Sid, it sounds like some sort of mistake," I offered, "like somebody hurriedly ran off a test pressing of something without lining up all the different tracks or something."

"I know what you mean," Sid agreed. "It's like there's half of the mix missing. Like there should be something else there to give what is there shape and make sense of it all."

"Yes. It doesn't sound like some experimental jazz avant-garde thing," I agreed, "where it's wrong for a reason. It just sounds . . . wrong."

"Musically wrong or morally wrong?" asked Sid, and I laughed because I assumed he was joking. But there was nothing, I realize in retrospect, about his tone to suggest that he found anything funny about the record at all.

"Where did you get it anyway?" I asked.

"Well, here's the funny thing. It was in a box you gave me when you were having a clear out around the time of . . . sorry, mate." Strange. I had no memory of the single, or how I might have come by it. It could have been sitting at the bottom of a box unplayed since the Eighties, or I could have had it only a few weeks when I started trying to purge the house. I couldn't remember. But there are big gaps, clouds in my memory that I wonder if I allowed in there myself, to protect me from yesterday, the pull of the past. Because that life is gone now.

At lunchtime I wandered out into the old town to buy rolling papers for Sid and I to have a quick smoke under the pier before I got the train home. Lhasa was sat on a bench looking out to sea, wrapped in a World War I great coat, throwing great handfuls of brown rice up to the seagulls that swarmed and swooped by the dozen around him. "Lhasa?" I said.

"Keeping in with our future masters," he confided. "One day soon our civilization will fall, but they will bring me fish. Or old chips from bins, at least. You well?"

"Well enough," I replied.

"A word of warning," he said, sealing a Tupperware tub as his seabird overlords wheeled away, "something's up. I know you think I'm nuts, but keep your wits about you. Friends in the occult community have been on the psychic blower."

"The occult community Lhasa, please," I laugh. "It conjures up visions of some kind of terrible retirement home, thirty old guys like you all spilling their Lemsip over a Ouija board."

"You may laugh, man, in fact, I hope you do. Hope it cheers you up, cunt. But the Northamptonshire chapter, they say it's in the stars that something ancient and ugly is coming out from the deep sea, round about now, and it's looking for a way in to our world. I'm taking no chances, look." And then he stood up, turned around and raised the long tails of the coat up over his head. Underneath the heavy material, Lhasa was wearing nothing but a one-piece rubber S&M gimp suit, zipped tightly head to toe.

"Left-over perv-gear from the old Torture Garden disco days, down the Clink by London Bridge, back in the Eighties when painful sex still seemed like a quick shortcut to spiritual enlightenment. How naïve we all were. I blame MDMA. But I'm taking no chances, mate. I'm zipped up tight and every orifice is plugged with freshly-frozen Alaskan pipelines. Nothing's getting in and nothing's getting out." And with that he stood and walked stiffly away.

Back at the shop, Sid's mood had lightened. A dealer he had never seen before had come in and offloaded a box of Sixties and Seventies singles, including some rare gems. The job lot's price had been pegged far below what Sid reckoned he could get for resale of five or six of the most choice sides present alone. I took off my coat and spent the rest of the afternoon helping him sort the stash, glad to have something to occupy me, more disconcerted by Lhasa's strange behaviour than I would care to admit. There was another white label seven-inch in the box, like the one Sid had claimed he had taken off my hands, which was still on top of the turntable lid.

I held the two records up to the light, the sun filtering through the spindle holes, making me squint, as I felt the weight of the heavy thick old vinyl in my hands. I could see from the shape of the grooves that they were not the same single, but they felt like two of a kind, twins separated at birth, and now they seemed to wobble in my grip, as if buzzing with pleasure to be back together at last. And suddenly I didn't want to hold the records anymore.

I put the new single down on the counter. Sid gestured to the turntable, but I declined to listen to the unmarked record, thinking it best to leave Sid to peruse it professionally after I had gone. I wasn't in the mood to be much help speculating about the provenance of another slice of grim abstraction, should the unmarked side prove to be as discombobulating as its fellow.

I always liked the twilight walk back to the station. We had never come to see Sid together. The music was my thing. And so the town held no mutual memories for me. I looked out to the sea and nothing stared back. At the support group, my fellow mourners frequently spoke of how they liked to visit places they had known with those they had lost, to bring them momentarily back to life alongside them. I wanted nothing of the sort, no triggers, no reminders. I wanted to be through this, to accept my loneliness as the new normal, to move through it.

Eventually I will leave the house, sell it, or rent it out, or burn it to the fucking ground if I have to, and live out my last years off the profits or the insurance money, in a place that I am not known, a place that we never knew, where I will not be spoken to or sympathized with. Sometimes in the evenings at home, or suddenly in a library or a quiet bookshop, I forget. I imagine I hear a footstep, or a breath. And I want it to stop. Because it is unbearable. If you are there, have mercy upon me, oh please have mercy upon me, and move on.

Later that night, as I pottered around turning off the lights in the now too many rooms, and locking the door to the now unvisited garden, Sid rang, to see if I made it home ok. And to say, "A strange thing. I played that white label. Just twangy guitar and some kind of chanting, like some Yo Ho Wha 13 off-cut, or Jandek, or Derek Bailey with some Chinese bloke tap dancing or some wank like that. But evil with it, you know. Super-fucking-early-Sabbath dense but properly evil, and unpredictable, and fucked in the head. Then a funny thought struck me. So I dragged the spare turntable out from the back and played it and your white label at the same time, cued 'em up to run together like fuckin' Grandmaster Flash or some hip-hop pioneer type in trainers, some black Detroit guy listening to Kraftwerk and Neu."

"And?" I asked, but I knew. I knew what Sid had heard, and what he was reluctant to describe. It was the sound of uncoiled lengths of ageless life, wet with poisonous lubricant, unfolding in the watery dark over and over, until finally flapping against rock and rolling mud, shuffling pebbles under the bulk of an all but immobile body, to haul it slowly from the sea, up onto the sand and shingle where it could not survive, unless its way forward had already been prepared. And Sid didn't answer me, because he worried that if he said what he had heard, I would worry about him, and he wouldn't want me to worry about him. "And?" I asked again.

"Well, it became something, the tracks, the two tracks together. I don't know what, but something."

"Did you like it?"

"No. I didn't fucking like it. Viv came in when it was playing and told me to take it off. Said she was going to puke. There were all these weird frequencies happening, caused by the juxtaposition of the two tracks I suppose, I don't know, that didn't seem to be there on either individually. Mad as it sounds, they seem to be part of a pair, those two singles. But of course, the bloke who came in, I can't remember anything about him and he didn't leave any details. There's just nothing about anything like them anywhere. Not on the web, not in that Vernon Boynson book, not in Paal Lundquist's thing, nowhere. I've been making calls. Tommy Junk didn't know anything. Nor Micky McLure from *Bathysphere Soundings Quarterly* down in Cornwall. I rang Blessed in Massachusetts, The Exposed Forcep, the godhead, the source. Woke him up. He was pissed off. Didn't know anything. Told me I was an asshole and I should get fucked and how was Viv, who I didn't deserve. You don't remember where you got it, do you?"

I didn't. I was sick of Sid, and Boynson, and the late Paal Lundquist, and Tommy Junk and Micky McLure from *Bathysphere Soundings Quarterly* down in Cornwall and Blessed The Exposed Forcep in Massachusetts and all those boring record-collector cunts, unchanged for thirty years. Why didn't they all grow up? What had any of them, or anyone, ever done for me? I went to bed.

I am not a superstitious man, as I said, but nonetheless, I woke in the small hours with a start. I said everything was the same. And it was. Except for one thing. I could sense a presence next to me, even without looking, like a change in the weather, when you can tell that tomorrow will be hot and dry, even without listening to the forecast.

But I knew that the presence, despite being in our bed, was not her, for she was in Abney Park, three years below ground, with generations of Salvation Army pioneers, and acolytes of Blake, and long-forgotten musical hall comedians male and female, and heroic fallen firemen and famous menagerists, not here beside me, not here, not now. But I smelt the smell of hair product and dental floss and coffee, and skin and blood and sweat and tears, and familiar perfume dabbed behind the ears.

And then I heard the soft in out of breathing, of a chest rising and falling, and the all but silent scraping of sheets as they pulled against the ebb and flow of the lungs, tight and then loose across ribs and hips. And then I felt the warmth, the imperceptible glow of the feint heat of a body, inches away. And then this body rolled in its sleep, and lay its left arm heavily upon me. I felt the tiny hairs brush the flesh of my neck, the fabric of a nightdress move against my shoulders, a murmur of breath upon me, and years falling away. And I wondered what deal I was being offered, and what I would be expected to do in return.

In the morning I made breakfast and we sat on the sofa in an easy silence. I turned on the radio. Various geopolitical cauldrons had boiled over in the night. Eastern tanks rolled West. Vast waves of walkers moved on foot North through

219

former Soviet satellite states. Severed heads in Syria. Bodies falling from buildings and boats sinking and people washed up ashore. I turn off the radio and switch on my old 1972 jukebox, for the first time in years, it having lain neglected in the corner for too long now. The Brogues' 1965 classic, 'I Ain't No Miracle Worker', comes on, always one of her favorites.

I don't ask her how many have come through, and what their plans are. We already have an understanding. I just sit back, drink my tea, and wait to see what will happen next. And Gary Duncan sings from the Wurlitzer. Something about how he'll be tender, and how he'll true. And how, if you ask him for all the love he has, he'll give it all to you.

ALAN MOORE

COLD READING

IN THE OLD black and white plate, the pool of shadow on the left of the ghost's face uncurled its legs to scuttle for the margin and the cluttered desk beyond. I shrank back in my seat and, no word of a lie, I genuinely felt it. It was over in a second when I realised it was just a garden spider come indoors out of the cold and had been camouflaged against the dark bits of the photo, but I really felt that sort of tingle up the spine that all my clients go on about, so I know what they're saying. I can empathise with them. It's not all acting.

Actually, to be perfectly honest, I think nine times out of ten it gives us what I suppose you'd call a supernatural feeling: something turning out to not be what you thought it was. I can remember, I was only six or seven when I saw my first and only ghost. I was with Mum and Dad in the lounge of a seaside pub at night, standing there glued to the glass doors and gawping out into the dark, not thinking of anything in particular. Just then I saw this man walking across the car park of the pub away from me. He wasn't any colour. He was all washed out and then I realised there were parts of him that I could see through. I could see the scrubby strips of grass, the bollards and the drooping lengths of chain that closed the car park in, through the black folds and shadows of his jacket. I thought, "It's a ghost! I'm really seeing one!" And then, and this was the most frightening bit, it turned its head and looked straight at me. It had two blurry faces, one of them just slightly offset from the other, and it smiled in at me through the glass from out there in the night, and then it spoke my name. It's like, I saw its lips move but I heard its voice as if it was right next to me, rather than outside in the car park. It said, "Ricky? Would you like a Fanta?"

Obviously, it was my dad, standing behind me in the lounge with his reflection superimposed on the dark outside. The business with two faces turned out to be caused by double glazing, but just for a second there, you know? I'd thought it was a ghost and that it proved all of the stories that I'd heard from other kids at school. I think it made me cry and when I explained why, about the ghost and everything, Dad told me off and said I was like an old woman, getting taken in by all that superstitious rubbish. Always very level-headed was my father, and I probably take after him in that respect, although I never really liked him much. I was much closer to my mum, but then that's very often how it is with boys, especially an only child. When Dad passed on I suppose Mum was my first audience, as well as being my most willing and my most appreciative. She thought the world of me, my mum. She gave a little gasp and filled up when I did his voice and said, "I always loved you, Irene."

Knowing Dad, it was a safe bet that he'd never told her that in life, and when I saw the comfort that I'd brought that woman, my own mum, that's when I knew I had a gift. That's when I knew what Ricky Sullivan had been put on this earth for. Oh, there'll always be the unbelievers and debunkers in the papers, on the telly or what have you and it does, it makes me angry when they say people like me are cold, unfeeling, just taking advantage and all that. I'm sorry, but if they could see the happiness on people's faces, if they really thought about the service me and others like me are providing, giving people strength to get on with their lives when they've just lost a loved one, well, they couldn't say the things they say. I'm sorry, they just couldn't. I don't have to justify myself.

I mean, do I believe all of the things that I tell people? In my heart, I can't say that I do. But then, what about priests? You can't tell me that all of them believe every last word of what they preach, but do they get called "ghouls in cardigans" or "Vincent Price, but camp"? No. No, they don't. That's because people recognise all of the reassurance and the comfort that religion brings to people, and it doesn't really matter if it's true or not. Or doctors - it's like doctors when they say that a placebo, that's like, what, a sugar pill? That a placebo can work wonders without any side effects, but that they can't prescribe them 'cause of all the medical red tape and ethics, health and safety, all that business. That's me. I'm a spiritual sugar pill, but I do people good. I'm sorry, but I touch their lives.

And yes, I suppose you could say that I've done very well out of it, got the mortgage on this house paid off last year, but that's not what I do it for. It's not the money. How can I explain? It's more the gratitude, the look on some poor widow's face and knowing that you've helped them. That, to me - what can I say? - that look's worth more than gold. That's my reward, right there.

Although this place is very nice, it must be said, with the old-fashioned furniture and all the books, the angel figurines along the mantelpiece, all that. It's mostly for the clients' benefit, same as the New Age music I've got on. It reassures them, makes them feel as if they're in safe hands. No, no, it's very comfortable. It's very cosy, and especially now that the clocks have gone back and we've got these cold nights. If I peer out of the window at the park across the road it looks like one of them old-fashioned fogs tonight, where you can hardly even see the trees. It just makes me feel all the warmer, with the central heating turned up, standing here in this new cardigan that one of my old ladies knitted for me. Said I hadn't charged enough for all the happiness I'd brought her, bless her, and she knew that I liked cardigans. A lovely lady. No, when I was little, what I liked best were the rainy, windy nights when I could lay tucked up in bed and think about all of the people out there in the cold, so that I could feel even snugger by comparison. I'm lucky in that that's what my whole life's like these days, very snug. Snug by comparison, you might say. Ah. There goes the phone. The landline, not my mobile, although even I have trouble telling them apart because the ring tone's very similar.

"Hello, there. You've reached Ricky Sullivan – the angel's answering service. This is Ricky speaking. So, how can I help you?"

"Um, hello. My name's Dave, David Berridge. Look, I've . . . well, I've lost somebody, y'know, recently, and I was just . . . I don't know. To be honest, I've been in two minds about if I should ring you up or not. I've never really been much of a one for all this, no offence, and I don't even know if they'd approve, the person that I've lost . . ."

Just judging from the accent he's a local man, probably lower middle class and in his, what, his forties? Early fifties? He sounds lost, as if his life's just fell to bits and nothing makes sense to him anymore. He's calling out for help, and

I've already heard enough to know that as clients go, this one is classic Ricky Sullivan. You can tell quite a lot about a person just from speaking to them on the phone. I'm writing down his full name on my jotter even as I'm talking to him.

"Mr Berridge, let me stop you right there. I prefer it if vessels of light - that's what I call my clients - if vessels of light don't tell me anything about themselves before they come in for a consultation, if that's what you should decide to do. That way I get a clearer reading of their aura, without any preconceptions, and it's fairer on them. What I always say is, if a person has a genuine psychic gift, why should you tell them everything? They should be telling you! That way, you can judge for yourself if I'm the real thing or not. That's only fair. We do get a few con men in this business, and that's why I insist that the special people who've been brave enough to seek my help are treated properly and given credit as intelligent adults. I'm sorry, but that's just the way I am. Now, if you should decide to come in for a consultation that'll be just fifty pounds, or it's a hundred for a house call. No need to bring any money with you, you can pay me when you get the invoice in a week or two, and only if you think that what I've done in contacting your loved one's worth that much."

I used to ask less, but I found that people are more likely to believe in something if they've paid more for it. Mr Berridge, he sounds half convinced already, though his manner's very shaken and uncertain. I expect that he's been through a lot. He ums and ahs a bit and then asks if he can come to the house and have a consultation, perhaps later, around eight or so? I tell him that's fine, and that he can call by earlier if he likes, I shall be in all evening. It's a little touch, but it makes everything feel more relaxed and casual. It puts people at their ease and makes them feel as though they're in control of things, and that's important when you've had a loss.

He thanks me and hangs up, and right away I fish out the old iPhone and look up the local paper's website, scrolling through the last two weeks' obituaries before I find the name that I've got scribbled on my notepad. "Berridge, Dennis, beloved brother of David, uncle of Darrell and Josephine, passed away quietly at home, November blah blah blah", and after that there was one of those poems that they must get from a book, like Best Man speeches. I'm not criticising. People are entitled to their feelings, obviously, but I just feel it's tacky and it's inappropriate; I'm sorry but I do, especially when it's about something as personal as someone's death.

So, anyway, a brother, then. I check and see if Mr Berridge is on Facebook, and it turns out I'm in luck. Just reading through the updates and then following up links to a few other sites, I've pretty soon got all the information that I need to make a good impression on the client when he turns up. From what I'm reading here they weren't just brothers, they were twins. It's hardly any wonder David Berridge sounded so shook up. They say they often share a psychic link, do twins, and when one of them dies it must be terrible. I can remember Ronnie Kray, the gangster, when he died and it said in the paper that his brother Reggie had sent a wreath he'd made out "To the other half of me". It must be dreadful, losing somebody so close. You'd be so vulnerable. Still, on the bright side, it makes all my prep work easier, only having the one birthdate to remember and with a good many details of their upbringing in common. And it says here they're identical, so David's Facebook photo will do me for Dennis, too: a very bland face with fine, mousey hair that's going grey and starting to recede;

a light dusting of freckles on the nose; lacklustre eyes and a slight overbite that makes his mouth look rabbity. He doesn't look as if he's got much to him, to be frank about it, although I suppose it might be a poor choice of photograph. That's why I always make sure Jenny, she's my press girl, I make sure that she runs all the pictures by me before sending them out anywhere. I don't want any more of me with that little moustache I used to have. I mean, I've never looked like Vincent Price, that's just ridiculous, but where's the sense in giving people ammunition? Anyway, clean shaven I look younger.

Oh, now this is interesting. Dennis Berridge had a blog, apparently. Hmm. Flicking through the recent entries, I'm afraid I have to say . . . oh, now, that's very negative. That's very harsh . . . I have to say he doesn't sound like someone that I'd have got on with. In the science stream at school, then working as a physics teacher until it all got too much for him and he took an early retirement this last April. He sounds like a very bitter man. He starts off ranting about the Americans, the Christians, how they're saying that the Bible should be taught alongside evolution in the schools. Well, I don't see what's wrong with that, with putting both sides of the argument. Oh, here we go. It's Richard Dawkins this and Richard Dawkins that. There's all the old stuff about homeopathy, how can it work with the dilution and the rest of it, and I expect . . . yes, here we are. "Why isn't Doris Stokes keeping in touch more often since she died? Surely she still has books to push?" That's low. I'm sorry, that's just low. I mean, the woman's dead and she can't answer back. Show some respect, that's all I'm saying.

Thinking back, that must be what his brother meant when he said that he didn't know if the departed would approve of him consulting me. No, no, I'll bet he wouldn't. I'll bet Dennis would regard that as a bitter irony, the thought of someone like me having the last laugh. Wouldn't he just!

I memorise all the important details – a Great Dane called Benji that both twins were soft on when they were eleven, things like that – and then I smarten up the front room for when Mr Berridge calls. There's not much that needs doing, just some little touches to create the proper atmosphere. I put the dimmers down a whisker and then light a joss stick. I'm not sure what kind of incense it is technically. It's that sort that smells a bit pink, if you know what I mean. I put a couple of my most impressive ghost books on the coffee table. There's the Elliot O'Donnell *Haunted Britain* where the spider gave me a fright earlier, and a great big thing full of airbrushed angels, just there lying casually around as if I read them all the time when actually I'm not what you'd call a great reader. Even *Haunted Britain*, I just got it for the pictures, really. They're very impressive at first glance. You take the monk, "PLATE II. PHOTOGRAPH OF A NOTORIOUS SOMERSET GHOST". It's a proper what I call old-fashioned spooky apparition, manifesting on the well-lit landing of a fancy house in Bristol. Only when you've looked at it a minute or two do you notice how the light that's falling on the monk is coming from a different side to everything else in the picture, so that you can tell it's a double exposure. And of course, you have to ask yourself what the photographer (a Mr A. S. Palmer, it says in the caption) would be doing setting up his camera and his lighting kit to take a picture of an empty stretch of landing. Still, like I say, it's effective if you only catch a glimpse of it.

Was that the doorbell? With the background music that I've got on now, *Rainforest Sounds*, there's some bits where it's very tinkly, like – what are they called? – wind chimes, and it's difficult to tell if someone's at the door or not. It's only half past seven so I shouldn't think it's time for my vessel of light yet, although I did say he could come early if he wanted. Even out here in the hallway, I can't make out if there's anybody there outside the frosted glass. It's probably just shadows from my hedge, but I expect I'd better check and see in case it's—

"Hello. Sorry, didn't mean to startle you. Would you be Mr Sullivan?"

God, Ricky, get a grip. First it's a spider, and now this. I've heard of being highly strung and sensitive, but this is being an old woman like your dad said. Still, I make a good recovery.

"Yes. Yes, I am. I'm Ricky Sullivan, lovely to meet you. I hope you've not stood here long, only I had some music on and wasn't sure if I could hear the bell or not. You must be Mr Berridge."

He's just like his Facebook picture, except he's a bit more drawn and crumpled-looking since he had that took, a bit more haggard, which is the bereavement, I expect. He's standing framed there in the open doorway, letting all the cold in. He looks up and manages a weary little smile. Bless.

"Mr Berridge, yes, that's right. And no, I'd only just turned up. I hadn't even had a chance to ring the bell. You must have had one of those feelings that you fellers have."

Well, there's a stroke of luck. He's half convinced and he's not even in the door yet.

"Oh, well, it's not much, but there's times when me having a God-given gift can come in handy. Anyway, come in the warm. We'll see what I can do to help you, shall we?"

He sidles in past me, still with that self-deprecating smile, and I shut the front door behind him. It's that cold outside that you can feel it in the hallway, even with the heating up.

There's no wind, and the fog's just hanging there like rubbed-out smudges on a pencil drawing. He goes through into the front room and sits down upon the sofa without taking his long mac off, which gives the impression that he's not anticipating staying very long. Well, we'll see about that.

"Mr Berridge, can I just say that when you walked in, I got a very strong impression. Stronger than I usually pick up off of my regular vessels of light. You've recently been separated from somebody, am I right? Not just somebody close, but someone who was so close to you that I can't even imagine what it must have been like. No, no, let me finish. I'm getting a letter 'D' and what I think might be a name? Denzel? Is that right? Wait a minute . . . no. That's not right. No, it's Dennis. Definitely Dennis. And the picture that I'm getting . . . no, that must be wrong. That can't be right. I'm sorry, Mr Berridge, but I think I'm going to have to let you down. I must be having an off night. I'm trying to get a picture of your loved one, but all I can see is . . . well, it's you, basically."

Oh, yes. That's got his attention. He looks up into my eyes, with that same rueful little smile, and shakes his head in wonderment.

"It's my twin brother. That's who I've been separated from. I've got to say, I didn't know if I should come to visit you like this, but, well, you're living up to all my hopes and expectations. So, can he say anything, my brother? Is there any message that he's got for me?"

I'm sorry, but I can't resist it, not when I've read all that rubbish on his brother's blog.

"Yes. Yes, there is. I'm not sure I can understand it properly, but I think Dennis wants to say that he was wrong. Does that make any sense? I'm sensing that he never thought there'd be an afterlife, and that he might have had some harsh words about those of us who do. Is that an accurate impression, that I'm passing on? He's saying he wants to apologise, and he knows better now. He says it's wonderful, the place he's in. He's telling me that he's been reunited with old friends. He says to tell you he's with . . . Benjamin, or Benji? Is that right? Is that somebody that you used to know?"

To tell the truth, I threw that last bit in just on an impulse, but I've hit the jackpot, so to speak. He's filling up. He's staring at me and his eyes are wet. The little smile he had is gone.

"Benji was . . . he was a Great Dane that we had when we were kids. Both of us loved him. But then, you know that already. Mr Sullivan, to think that you could bring up a beloved childhood pet like that . . . you're truly unbelievable. If I had any doubts about what kind of man you were before I came to see you, they're all gone. And what you said, how Dennis was always so sure that there was no life after death and having to reluctantly admit that he was wrong, that all rings very true as well. That's very much what Dennis used to be like. Very much the cold-eyed rationalist. It must have took him by surprise, his current circumstances, but if I know him he'd see the funny side as well."

The little smile's come back again. I'm not one to brag, but I think we can chalk up this one as a victory for Ricky Sullivan. I'm wondering, if I offer a cup of tea and biscuits perhaps we can chat about his brother for a while and then I'll see him out, ching, fifty quid, but no, he's off again.

"Am I correct in thinking that you said you'd do a house call for a hundred pounds? I wasn't certain earlier that it would be the proper thing to do, but like I say, that business about

Benji, you've convinced me. You're the right person to do this with. I mean, surely you'd get a clearer message, wouldn't you, if we were in the actual house where Dennis lived?"

I'm nodding from the point where he mentioned the hundred pounds. Well, I must say, I hadn't thought this sounded very promising when David Berridge rang up earlier. He sounded so nervous and hesitant I wasn't even sure that he'd turn up, but listen to him now after he's had a dose of what I call the Ricky Sullivan effect. He's like a different person. He's more confident. It's like he's made his mind up. I think that's a measure of the magic I bring to a situation, just my personality.

"Well, yes, I'm sure that it'd make things clearer. More vibrations with a visit, obviously. Were you after making an appointment, or was it tonight that you were thinking of? I mean, I don't mind. With the bookings I've got coming up, tonight would actually be quite convenient."

Meaning it's better from my point of view if we go now while he's still feeling the enthusiasm, rather than giving him time to change his mind. But no, he's nodding. He looks eager.

"No, tonight is good. Tonight is perfect. It's not far. We could be there in twenty minutes."

This is turning out to be a very profitable evening. For the house, I've still got plenty of material I haven't used, their parents' names and so on, so I can give him his money's worth. I can give him a proper visitation. I wonder if I dare do his brother's voice? It's a safe bet that they'd sound very like each other, but you never know. His brother might have had a stammer or a lisp or something. We'll see how it goes, play it by ear. He stands up from the sofa with his hands still jammed deep in his raincoat pockets . . . he's not took them out the whole time that he's been here. He must be feeling the weather even worse than I am . . . and I take my scarf and leather coat down from the peg out in the hall so I can let us out. It cost a lot, the coat, but you should see it on. It makes me look much taller and much more mysterious, like somebody from out *The X-Files* or *The Matrix*.

I shepherd him out the door, and while I lock it after us I hear the phone go. It might be another client, so my natural impulse is to pop back in and answer it, but no. I'll let it go. The answerphone will pick it up, and anyway, if I'm that interested I can always call the landline when I'm out and see who left a message. When I put my keys back in my pocket I have a quick fumble and make sure I've got my mobile, safe inside a kiddie's knitted bootie, which is what I keep it in. I turn round and venture a breezy, "Right, shall we be off?" but David, Mr Berridge, is already out the open front gate and away along the street, so that I have to hurry to catch up with him.

Oh, but it's bitter out tonight. It strikes right at you through your cardigan. I don't think that I can remember a December quite as cold as this since I was little. It's the kind of cold that takes you back, and with the fog it's dreadful. I'd forgotten, but it has a smell to it, does fog. It's like damp smoke or something; it's less of a smell than it's a miserable musty feeling in your nose. And there's a sort of cold burn in your airways when you breathe it. To be honest, I'll be glad to get the stuff with Berridge over with so I can get back home. It's, what, just after eight now. Twenty minutes there and twenty back, another twenty for the business, I could probably be back in time for QI. I'll admit, the humour isn't always to my taste but you can find out all these interesting little facts, like how the sea slug's actually a form of cucumber if I remember right.

Isn't that fascinating? If only these sceptics, all these types like Mr Berridge's late brother, if they could just open up their eyes and see how marvellous and inexplicable God's wonders really are, like with the nature and that, then perhaps they wouldn't be so smug and certain when it came to voicing their opinions. Because that's all that they are, opinions. None of us can really know for certain, can we, what awaits us on the other side? I must say, I wish Mr Berridge would slow down a bit. Still, he's keen. That's the main thing.

We walk down the road beside the park and then cross that dual carriageway that's at the bottom end. It's funny, but for saying that it's so near Christmas, there's hardly a soul about. Must be the weather, keeping them indoors. Or the recession. People always look so worried and so tense this time of year. It's very stressful, isn't it, trying to live up to everybody's expectations? Not that I find it a problem, Christmas. To be honest, I always look forward to it. I mean, ever since my mother passed I haven't really anyone to buy for, so it's not a great expense. I know that for some people it's a very lonely time, and that it's when you get most of the suicides and that, but speaking personally I always find I get a little bulge in clients and consultations around January, so it's an ill wind and so forth.

There's kebab-shop neon and occasionally a set of headlights burning through the fog. We walk along by the dual carriageway for a few minutes, then we cross another main road that runs off downhill. I'm too puffed keeping up with him to make much of a go at conversation, but it's not like there's an awkward silence. We're just eager to get where we're going, for our different reasons. He's thinking about his brother and I'm thinking about Stephen Fry and that hundred and fifty quid.

You know, in all the years I've lived where I am now, I've never had much cause to come down this way previously, and never as far as this. It's what I think of as one of the rougher neighbourhoods, where most of it's all tower blocks but where you'll get the odd building going back to Cromwell's time or even earlier. I don't know why they don't just pave it over, put a precinct up or something, with some nice pavement cafés. It's probably the riff-raff down here with their tenant's rights and everything that's stopping it from happening. I know that this sounds awful, but if we have a bad winter, what with all these cuts, it might thin out some of the obstacles around these parts and end up being the best thing that's ever happened to the district. There. I'm sorry, but I've said it.

If you want the honest truth I think it's areas like this that are the real ghosts, aren't they? Mouldy old things, dead things from hundreds of years ago that have no right to still be making an appearance in the present day, with all their creaking woodwork and their rattling chains. These terrible young men with their pale, undernourished faces and their hoodie tops, like apparitions, like the monk in Mr A. S. Palmer's photograph. Shrieks in the night and phantom bloodstains on the paving slabs outside a takeaway that will have disappeared by the next afternoon, it is, it's like a Gothic novel. And just like a ghost, a neighbourhood like this will hang around for centuries with all its flapping rags and its depressing atmosphere. It's an accusing presence, making everyone feel guilty about things that happened before most of us were born. It's not our fault if people were too lazy to make something of themselves and find a better place to live. Leave us alone.

Oh, look at that. A great big lump of dog's mess on the pavement. That's disgusting. I'm lucky I spotted it, what with the fog. If Dennis Berridge had to live round here, all I can say is that he can't have been much of a physics teacher. Or perhaps he was, but never got on in the education system as it is now. Either way, it must have made him bitter that somewhere like this was all he could afford. Reading his blog, I sensed he was a very angry man. You'll often find that people who say nasty things about spiritual healers, which is how I see myself, you'll often find that it's their own frustrations and their failures that they're really cross about, deep down inside. His brother David here, though, seems much more contented in himself, more open-minded and more likeable. Walking a pace or two ahead he turns and glances back across his shoulder at me with his funny smile that, frankly, in the useless lamplight that they have down here, is looking a bit ghastly. Doesn't look like a vessel of light, let's put it that way, but you must remember that he's had a blow, the poor soul.

"Not far now. Dennis's house is just along the end here."

Well, thank God for that. If we'd have had to go much further, I think I'd have wanted rabies shots. I'm sorry, but I would. This street we're on, it's like a terraced row with little badly-kept front gardens, most of them with the gates hanging off or missing altogether. David takes a right turn up the pathway of a pebble-dashed affair and I follow behind him. The house looks to be in a better condition than the other properties along here, although not by much. It's shabby, and the paint's all peeling off round the front doorway, but at least its windows aren't smashed in and patched with plasterboard like that house that we just passed two doors down. Someone had drawn a willy on its wood fence with black spray-paint and it's had, you know, the stuff, the droplets coming out the end. Who wants to see that? They've got ugly minds, some people. Ugly minds.

"I'll tell you what, I'll just check round the side to see that all the windows and back door are still alright since Dennis died. He kept a key under that flowerpot, next to the front doorstep there. Let yourself in, and if they've cut off the electric there's a big torch in the passage, just inside the door."

This is a bit irregular but, still, a hundred pounds. I have a job finding the plant pot in the dark and then my fingertips are that cold that they're numb, so I've only just unlocked the door and found the torch that Mr Berridge mentioned when he's back from his inspection, standing there behind me. I can't see his face in this light, but I know he'll have that weary, gormless smile showing his rabbit teeth, that little overbite he's got. I switch the torch on and it throws a puddle of tea-coloured light along the passageway, so I can see the bottom of the stairs. I think that's . . . no. Is it? I think that's the old-fashioned stair rods showing, brass ones like they used to have. That's shameful. You're not telling me a science teacher couldn't have afforded to splash out on fitted carpets?

Mr Berridge slips in past me, and I notice he leaves me to shut the door behind us, thank you very much. Born in a field, as my mum used to say. Not that shutting the door has made a scrap of difference to the cold. If anything, its colder indoors than it was outside and there's that smell, the smell of other people's houses. With the better sort of residences you don't notice it, they all just smell of Glade or something, mine does, but in poorer people's houses you can smell all the fish fingers and the dirty socks going back years, like it's accumulated in the furniture. I try the light switch in the hall, but nothing happens. I doubt that the council would cut somebody's electric off so soon after they'd died, so probably what happened was he hadn't paid his bill. I think it's better if I hurry things along a bit, get to the business, so to speak. I don't want to spend too long here.

"Well, now, this is very atmospheric, Mr Berridge. Very atmospheric. I can almost feel Dennis's presence, as if he were right here next to me. I sense that he's concerned about you, worried that you're suffering needlessly over his death. He's saying that he doesn't want you to be hurt."

I angle up the torch beam from where it's been playing over the unappetising wallpaper and the chipped skirting board and there they are, the goofy teeth and mournful smile as he considers.

"Yes, that sounds like Dennis. We were always ever so protective of each other, being twins. If either of us were in any trouble or had someone picking on them, then the other would be on it like a ton of bricks. Dennis particularly. Out of us two, Dennis was always the bloody-minded one."

Why am I not surprised? Anyone who can fume for pages about chiropractors and the like is hardly likely to be someone normal who just lets things go. I'm frankly glad I never met him. He sounds like a nightmare.

"He sounds like a lovely, very caring man. Just let me ask you, was there a possession or an object Dennis was especially attached to, something I could touch? I find it often makes the contact stronger, that's all. It could be a favourite pair of slippers or a record he was fond of. Literally, it could be anything. Just something so I can make a connection with him."

There's the smile again. It's probably the torchlight bouncing round this narrow passageway, but it looks almost pitying, or even condescending. Oh, it's very cold in here. It's icy.

"Well, if you want something so you can connect with Dennis, I think if I popped upstairs a minute I might come back with the very thing. Go in the living room and make yourself at home."

He turns and walks towards the stairs, then he looks back at me, and . . . no. No, his voice is very faint and I can hardly make it out. He's asking if I'd like . . . don't know. A cuppa? Is he offering to make a cup of tea? I shake my head, smiling politely.

"No, no, I'll be fine. You go ahead and I'll wait in the living room."

He turns and walks up the stairs very casually for saying there's no lights on, although obviously he's more familiar with the place than I am. I'm guessing he's spent a lot of time here.

I push the door open and I sweep my torch around the living room. God, this is a depressing little hole for somebody to spend their final years in. There's three bookshelves, mostly science and science fiction from the look of it, and there's no television. Two sagging armchairs with one each side of an old three-bar fire. I've not seen one of them in years. Upstairs I can hear Mr Berridge walking back and forth as he looks for whatever piece of sentimental tat he's going to bring back down for me to go into my Vulcan mind-meld with. It'll be Richard Dawkins' autograph, I shouldn't wonder. If he's going to be a while then I suppose I could risk sitting on one of the chairs and rest my feet after that walking. I hope he's not long. It's twenty-five to nine already and I'm going to miss the start of QI unless Mr Berridge gets a move on. Sitting in the dark like this, well, it's not how I like to spend my Friday evenings, put it that way.

Oh, hang on, there was that call I had when I was just

locking the front door, wasn't there? While Charley Boy's up-stairs having a weep over his brother's keepsakes I can at least check on that and see if there's another client in the pipeline. Honestly, my fingers, fishing out the bootie with the iPhone in from my coat pocket, they're half frozen. If it gets much colder they'll be falling off.

Dialling the number and the suffix that connects me to the answerphone takes ages. Clump-clump-clump upstairs, the footsteps through the ceiling. Thinking back, it didn't sound like "cuppa", what he offered me when he was just about to go up. It was more like "phantom" or a word like that, except that doesn't make— ah! Here we are. The girl's voice tells me I was called at eight o'clock and then there's the long pause before it plays the message.

Fanta. That's what he said. "Ricky? Would you like a Fanta?" But why should he—

"Mr Sullivan? I'm sorry, this is David Berridge. Listen, I've been talking to my wife and, well, I'm sorry, I've had second thoughts about coming to see you. I don't think it's anything that the departed would have wanted. I'm sorry to cancel the appointment and I hope I haven't, like, put you out or anything. Anyway, thanks again, and sorry. Um, you take care. Bye. Bye . . ."

What? Is this . . . is he playing a trick or something, calling from upstairs, just some mean joke to make me . . . no, he didn't call. It's me who called, what am I thinking? It's the landline, isn't it? The landline at my house. I called and it said eight o'clock and he was with me then, outside my gate. There must be, I don't know, there must be something that explains this, calm down, Ricky, something I've not thought of, and in just a minute I'll be laughing at how daft I am. Because if

David Berridge, if he rang at eight to call it off, if he's still sat at home, then . . .

Up above me on the landing there's a creak. Somebody's coming down the stairs.

I'm sorry.

I'm so sorry.

ALICE LOWE

PAEDO

THE FIRST TIME he came into his room, in the dark of night, out of the wardrobe. A crack would appear, widening. A hand, then half a pale face and one eye, checking to see if Michael was asleep. He never was. Michael clutched his He-Man duvet to his chin, gulped. But did not scream out. Could not. Then The Man would come into the room. All the time maintaining eye contact. The eyes watering horribly. A horrible recognition, as if they were somehow related. And they were related, in the secret knowledge of what would happen next.

At some point, Michael would fall asleep. A deep dark slumber. Blurring the boundaries of dream and day. In the morning, Tony the Tiger and other childish things would help him forget everything that had happened in the night. The brightness of the morning pushing out the vision of that long, pale, oval face, the round, staring, green eyes, like a Jenga brick smoothly ejected and joining the other brightly coloured toy-junk scattered on the floor. Memories are like that in childhood, aren't they? The sharp painful ones mixed in with the fluffy toys.

In the morning, a hamster had appeared. Caramel and white. Scrabbling around in the corner of the room quite happily.

Must have been the neighbour's, escaped in the night. Michael was good at keeping secrets, so he kept him. In an old fish tank lined with *The Beano*. He didn't give him a name.

Michael was good at science. He had lots of science kits, mouldy crystal gardens growing in jars, Meccano constructions; an Amstrad computer. He captured frogs in jam jars and vowed to keep them kindly. He was even saving up for one of those glass balls where you can keep pet electricity and stroke it whenever you want. One day, he would find a way to stop The Man once and for all. He'd build a machine. That would blast The Man back into the wardrobe, hair standing on end, a frightened frazzled look on him, smoke coming out of his wicked charred fingers. His penis shrivelled like a burnt prawn on a barbecue. Punishment. Michael day-dreamed about this in science class. Giggled out loud. A couple of the girls whispered about him. Horrid. How could they understand? Only he understood. Only he. And perhaps The Man. Michael didn't have friends per se. But then, he was trapped. Trapped in a glass ball. A hamster in an old fish tank. With only one person who really visited him. And he wanted it to stop.

So he began to steal from the school. Michael was a patient child. He was able to recognise that with maturity would come improvement in his skills. An instrument here, a gas cylinder there. He could conduct his private experiments in his bedroom. "What are you doing in there, Michael?" his mother said, after a loud bang and green gas creeped out of the bottom of his door.

"It's an experiment mother!" he yelled. The frog was quite dead. He examined its guts. The glassy gaze of its remaining eye. But somehow he wasn't satisfied. It didn't erase the pain he felt. The indelible pain. As if someone had scratched a compass upon his mortal soul. And written their name across it. Badly.

That night The Man visited him again. Creeping across Michael's town-map rug like a rolling fog, tiptoeing over the printed streets and houses like a polite Godzilla. How Michael hated this politeness. How dare he be so careful, so considerate when he was violating him so brutally? The Man lifted a long thin finger to his lips. 'Shh'. His politeness stank. If Michael could, he would explode The Man and burst his round eyes, gladly smear the walls with The Man's smarmjuice, garland the bunk bed with his guts, put a Bunsen burner under his testicles and watch him moonwalk in agony . . .

But Michael simply shrank in terror as once again The Man enveloped him. And then sleep. Betraying him terribly.

"You're a weirdo," his sister announced to him over breakfast. "Everyone says so," as she dug and twisted into the Weetabix. "You've got weird eyes."

"Jane! Don't talk to your brother like that," said Mother, distractedly using her Braun Automatic on her perm while hovering over the sink. Michael looked at Jane with his weird eyes. Why didn't The Man come out of her wardrobe? That would certainly wipe the smile off her face. Why him? Why him? Girls were repulsive, he decided. There was no understanding. About as alien as frogs. If they weren't ignoring you, they were snickering about you in clumps. No honesty there. No direct contact. He'd prefer if one just punched him in the face. But no, these little scathing skimming blows taking chips off you, like being a pencil in a sharpener. But he was getting sharp. Oh how sharp he would be.

He threw the biro into his pencil case. Into his Air sports bag. Along with a soldering iron and a couple of circuit boards. From the CDT workshop. Looking around to see if anyone was watching. Only one ginger fat child, biting his lip and saying "Ammmm." This was shorthand for, 'that's naughty' and implied, 'I will now tell a teacher'. The now-thirteen-year-old Michael stared him out. No ginger child was a match for Michael's stare. An incipient moustache was thinking of breaching the trench of his lip. And his jaw was lengthening due to the hormones bustling to crowd his system, like football hooligans surging over the turnstiles. The ginger kid backed down. All too aware of the natural order. Not until he was thirty-two and a successful journalist, would he truly escape the unfortunate nature of his ginger sub-species classification at school. But for now, he was well scuppered. He knew it. Michael knew it. And even though Michael was sub-species 'science nerd/weirdo', he still had more power.

In fact, Michael was an unknown quantity. Teachers found him a puzzle. At times brilliant, at others disinterested. A nice background, normal family. "Where has it come from?" mused Miss Harding, the well-meaning English teacher with dangly earrings and a dangling bleeding heart on her sleeve. Oh where did it come from? The internalised . . . destructive energy? Had something happened to him? Or did it just come from within him? It was like a black hole of emptiness existed within him that could at any moment . . .

"Oh shut up, Jan," said Mr Bennett, the P.E. teacher. "You're not a psychologist. He's just becoming a teenage boy.

And they all do that. Turn evil. There doesn't have to be a reason for it. They do it to themselves. About twenty times a day. I did when I was his age."

"Nigel!" exclaimed Miss Harding.

"What?" replied Mr Bennett, crunching a pepperami. "Self-abuse is better than abusing others, eh?" He shrugged and held his hands out like a cod-Italian actor advertising pizza. Whaddaya gonna do? Miss Harding shook this off. She wore her romantic notions like a shawl.

"These tortured types. They just get me . . . here," said Miss Harding, involuntarily squeezing her own breast. She drank her chai and resolved to help Michael, even if he shot her in a killing spree. She could see the headlines now and they were very favourable towards her. She knew which photo of her she hoped they'd use. That one in Marrakesh where someone had said she looked like Anthea Turner.

The Man would visit tonight. Michael felt it in his bones. He looked in the mirror. At the bum fluff coating his still pudgy cheeks, at the last childish roundness of his face. Would The Man still visit him when he was no longer a child? When all traces of childishness had gone? He felt instinctively not. He'd read about these monsters in the papers. They only had sick fetishes for certain things. A certain age. A certain gender. A certain . . . type. Perhaps he'd brought it upon himself? This thought had him sweating and his eyes watering, anger swelling in him. He slammed his fist into the mirror, the Panini stickers quivering in terror. No. No. It was not his fault. He couldn't help the way he was. And he wouldn't let this happen to him anymore. Or to anyone else. He would no longer be the victim. He would be the punisher. But he was running out of time. More time. More time. He needed more . . . time.

As The Man visited him that night, Michael took his mind to another space. Played a video in his head. Of something, anything. Old Tom and Jerry cartoons, *Happy Days*, the Midlands news with Sue Lawley, a fluff piece about goats, *The Young Ones*, 'got myself a crying walking sleeping talking living doll', the chart countdown on *Top Of The Pops*. Every now and then, pain punctured through, creating a glitch in the video. Pain. Pain writes itself indelibly, making itself part of you. You can't erase it. Once pain has been done to you, you can't take it away. He would never want this inflicted on anyone else if he could prevent it. Some poor child whose life would be damaged forever. But back to the tape. The video. The laughter track, the loud music, the bright happy images. Rewind. Rewind. If he could just rewind. If he could just rewind time
And so the plan changed. A time machine. Blood and guts of his tormentor wasn't enough. He wanted to erase the pain. Of the child Michael. Poor little Mikey. He would go back in time and destroy The Man before he had a chance to perpetrate his wickedness, at the very scene of the crime. He'd rescue himself! He was already drawing up the plans. Others had failed. Sure. But they didn't have the reserves of plutonium-like rage that seethed inside him. A nuclear reactor. It was just that no one had flipped the 'on' button yet. He sketched in his notepad fervently. Sitting on the school bench in the furthest corner of the playing field, under an oak tree. Graffitied heavily with 'Leanne 4 Bradley', 'Sam Cooper hearts Sunny Sandhu', 'Hannah + Chris Chalker'. This was where all the girls came to lose their virginity, usually to a finger. Here or the graveyard.

Michael + Michael, Michael thought to himself, by himself. Heavy breathing down his neck. Michael flinched, turning quickly. The Ginger kid, with a sniffling cold. "What are you doing?" said the Ginger kid, sitting down next to him with a trust Michael despised. Sort of reminded him of himself. The born stupidity, like a fucking trusting hamster.

Michael lifted his finger to his lips "shh."

"Is it a time machine?" said Ginger excitedly. "Because we were talking about time loops in physics, and whether you can ever change the past or whether what will be will be, even if you think you've changed it . . . !" The Ginger babbled. Perhaps thinking he'd found a kindred spirit. Michael shot out a hand, one elongating daily with puberty, and put it on Ginger's knee, stroking it ever so gently. Michael gazed into Ginger's eyes. A silence. The Ginger froze, like a fat squirrel, then bolted away across the field as fast as his chubby little legs could take him.

"Some people are born victims," chuckled Michael to himself. There distilled a vague steam of disquiet, rising inside himself. An internal science experiment.

"Do you want to talk, Michael?" said Miss Harding. Raising her eyebrows into a tent of concern, and cocking her head like Lady Diana visiting an AIDS patient. Michael frowned at her. His head was full of calculations, and he was desperate to get home and try out the prototype. But he was trapped here. After English. "You know. You're going through a lot of changes," said Miss Harding, rubbing his back. Michael flinched at the contact. "It's quite normal. To feel what you're feeling."

"Is it," said Michael blackly. He didn't ask if it was normal to have fantasies about time-travelling in order to murder your childhood abuser before they get a chance to abuse you. I mean, what's the 'problem' with that anyway? It's the perfect crime, in many, many ways. Circular, neat. No one gets hurt. Except the criminal. Who deserves it. There were some Hamlet quotes about incest on the wall, done in bubble writing, next to a big picture of Glenn Close, who had played Gertrude. Hamlet was a dick, thought Michael. If you want to shag your mother, just shag your mother, there's no point fretting about it. You can't change who you are.

"Look," said Miss Harding, stroking his knee, "you'll have these urges you can't quite understand yet. And because they're unfulfilled, you'll feel anger." Too right, thought Michael. "But Michael, you have to understand that these urges are not wrong. They're right. It's right to act on them." Now Miss Harding's face was quite close to his. He could smell her perfume, a mixture of patchouli oil and Marks and Spencer's magnolia bodywash. "Remember," she murmured, "self-abuse is better than abusing someone else." He could feel her breath now. "Unless you can find . . . a willing participant." It was almost as if she was leaning in to kiss him. Her breath smelt of soya and halitosis. But she was pretty. A pretty face. Eyes half closed in ecstasy.

But all he could see was The Man. The Man's face. He lurched away, the chair falling with a clatter. "Michael!" cried out Miss Harding, masturbating her emotions hard. "God, teaching is hard!" she groaned to herself. As Michael flickered out, just one eye and a hand clutching the door, looking back at her before he left.

In the playground, unnerved, he dawdled to watch the younger boys playing football. An uncomfortable snake of realisation unfurling in the pit of his stomach. His one true love, the time machine, was waiting for him at home. But he couldn't drag his eyes from the boys. The boys' legs. The boys' arms. The boys' taut young stomachs.

"I'll never let this happen to another child," he chanted to himself, putting on a jumper from the MFI drawer in his bedroom. The hamster, Mark XIV, was quite gone. No blood. No singed fur. No sign of him. Not a whisker. The time machine had been successful, as far as he knew. He'd programmed the date. The first time he used his He-Man duvet, two days after his eighth birthday. What would he wear? What would it be like to come face-to-face with his attacker? What would he do? Two of him in the same room. The helpless child version of him. And now this stronger, adolescent version of himself. He was no victim. Seventeen now, looked older, and long of limb. Yes, about the same height now, he reckoned. He'd take him easily. But quietly, cautiously. He wouldn't be caught out. The Man would meet his match. He flipped the 'on' switch. The machine began to charge again.

Downstairs his mother and father watched *Ready, Steady, Cook*. Oblivious to what was happening upstairs. Michael's sister Jane was in the bath. Trying to get rid of a particularly persistent verruca that had been with her on her right foot since 1986. Trying to dig it out with a nail file. Over a brown towel. She'd caught it swimming at Solihull swimming baths. No one knew who the perpetrator was, and it was unlikely he would ever be caught now. Sometimes these things can be blamed on others. But sometimes you've no one to blame but your own sick soul leaking at the edges. You just have to try and scrub it off with a pumice stone. Or something called 'Verruca-Blast' or whatever. Doesn't work. Still there. Growing inside you.

Darkness. The high-pitched scream of the generator gone now. A different environment entirely. It surely had worked. The time machine. The smell of soft, not-yet acrid, childish sweat mixed with sherbet-candy sweetness, Wham bars and stale Marmite. Michael sniffed. The comforting smells he loved. In a place he'd always want to return to. He reached out with his hands. Felt fabric. Slick. And what's this? A duffel coat toggle. A scrunched tissue in a pocket.

Slowly, cautiously, he pushed open the door of the wardrobe. A hand. Half a face. An eye looking out cautiously. Where was the monster? The monster who would ruin his life but no one else's if he could help it? This was the monster's portal but he was not in it. Yet. He tiptoed out, over the town map rug. Stopped in his tracks. The little Michael. Himself. In bed. But wide awake. Staring back at him. A look of recognition. As if they were related. And they were related. In the secret knowledge of what would happen next. And he had known. Michael. Deep down. That morning, when he saw his adult face, looking back at him in the mirror. And he knew what he was, and that it could not be changed.

"I'll never let this happen to another child," Michael promised himself. "Only me. Only me." As sobbing he approached the bed.

WHO'S WHO

JAMES ACASTER is a 31 year-old stand-up comedian. He lives in London but is from Kettering. He can play the drums and loves ice cream.

CLARE FERGUSON-WALKER has been working as a stand-up comedienne and performance poet for the last 5 years. She has won numerous awards for poetry and regularly supports John Cooper Clarke. Her 5-star Edinburgh show *California Scheming* is currently touring the U.K. She is a life-long horror fan and has spent far too much money buying old horror comics on Ebay. Clare lives in Wales with her husband and two children.

TOBY HADOKE is a writer, actor and comedian. His hit shows *Moths Ate My Doctor Who Scarf* (which received a Sony nomination when it transferred to radio) and *My Stepson Stole My Sonic Screwdriver* toured the world and were performed at the West End. His radio play *The Dad Who Fell To Earth* was a finalist for Best Comedy at the 2016 BBC Audio Drama Awards and he has appeared in television is everything from *Phoenix Nights* to *The Forsyte Saga* via *Coronation Street* and *Holby City*. He has written for the *Guardian* and the *Independent* and presents The *7th Dimension* on BBC Radio 4 Extra.

NATALIE HAYNES is a writer and broadcaster. Her books include *The Amber Fury* and *The Ancient Guide to*

Modern Life. She co-presents *The Seventh Dimension*, the sci-fi/horror strand on BBC Radio 4 Extra.

RUFUS HOUND is currently an actor. He is not currently a panel-show turn, a TV presenter, a stand-up comedian or proud of himself.

ROBIN INCE is a multi-award winning comedian and author. His book, *Robin Ince's Bad Book Club* was based on his tour, *Bad Book Club*. More recently he has toured *Happiness Through Science*, *The Importance of Being Interested*, *Robin Ince Is In And Out Of His Mind* and *Blooming Buzzing Confusion*. Robin is currently hosting *Book Shambles* with Josie Long.

ELIS JAMES started performing stand-up in 2005. You might have seen him at a gig, or in *Crims* (BBC3), *Josh* (BBC3), or heard him on the *Radio X* show he hosts on a Saturday morning. He is also a regular guest on *The News Quiz* (Radio 4), and in 2015 he wrote a stand-up show in Welsh for S4C. He has done stand up on Russell Howard's *Good News*, *Live at the Comedy Store*, Dave's *One Night Stand* and *The Rob Brydon Show*. He has an MA in Modern History, and likes to unwind by reading about coal mining or listening to podcasts about football.

STEWART LEE is a comedian, writer and director. In the 90s he worked with Richard Herring and has since gone to co-write the libretto of Richard Thomas' *Jerry Springer: The Opera* which found itself in the centre of a media meltdown (although the critics loved it), and a new series of *Stewart Lee's Comedy Vehicle* which has been recently filmed.

JOSIE LONG is a comedian who won the BBC New Comedy Awards at 17, as well as being nominated for the Edinburgh Comedy Award for Best Show three times. She has co-founded the Arts Emergency Service, written and produced two short films and appears regularly with Robin Ince on podcasts, the latest being *Book Shambles*.

ALICE LOWE is a writer and actor. She co-wrote and starred in the cult film *Sightseers*, directed by Ben Wheatley and has appeared in the cream of British television, including *Garth Marenghi's Darkplace*, *Sherlock*, *Inside No 9* and *Horrible Histories*. She has recently directed her first feature film, *Prevenge*.

JASON MANFORD is one-time comedy-club glass collector who has become an all singing, all dancing, sometime opera singing stand-up comedian with an obsession with urban legends. He is somewhere between Bruce Forsyth and Dennis Wheatley; when the devil rides out he uses a soft shoe shuffle.

ALAN MOORE is Britain's greatest comic book writer. Living or dead. It really is as simple as that.

ANDREW O'NEILL is an occult comedian. He has appeared on *Never Mind the Buzzcocks*, *Saxondale* and is in a band called The Men Who Will Not Be Blamed For Nothing

KIRI PRITCHARD-MCLEAN recently burst onto the scene in 2013 and since then has won three awards, the most recent being Chortle Award's 'Best Newcomer' for writing *Gein's Family Workshop*. Kiri has also written for *Crackanory* and her show, *Kiri Pritchard McLean's Racist, Sexist Comedy Show* has received rave reviews.

JOHN ROBERTSON is a comedian, TV presenter and the creator of interactive horror show *The Dark Room*, the world's only live-action videogame. An award-winning stand-up comic, crowd surfer and recreational sadist, his career includes understandable successes like going viral in 2012, racking up 4,000,000 YouTube views and stranger ones, like faking a seizure on talent show *Australian Idol*. From 2014-2016, he presented 105 episodes of Challenge TV's *Videogame Nation*. He lives in London and will do a surprisingly large number of things for money.

ISY SUTTIE is a writer, actress and comedian. She is known for her portrayal as Dobby in the cult comedy *Peep Show*. Other credits include *Isy Suttie's Love Letters for R4*, appearing in the *Knightmare* revival, and her first book, *The Actual One*, was recently published to critical acclaim.

ACKNOWLEDGEMENTS

THE EDITORS WOULD like to thank everyone who has bought, written or talked about this book. They would also like to thank those who came to the Bloomsbury show or any of the *Dead Funny* double bill nights. They would also like to thank Salt for their continued support.